December's
Thorn

BY PHILLIP DePOY

THE FEVER DEVILIN SERIES
The Devil's Hearth
The Witch's Grave
A Minister's Ghost
A Widow's Curse
The Drifter's Wheel
A Corpse's Nightmare

THE FLAP TUCKER SERIES
Easy
Too Easy
Easy as One-Two-Three
Dancing Made Easy
Dead Easy

ALSO BY PHILLIP DePOY
The King James Conspiracy

DECEMBER'S THORN

PHILLIP DEPOY

MINOTAUR BOOKS

NEW YORK

DECEMBER'S THORN. Copyright © 2013 by Phillip DePoy. All rights reserved. Printed in the United States of America. For information, address St. Martin's Press, 175 Fifth Avenue, New York, N.Y. 10010.

www.minotaurbooks.com

ISBN 978-1-250-01198-5 (hardcover)
ISBN 978-1-250-02600-2 (e-book)

First Edition: January 2013

10 9 8 7 6 5 4 3 2 1

ACKNOWLEDGMENTS

Grateful acknowledgment is made to Janet Reid for her generous enthusiasm, to Keith Kahla for his constant brilliance, and to Dr. John Burrison for introducing to me, many years ago, the conjunction of Jung and folklore. I also hereby acknowledge that Lee Nowell is a better playwright than I am, and the best first-reader in the known universe.

If you cannot get rid of the family skeleton, you may as well make it dance.

—GEORGE BERNARD SHAW

1

The past lingers all around us, a clear winter's light, and a shroud.

Five nights before Christmas, a stranger came to my door. She was dressed in widow's black, pale and gaunt, and appeared to be half-frozen by the icy rain. The night behind her was starless, and the moon refused to shine. It was a pretty face, in some way, despite an overwhelming sorrow in her eyes. She said nothing. She stayed in the doorway, a granite angel, a cemetery decoration.

I stood transfixed, for a second. I'd been asleep on the sofa and my mind was clouded. I was still dressed: flannel shirt, gray sweater, black jeans, construction boots. Then I remembered my manners. "Please come in," I said. "You must be cold."

"I'm not," she said, stone still.

Her voice was melodic, a surprise. It didn't remotely match her face, or her clothes—or her spirit.

"Do you know me?" she said.

I blinked. "I—I'm sorry," I stammered. "I don't. Should I?"

She held out her hand, and in it there was a golden ring, a wedding band.

"It's me, Fever," she said, her eyes rimmed in red. "It's your Issie. Your wife."

I don't know how long I stared at her, hand on the doorknob, before I stepped aside.

"Please come in," I said as gently as I could.

She drew in a breath, nearly a sob, and crossed over the threshold into my home. She didn't look right or left. She took three strides and stopped, eyes closed.

"It smells like home," she said.

True enough. A warm fire in the stove at the hearth, a hint of cloves from dinner's steamed pumpkin, and the bold, dry evidence of rosemary and lavender hanging in the rafters in the living room all combined to sanctify the air.

"Why don't you sit down by the fire?" I asked her.

She acquiesced without a word.

It's difficult to recall my exact emotions at that moment. I may have thought I was dreaming, or misunderstanding what she was saying, or even that some lonesome winter's ghost had wandered my way. I was trying to wake up, but my stupor had been complete, and even my own living room seemed strange, somehow different, as if I might have been transported to another reality—a reality in which some other version of myself was married to the cemetery angel.

She sat on the sofa close to the fire but didn't look at the hearth. Her eyes wandered. She seemed to devour the contours of the room, the sofa, the rugs, the large picture window. Her eyes paused at one of the older quilts hanging on the wall, then she stared out the window with something akin to longing, as if being indoors was difficult for her, as if she were an elemental wraith, and not a human being at all. I followed her gaze. The icy rain was turning to snow and beginning to collect on the porch.

"Snow," she said softly, and again the melody of her voice, a single perfect velvet note, surprised me.

I did not sit down. "Would you like some coffee or some tea? To warm you up?"

She shook her head.

"Well," I told her, "I think I'll have something."

I turned toward the kitchen. The pots from dinner were still on the stove. The dishes were in the sink. I turned on the light.

"Oh!" she said, alarmed.

I turned back to see her, and she was squinting and turning away from the harsh light of the kitchen. The glare from the overhead fixture seemed to be hurting her. I switched off the light instantly, and she sighed.

"Sorry," I said, watching her.

She did not respond, except to wander into my kitchen.

I moved to the espresso machine, but I was suddenly afraid that its loud grinding would frighten her. It was becoming clear to me, as I began to wake up more fully, that it would be best to keep her calm. So I took out the kettle and found a bit of tea in the same cabinet where I kept the coffee. Tea was pushed to the back, a second-class stimulant.

In short order, however, the kettle was on the stove and two cups were on the kitchen table, each with its bag of pomegranate black tea: a blend of tea leaves, calendula flowers, and pomegranate. That tea was a gift from my fiancée, Lucinda, who was, at that precise moment in her own home not far away, finalizing plans for our spring wedding.

Exploring that thought for only a moment proved as effective as caffeine, and I was much more awake.

"What did you say your name was?" I called to my fragile visitor.

"I don't wonder that you're angry with me," she answered softly. "But you know my name. You know my name full well."

"Essie?" I repeated.

"No." Her voice grew hard, though it managed to remain melodic. "Issie is a diminutive, to be certain, and one not used all that often, but how else does a husband refer to a wife?"

I could feel that I might be about to say or do something confrontational and, ultimately, rude, even though I realized it would be the wrong thing to do with someone so delicate, so obviously troubled. There was no telling how she might react to being told that she was out of her mind. Still, confusion was turning to irritation fairly quickly. I wanted to say, "I have to tell you that I don't know you, and I don't know what you're talking about."

Here's what I did say: "How did you get here? I didn't hear a car. Did you come by yourself? Is there someone with you?"

She looked away. "I thought you might ask about that."

The whistle from the kettle startled us both. I turned around quickly to take it off the heat and switch off the gas flame. When I turned back around, she was standing.

"Please don't be angry," she said, almost whispering. "Any more angry than you already are."

"I'm not angry," I began.

"I know that you are, and you have every right to be," she interrupted me. "But let me tell you this news and then everything will be out in the open. Then we can say whatever else there needs to be said. Please?"

"News?" I asked, completely at sea.

"I'm here to tell you," she said, but then she stopped and seemed to have lost her train of thought. "I think I would like some tea after all."

"Yes," I said quickly. "Absolutely. I have your cup right here."

As quickly as I could, I poured the hot water into the nice white cups. Scented steam rose up.

"I smell pomegranate?" she asked.

"Right," I assured her. "Good guess."

She took up her cup and saucer. "Shall we go back in by the fire?"

She returned to the living room and I followed. She sat on the sofa. I sat in one of the chairs across from her, back to the window and front door, facing the sofa and the stairway to the bedrooms— not my usual seat. I was uncomfortable with my back to the door.

I worried that someone would barge in without my seeing them coming. I tried to reassure myself that innate paranoia and the strangeness of the situation were mostly to blame for that fear.

"All right," I said, trying to settle into my seat, turning a little so that I might see the front door out of the corner of my eye. "What news is this you have for me?"

She opened her mouth, and then closed it. She cast her eyes down. She licked her lips once. She took a sip of her tea, and then set the cup and saucer down on the table between us.

"I don't know how to say this," she finally said.

"Best to just blurt it out," I encouraged her. "Then we can examine it however you like."

I had no idea what I was talking about.

"Well, then," she said.

She placed her hands in her lap. She took a deep breath. Her eyes rose to meet mine, and they were filled with anguish.

"Here is my news, Fever," she said, wincing. "There is a child."

2

I sat silently, contriving and then dismissing responses and questions to her flat statement.

At last I came up with the perfect, well-thought-out question. "What child?"

"He has your eyes." The stranger sipped from her teacup. "This tea is delicious."

I wanted to say, "It was a gift from my fiancée."

I did say, "Yes. Pomegranate."

"Do you want to know about him?" she asked primly.

I shot a glance toward the door. "About the child?" I had a sudden fear that the child might charge into my home.

"He's quite precocious, of course," she told me. "Like his father."

"Precocious," I repeated, unable to take my eyes from the door.

"Fever," the woman said gently, "look at me."

Reluctantly, I did.

"I've come to apologize," she said firmly, "and I want you to hear me out."

I leaned forward and looked deeply into her eyes. I spoke as soothingly as I could considering the irritation and, admittedly, good bit of fear I felt.

"Look," I said, "this has gone far enough. I'm going to call some people who might be able to help you. Just sit tight."

I set my tea on the coffee table and stood so quickly that it startled her. I ignored her discomfort and strode very deliberately to the phone. I hadn't quite thought it through when I found myself dialing Lucinda.

The phone rang a very long time. I finally caught sight of the clock in the stove. It was almost midnight. At last Lucinda answered.

"Hello?" she managed to mumble.

"Hi, sorry. I have a situation."

"Fever?" She struggled to wake up.

"There's a very disturbed woman in my house," I whispered, "and I'm not certain what to do. It seems clear that she's out of her mind and possibly dangerous."

"Fever?" she said again.

"Yes, please wake up. I am in the middle of a difficult— a potentially very difficult situation."

"There's a woman in your house at this hour?" She was beginning to rouse herself. "Who is she?"

"No idea," I assured her. "She just appeared. I'd fallen asleep on the sofa."

The stranger materialized in the wide doorway to the kitchen.

"I'm talking to someone who can help you," I told the woman.

"What the hell is going on over there?" Lucinda growled.

I could count on a single hand the times I'd heard Lucinda use a four-letter word, even one so mild. This particular usage did not bode well, I thought.

Before I could think how to calm the little play that was transpiring in my kitchen, the strange woman charged toward me, grabbed the receiver out of my hands, and hung up the phone.

"Who was that?" she demanded to know, her voice, for the first time, shrill and grating. "Was that Brenda Gain?"

"Who?" I asked.

"I know I don't have a right to be jealous," the woman said, still seething, "but you could at least have the good manners not to call up my rival when we're in the middle of an important conversation. I'm trying to tell you something important. Something you'll want to know. I'm afraid, Fever. I'm afraid for all our lives. You have no idea what my mother is capable of. Or the boy, you don't know what he might do."

I could see that she was becoming increasingly hysterical and irrational. Despite the chill in the room and the snow outside, I could feel beads of sweat along my hairline.

"All right," I said, "all right. Good. Yes. Maybe we should call for help. I could call the sheriff."

"The sheriff?" she repeated, stumbling a bit in her forward panic.

"Yes," I said encouragingly. "That may be just the thing. He could protect us. From your mother. And the boy."

"No, he couldn't," she said firmly. "But he could kill them. He's the law. He could do that and get away with it. Maybe that's what we should do. The sheriff could at least kill my mother."

The phone rang.

My hand shot out to pick it up.

"Yes?" I said quickly, desperately wishing for the voice at the other end to be Lucinda's.

"Fever, all you all right?" Lucinda said into the phone, unable to hide the concern in her voice.

"Thank God you called back," I whispered.

"Sweetheart, are you awake?" she asked me.

It seemed an odd question.

The stranger moved to grab the phone out of my hand again.

"No," I said to the stranger immediately, "this is the sheriff's assistant—who is going to call the sheriff right now. He'll come to my house. He'll help you. He'll sort this all out. I don't think there will be any need to kill your mother—or anyone. Just try to stay calm."

"Oh, dear," Lucinda said, the tone of her voice changed entirely. "Okay. No idea what's going on over there, but I'm calling Skidmore."

"Yes, please," I said, "and now. It's an emergency, as you might well imagine."

"Right now," she said, and hung up.

"There," I said, trying to smile. "Sheriff's on his way."

"Wait, how did the sheriff's assistant know to call you?" my visitor asked.

I only hesitated for a second.

"The sheriff is one of my best friends," I explained. "His office monitors all of my calls. It's not hard to do. We have a central switchboard for the whole town—and it's a small town. You know how they are."

This bizarre explanation, miraculously, seemed to satisfy her.

"Yes," she said, returning to her more melodious tones, "Blue Mountain is a lovely town. I've wandered around the main street area before coming here. I never expected it would take me so long to walk from the town up the mountain to your house."

"You walked up the mountain?" It would have taken her hours to walk that far.

"I've walked farther than that," she said, as if she were telling me a secret.

I took a moment, then, to truly look at this woman. She was, I guessed, about my age, and would have been very pretty were it not for the obvious aura of insanity. She stood a good six inches shorter than I. Her lips were parched and cracked a bit from the cold, and betrayed no lipstick at all. Her dark hair, almost a match for the color of her dress, was pulled back behind her head. Her face was porcelain white. Her black dress reached below her knees, and she wore black tights and black boots with flat heels.

She was wrapped in a quilted cape or shawl. She wore no hat. She did have on gloves, black fingerless gloves that were made, it appeared, of very soft leather. Her fingers were bone fine and delicate, almost blue.

"Why do you stare so?" she asked at length.

Then, unexpectedly, she blushed. Her eyes rose to meet mine and her demeanor began to trend, uncomfortably, toward the seductive.

Against all better judgment I blurted out, "I don't know you. I've never met you. I don't know who you are. I don't know why you're here. I only want to get you some help. Do you understand that?"

I instantly knew it was the wrong group of sentences to say. The expression on her face changed from slightly flirtatious to monstrously wounded.

"No," she whispered. "Don't deny me, Fever. God. Don't do that."

"Look," I began, "let's go back into the living room."

"You've called the sheriff to have me taken!" She stepped suddenly backward, away from me. "You mean to deny me! You can't be that cruel! I have to go."

"Wait—wait," I stammered.

But it was too late. She was flushed with panic. Her face red, her eyes filled with tears, she shot to the front door. Her expression had changed again, in a flash. She wore a mask of almost pure rage.

"You'll regret this." Her words stabbed and sliced the air like a dagger. "The same potions and medicines I used to save him twice? I can use them to kill you. Slowly. No one will know. Until it's too late."

She pulled open the door. Snow and a shock of frigid air rushed in.

"Wait," I said again. "Save who? What potions? I don't understand."

She stepped onto the porch. I was already shivering from the cold wind, and snow was beginning to collect on the floor.

"I never expected this from you," she said. "Not you. I know we deceived you. I know we broke your heart. I know you have a right to hate us. But to pretend you don't even know me at all—I would not have thought you capable of that. Not the Fever Devilin I knew so long ago."

She turned oddly, a pirouette, a dead leaf in the bitter wind, a collapsing rag doll, and then flew down the porch steps and into the midnight yard.

"I'll be back," she said, fading into the darkness. "And when I come back, it won't be to reconcile. It won't be to apologize. My return next time will be your tombstone. You should have listened to me. You should have heard what I had to say. Now, you're dead—your life is done. Cold clay, Fever. That is your only future now. That is what I'll bring the next time I come back: the frozen ground to dig your grave!"

And she was gone into the night.

I leapt through the doorway and bounded down the stairs into the snow and wind. I chased after shadows for what seemed an hour, but could not find her. Shivering and soaked, I gave up and retreated to my living room. I was standing over the fire, hands trembling, when I saw the flashing lights coming up the road toward my house.

3

To be sure, my life on Blue Mountain had always been strange. As the only child of carnival performers. I'd been on my own quite a bit. A freakish IQ and a morbid interest in ancient worlds had alienated me from most people my age. Aside from Skidmore Needle, who had become the town sheriff, and Lucinda Foxe, who had become my fiancée, I had no genuine relationships there, not even with the ghosts of my father and mother, who still wandered the house.

I'd thought to escape, at age sixteen, to the university life. That had worked perfectly for a while: I became the head of my own folklore program at the institution from which I'd graduated. But times being what they were at the beginning of the 21st century, there was little undergraduate interest in the perfect construction of a ladder-back chair made with tools a thousand years old, or the flood mythologies of Seminole tribes in certain parts of a swamp.

So, my program unceremoniously closed, I had little choice but to return to the place of my birth, an empty home on a cold mountain. I was welcomed back to the house, which had sat empty for several years, by a dead body on the front porch. I pulled into the yard to open the house, and there it was, mouth open, legs splayed, dressed in a dirty tan raincoat. It would only be the first of many such grim encounters on Blue Mountain.

Luckily Skidmore, still a deputy then, had been there to steady me. Since then he had saved my life more than once, and I his.

Unfortunately, on this particular evening so close to Christmas, he did not believe a word I was saying.

He hadn't bothered to dress in his police uniform. He'd pulled on a sweatshirt and hunting clothes. His hair was uncombed and his stubble was evident—a rarity in a man who sometimes shaved twice a day. He sat in the chair nearest to me while I stood over the fire, unable to get warm.

We had been talking for nearly a half an hour when the headlights of another car pierced the snow-raked darkness, and a second car pulled onto my lawn.

"That's probably Lucinda," I mumbled. "Wouldn't you think?"

Skidmore glared in silence while we listened to the car door slam, the single-syllable growl of complaint against the cold, and footsteps on the porch. The door opened very aggressively, and Lucinda Foxe burst into our world.

She stood, shaking snow from her dark green cardigan and wiping her boots on the indoor mat. She shook her head and muttered. Her hair was wet and she had no makeup on her face. She was astonishingly beautiful, despite her obvious pique.

At last she said, directly to me, "What the hell, Fever?"

"That's the third time she's cursed tonight," I said to Skidmore. "I'm glad you're here. I may need police protection."

"Don't look to me for help," Skid said, holding up his hands. "I side with her."

"Are you going to tell me what happened, or do I have to ask the nice sheriff to shoot you in the foot?" she wanted to know.

"I've just been telling Skidmore," I began.

"Start over," she interrupted. "I want to hear the whole thing."

She glided toward the other chair across from the sofa and collapsed into it with such a combination of grace and disgust that I thought she might have practiced it at home a few times before coming over.

"I fell asleep on the sofa," I told them both, feeling I had said the words at least a hundred times, "there was a knock on the door. I answered it. A woman, a total stranger, came into my house, told me she was my wife, apologized for something but I don't know what, then wanted Skidmore to kill her mother, *then* decided she would come back later to kill me—with potions. And then she vanished into the wintery midnight."

I sighed, realizing that my little speech sounded more like a dream than an actual event.

"Could this be any sort of after-effect of the coma?" Skidmore asked Lucinda, as if I weren't in the room.

"Could be," she said, a little more gently than she had spoken before.

A year ago, I'd been shot by an intruder in my own home. I'd been in that coma in the hospital, where Lucinda was the head nurse, for three months. So December was shaping up to be something of an uncomfortable month for me in general.

"Fever," Lucinda said very softly, "is there any possibility that this could have been a bad dream? When you were in the hospital, you had lots of dreams that seemed real, remember?"

"Yes," I said, a little more impatiently than I wish I had, "I remember, but this was nothing like that. Every time I woke up from one of those dreams in the hospital, I always realized they were dreams. I'm awake now—or *if* I'm awake now, which I think I am, then what happened was real. It was as real as this is, anyway— this conversation I'm having with you. I mean, you didn't hear her in my kitchen? She was the one who hung up the phone the first time!"

"He's still not awake," Lucinda said to Skidmore.

"He's not awake?" Skid asked, leaning forward.

"I'm awake," I protested. "Damn. Come into the kitchen, I'll show you the teacup she had in her hand!"

"I've done some research," Lucinda went on, ignoring me, "and I've talked with Dr. Nelson a number of times. Fever hasn't really been completely right all this whole year. Dr. Nelson reminded me about something called a *fugue state,* where a person can move around and talk but they're not completely aware of the real world. Sometimes it's a result of a partial seizure. Sometimes it's associated with trauma or even some generalized medical condition."

"What's it called again?" Skid asked.

"Fugue state," I answered, increasingly irritated. "And it's not what's happening to me. I haven't had a dissociative pathology or memory loss or a personality change. What I had was a strange woman in my house who wanted to kill me."

"I thought you said on the phone that she wanted to kill your mother," Lucinda said calmly.

"No," I snapped, "she wanted to kill *her* mother. She wanted Skidmore to kill *her* mother."

"And then she wanted Skidmore to kill you?" Lucinda pressed.

"No! Damn! She got upset with me when I told her that I didn't know who she was, and she said that she would cook up potions to kill me and no one would ever know."

Skidmore and Lucinda stared silently. It seemed an evening for a lot of that. Skidmore shook his head.

"But this woman vanished," he began. "You chased after her, but she was gone."

I hung my head. "I realize how this all sounds."

Lucinda reached into one of the side pockets in her cardigan. "I brought you a little shot, sugar," she began, "and I'll stay here with you tonight."

I'm not certain why I reacted so badly, but I nearly jumped backward, and felt an instant panic.

"I don't want a sedative," I said sharply. "I wouldn't mind if both of you stayed with me for the rest of the night, but I want to be wide awake."

Lucinda held the syringe in her hand, not moving. "You don't think you need your sleep?" she asked. "You know you haven't been sleeping well for a while."

"I've been sleeping just fine," I assured her.

But it wasn't true. I'd had vicious bouts of insomnia since coming out of the coma. So much so that I'd fallen asleep on the sofa more times than I wanted to think about because I hated the idea of going to bed—to a sleepless, angst-ridden bed.

"Fever." That's all Lucinda had to say. But in those two syllables were a soliloquy, a declaration of love and care, and a clear testament to her absolute conviction that I should take the shot she'd brought me.

"I can barely stand to climb the stairs and face my bedroom," I admitted. "What did Ahab say about sleep? 'That bed is a coffin, and those are winding sheets. I do not sleep, I die.'"

"What's he talking about?" Skidmore whispered to Lucinda.

"I don't know, exactly," she said.

"Not in the novel, maybe," I said in a misguided attempt to explain myself, "but it's in the movie, that quote. With Gregory Peck."

Lucinda stood up. "I told you," she said to Skidmore. "He's not completely awake."

I took another step backward, away from her.

"Look," I said. "I do have significant anxieties— I mean, in general. I do have sleepless nights, and the coma was definitely a traumatic phenomenon in my life. But I'm not in a fugue state right now and I'm not dreaming, and I'm not out of my mind. I have to stay awake."

Skidmore stood, too. "Well," he said, closing a small notepad that he'd been holding. "I have a description of the woman. She won't be hard to spot. Lock all your doors. Lucinda's going to stay with you. I'm going home to bed. Because I *don't* have trouble sleeping—except for certain people calling me in the middle of the damn night."

He pocketed his pad, pulled his coat around him, and headed for the door.

"You don't think we should go look for her now?" I asked, a little weakly. "She's out in this weather, not dressed for it, no car or shelter—shouldn't we be trying to find her?"

"Are you afraid of her," he asked me without looking back, "or worried about her?"

He pulled open the door.

"Both," I answered, as if that should have been obvious.

"Good night, Fever," he said, stepping onto the porch. "I'll talk with you again in the morning."

He closed the door behind him.

"Look," Lucinda said in her best nurse's voice, "I'm not going to wrestle with you to make you take this shot. But it's the same sedative we've been giving you since you started this insomnia business. Couldn't you use a good night's sleep, for once, sweetheart? And I'll be right here with you when you wake up in the morning."

I looked at the doorway where the strange woman had stood, and the spot on the sofa where she'd sat. I glanced into the kitchen at the dish drainer in the sink where her teacup was drying. Already I was forgetting exactly what she looked like, and the sound of her voice. Was it possible that she was, in fact, some sort of dream-state hallucination?

Then my eyes met Lucinda's.

"Okay," I said softly, rolling up my sleeve. "I guess I could use a good night's sleep at that."

"There you go," she said, moving my way, taking the cap off the syringe. "Everything looks better in the morning. It always does."

I don't remember a thing that happened after that, not walking up the stairs, not getting into bed, not sleeping, not dreaming. Nothing. I slept like the dead.

4

The next day was blinding. Snow was everywhere outside. Some-one had opened the bedroom window, the sun was pouring in, and my eyes were entirely unable to focus.

I was alone, but I could hear voices downstairs. As my head began to clear and my eyes became accustomed to the searing light, I realized that someone had straightened up my room. Lucinda usually left things as they were when she stayed over, but apparently she had thought to wrest order from chaos—or at least to try.

The chair beside the window, usually drowning in books and papers, was vacant. The shelves were tidied. The curtains were tied back, artfully, and the window shade was all the way up. That much light revealed that someone had swept and dusted my oth-erwise spare and simple quarters.

None of this cleanliness was typical of Lucinda, or anyone I knew, so I listened a bit more attentively to the voices down the stairs. They were in the kitchen. Two people talking—possibly Skidmore and Lucinda, but they were keeping their voices down. This was also uncharacteristic—of either. The final disturbing factor was the clock on the bedside table. It seemed to say that it was two o'clock. The sun was obviously out, which would suggest that it was two o'clock in the afternoon, but that was clearly impossible. I had never slept past seven in the morning in my entire life.

Then, slowly, I began to remember some of the events of the previous evening.

I threw myself out from under the covers and found that I was still in my clothes, sans shoes.

I had no recollection of coming up the stairs, getting into bed, but I did remember that Lucinda gave me a shot.

I checked my arm. There was a red, swollen mound where I'd had a slight reaction to the injection. I felt very odd. Unaccustomed to what might have been twelve hours of continuous sleep, I couldn't quite trust anything I saw. Everything looked strange.

Then, unfortunately, of all things, I remembered a sensation from the previous evening: the fear that I might somehow have been shifted to an alternate reality, one wherein I was kempt, married, and accustomed to sleeping twelve hours in my clothes. That fear threatened to expand to terror, so I called out.

"Hey!" I stood up. "What time is it really?"

The voices downstairs stopped talking for a moment, then both people laughed.

"So," Lucinda called, "you're awake."

Lucinda's voice—thank God.

"I'm awake," I answered, slipping into my boots and moving unsteadily toward the door, "but I might need to be carried down the stairs. What was in that shot?"

"You big baby," she called out cheerfully. "I gave you a tiny little bit of zaleplon, that's all."

I stumbled through the bedroom door and into the bathroom. Moments later I managed my way to the top of the stairs. I stared down at the living room, which had also been straightened up. Hand on the banister, I began to descend. The staircase looked a hundred yards long.

"The stuff you gave me, what is it?" I mumbled loudly.

"Lord." She came through the double archway to the kitchen and stood at the bottom of the stairs. "It's a non-benzodiazepine hypnotic. Makes you sleep."

"Yes," I agreed, lumbering down the stairs. "It certainly does that. I don't think I've slept for twelve hours straight in—ever."

"You needed it," she said.

"You cleaned up every room in the house?" I asked groggily.

"Yes. Come on in the kitchen, I'll set you up with some of that espresso you drink as if it's water." She disappeared back into the kitchen. "You should probably consider how that might affect your ability to sleep, all that espresso every day."

"It doesn't affect me the way it does other people," I growled.

I eked my way unsteadily down the steps and achieved the more stable floor portion of the lower level of my home with some difficulty. I rounded the doorway into the kitchen and was about to hold forth on the virtues of espresso when I caught first sight of the person at my kitchen table. It stopped me in my tracks.

"Oh," I said, because I couldn't, momentarily, think of anything else to say.

The woman at the kitchen table would have taken anyone's breath away. Her hair was completely white, a perfect match for the snow outside. Her face was astonishingly beautiful: clear dark eyes, vaguely olive skin, high cheekbones, soft features—the kind of face that always seems to be smiling in addition to whatever other expression it might be wearing.

"This is Dr. Nelson," Lucinda said, fussing with my espresso machine. "You have company. That's why I cleaned up."

I couldn't take my eyes off the woman at my kitchen table, and her gaze was equal to mine. She was dressed in a weathered, rust-colored jacket and sturdy khaki pants tucked into what looked like Russian military boots.

"Hello," she said.

"God. Yes. Excuse me," I stammered. "Hello. Sorry."

"You should sit down, sweetheart," Lucinda told me gently.

"Nurse Ratched, here, dosed me with horse tranquilizer last night," I explained, wheeling my way to a chair at the kitchen table, "and I'm not entirely certain about— about anything, actually."

Lucinda turned around, cup of espresso in hand. "Probably the wrong way to start off with the head of psychiatric studies at a certain state institution."

I think I blinked. "What?"

"I'm Ceridwen Nelson." Her hand shot out. "I'm a psychiatrist, and I'm sort of in private practice now, actually. Lucinda called me."

I took her hand, absolutely perplexed. "I'm sorry, your name is . . . ?"

"Ceridwen," she repeated, "with a hard C. It's Welsh or Celtic."

"I know," I assured her. "Ceridwen is a fertility goddess, a poetic muse, and even, sometimes, considered to be the Lady of the Lake in the Arthurian cycle."

She tightened her grip on my hand reassuringly. "Even groggy from the Sonata, your command of your discipline is impressive. Lucinda told me that would be the case."

"Sonata?" I answered weakly, letting go of her hand—with a bit of reluctance.

"That's the company name for the hypnotic I gave you," Lucinda said. Then she took a seat at the table and set my cup of espresso before me.

I stared down at the cup for a second, uncertain how to proceed. Then it came to me: drink the espresso. Maybe a few gears in the broken engine of the brain will engage and something will make sense. So I drank it down in one gulp.

"Dr. Nelson," I began.

"Ceri," she insisted, "if I can call you Fever."

I sat back, beginning to see what was going on.

"That depends," I said, as much to Lucinda as to Dr. Nelson. "Are you here to help me with the troubled woman who came to my house last night, or are you here to help Nurse Foxe convince me that I was dreaming?"

Dr. Nelson's smile grew brighter. "Which would you prefer?"

"Which would I prefer?" I snapped back.

"How about this," Dr. Nelson said, before I could get anything else out. "If the woman is real, I'll help her. If she's not, I'll help you."

"Either way, Fever," Lucinda said soothingly, "she's here to help, all right?"

I could tell that Lucinda was just indulging me, that she was certain the previous night's visitor had been, in fact, a dream—a lingering result of my coma. But Dr. Nelson was less transparent. She seemed genuinely committed to the concept of objectivity. She might actually have been willing to entertain either reality.

That notion calmed me down. I took a deep breath. The cobwebs in my cortex were clearing, and the day was, in fact, very beautiful outside. Lucinda had called Dr. Nelson out of love and concern. How could I object to that? And Dr. Nelson had come—why? Because she liked Lucinda? That wouldn't be hard to imagine. Everyone liked Lucinda. Because I would make an interesting and possibly publishable case study? Likely. Because she actually wanted to help another human being? That remained to be seen.

So I resolved to play along. After all, it would give me a chance to ascertain Dr. Nelson's true motives, and if it became apparent that she actually could help the troubled woman who thought that she was my wife, then it would be a great service to all.

"Thank you, Dr. Nelson," I told her, attempting to sound a bit sheepish. "I know you'll forgive my current state. I had something of a shock last night, and I've never slept so long in my life as I did after that. I'm a little at sea. But I'm very grateful for your help, really."

"All right, then." The doctor's smile remained. She sat back.

It was clear that she was already on the job, and not at all willing to show me what was on her mind.

"Good," Lucinda said, patting my hand. "Now I have to go home, change, and go to work. You'll be fine."

She stood.

I looked up at her. "I really love you."

Her head twitched, ever so slightly. "Bold talk in front of a stranger," she teased.

"Lucinda Foxe has saved my life in several ways, Dr. Nelson," I announced, "despite the fact that I am generally not as vocal about my feelings as I should be. You are currently witness to a somewhat sad attempt to rectify that deficiency in my character."

Lucinda put her hand on my cheek. "He's just showing off in front of company," she said, looking at me but speaking to Dr. Nelson. "I wonder why."

With that, Lucinda nodded to us both and was gone, in very short order, out of my front door.

5

I have no idea how long Dr. Nelson and I sat in my kitchen, silent, never achieving eye contact. It seemed like an hour.

At last she spoke. "I don't mind sitting here like this all afternoon," she told me, and seemed quite genuine. "I have kind of a hectic life elsewhere, and it's very nice for me to have to be still. Very nice. But eventually Lucinda is going to ask one of us what we did today, and I think it would be better if we had more to say than 'nothing.'"

I smiled. "Well, you're right about that. And I'd get the worst of it. I think she actually likes you at the moment."

"Well," Dr. Nelson said, "if you want her to like you again, you're going to have to explain your wife. Aren't you supposed to be marrying Lucinda this spring? How's that going to work?"

"That's not funny." I finally looked at her.

"It's a little funny." She smiled.

"Proving the adage that comedy is something that happens to someone else."

"That's an adage?"

"Actually I think it's better than an adage," I affirmed. "I'm pretty sure it's in Aristotle's *Poetics*."

"All right, so much for banter." She sat up. "This woman you saw last night, is she real or not?"

"What?" I found that my voice sounded shocked.

She stared. "Good. You're not sure. That's actually good."

"I'm not sure?" I scowled. "Of course I'm sure. She sat in my living room. She drank my tea."

I pointed to the pair of teacups in my dish drainer.

"Maybe." Dr. Nelson sat back. "But your initial reaction to my blunt and sudden question was to be startled. Most people react with a bit of anger if they're certain they're right, or with a touch of fear if they know they're wrong—or they've been lying."

I took the merest of seconds to reflect, and saw the merit of her gambit.

"I'm not sure," I admitted, staring at the top of the kitchen table.

"Good," she said again. "That's a perfect place to start. Lucinda filled me in on the coma, the dreams, and the traumatic events of the first part of this year. What she couldn't tell me is exactly how you're feeling now. She thinks you deliberately obscure your emotions. And, to your credit, she thinks you do that to spare her any extra anxiety where you're concerned."

"Extra anxiety?"

Dr. Nelson's smile grew bigger. Her face seemed to be filled with light. "My research in this case so far has revealed that everyone you know is worried about you."

"I—I'm a *case*?" I stammered. "You've been talking with people? About me?"

"Yes." That's all she would say.

"And they're worried about me?"

"Yes."

"Who, exactly, is worried about me?" I leaned forward.

"In no particular order," she answered, "Lucinda and most of the people at the hospital where she works, Skidmore Needle and everyone in the sheriff's office, your English professor friend Dr. Andrews . . ."

"Stop," I said, holding up my hand. "You've been asking all these people questions about me?"

"Yes."

"Stop saying *yes* that way."

"Okay."

I cocked my head. "You're exasperating."

"I don't mean to be," she said, but her voice sounded very amused.

"Is this some sort of interview?" I guessed. "Are you deliberately trying to provoke me, hoping my subconscious might slip out and, I don't know, explain everything?"

"Gee, wouldn't *that* be great." She put her elbows on the table. "But I don't see how I'm provoking you."

"Look," I said, determined to change the tenor of the scene, "I fell asleep on the couch last night. There was a knock on the door. I woke up, got up, and there she was: a deranged woman in black, a stranger claiming to be my wife, and then wanting to kill her mother. She left quite angry with me, and threatened to be back."

"Wait," she said, a little less amused than before. "She told you she'd be back?"

"Yes," I insisted, "I reported that to the sheriff last night. She said she'd come back and poison me."

"That's kind of good news." She looked out the window. "Either a real woman will come back to this house, or you'll hallucinate again. Either way, this could be put to rest immediately. All we need is for someone to stay with you all the time until something happens. That person will confirm the truth of the matter."

"You think someone should stay with me around the clock until this woman comes back?"

She nodded. "I do."

"Who might that be?" I asked.

"Me. That's what Lucinda asked me to do, in fact. I'm glad we've arrived at the same conclusion, you and I."

I pondered. Before we'd begun the peculiar dialogue, I might have been uncomfortable with the notion of spending too much time with Dr. Nelson because, if I were to be completely honest with myself, I'd found her attractive. But now that we'd had a chance to get to know one another a little better, any threat of further attraction seemed unlikely.

In fact, Lucinda had too many responsibilities at the hospital, and Skidmore could hardly afford to assign a deputy to be my constant companion. And just like that, it seemed the best idea in the world to have Dr. Nelson stay with me until my phantom wife returned.

"If you'd be willing to stay here with me," I said, my voice a little softer, "I would, as it turns out, be very grateful."

"Interesting," she said. "I could actually see your thinking process on your face while you were coming to that statement."

"You could?" I asked.

"Most people are transparent," she told me. "They don't think they are, which is cause for a lot of entertainment. If you really watch someone, really engage with them, really look into their eyes, you can always tell when they're telling the truth, when they're lying, when they're holding back, when they're sad or angry or upset."

"You mean that *you* can," I said. "You can tell all that."

"Anybody can do it," she said with a rather grand wave of her hand. "They just don't know they can do it."

"I don't know if I agree," I told her, "but I'm willing to investigate further. For example, the truth of all this—I mean your visiting me here today—is that Lucinda wanted you to come and observe me in my native habitat to see if I'd gone completely off my rocker."

She slapped the table lightly. "See? You can do it, too."

"I'm right."

"You're partly right. Lucinda is afraid, after last night, that there may be lasting damage from your coma."

I tried not to let that sink in too deeply, and I spoke out loud before I'd thought it through.

"If that's the case," I said softly, "Lucinda might want to call off the wedding."

Dr. Nelson blinked. "No. She's afraid you might blame her, because she caused your coma, about which she feels guilty, and she's afraid that *you* might call off the wedding."

I looked up. Dr. Nelson's face was nearly beatific. I couldn't help but smile.

"Gee," I said, "we really are a pair, Lucinda and I. Difficult to say, really, which one of us needs your help more."

She shook her head. "Oh, you need it much more. You're lots more messed up."

Again, I cocked my head. "Is that the right thing for an analyst to say?"

"I wouldn't know," she said happily. "I'm not exactly an *analyst*."

"All right, then." I rolled my eyes. "What would you call yourself?"

"I hardly ever call myself anything," she shot back. "But that's not really what you mean. You want to know what I think my job is here at the moment. Am I a babysitter, am I a psychiatrist, am I Lucinda's friend—right?"

"Right."

"Then I'd say that I am exactly like you, Dr. Devilin. I'm a well-educated oddity, someone who's interested in finding something out. I'm investigating. I want to know what happened. I want to solve a riddle. I find the research interesting completely on its own merits, without regard for subsequent achievement or goal. Isn't that about what you've been doing since you came back home to Blue Mountain however many years ago?"

I had to admit that she seemed to be saying something very true. I just didn't know how to respond, because her speech had set off a wildfire of personal reflection.

So I said, "Let's suppose that's true. Then why do we do it, you and I? Why do we chase all around looking to answer these inexplicable phenomena? What are we actually looking for?"

"Ah," she agreed, "that's really the question, isn't it?"

And then we sat in silence once more.

6

Dr. Nelson stood up eventually and went to the espresso machine. She tapped it and pushed a few buttons. Nothing happened. She exhaled, exasperated, and looked as if she might hit it before I got up to help her.

"I can get it," she said, a bit defensively.

"Had we but world enough, and time," I told her, "but you want espresso now, I think."

"All right." She sighed. "How does this thing work?"

"Simplicity itself," I told her.

I pushed a certain button and the machine began to growl. I took the cup from her hand and put it under the spigots. Almost instantly the cup began to fill.

"Voila," I said. "It's easy when you know how."

Before I could say anything else to taunt her, my kitchen window exploded and a bullet flew past our heads.

We both ducked, and neither of us made a sound. I noticed, with no small admiration, that Dr. Nelson had kept hold of her espresso cup. She hadn't spilled a drop.

"What was that?" she demanded to know.

"I think someone's fired a rifle into my kitchen," I said.

A second shot rang out, blasting a hole the size of a baseball in the tiles above my sink.

"I think we should keep down, don't you?" I whispered.

She tossed back her espresso and set the cup on the counter beside the machine.

"Okay," she said.

"I'm going into the living room to have a look out the front door window. It's shielded by the porch awning and harder to see into from the yard."

Without waiting for her to respond, I dashed for the front door. It had been replaced several times since I'd moved back home, and this particular door was a style that was sometimes called "craftsman"—strong oak in panels, a triptych of windows. I waited for more shooting, but silence ensued.

I rose slowly and took a quick peek out the window. I half-expected to see my ghostly bride—I may even have been hoping to see her, just so that I could prove to everyone, including myself, that she was real.

What I did see was, if possible, more unnerving. Standing in my yard was a boy of ten or twelve years, dressed in white snow camouflage, reloading his rifle.

I thought for a second that I might be seeing things—again.

"Dr. Nelson?" I said softly.

"What?"

"Could you come in here, please?" I moved away from the window for the moment.

"Why?"

"I want to see if you see what I see," I told her.

"Is it her?" she asked excitedly. "Is it your ghost?"

I could hear her moving quickly, and then she appeared, crouching low, right next to me.

"No," I answered. "It's a young boy."

"What?" She stood up.

I moved away from the window. "Be careful when you look out. I saw him reloading. He has a hunting rifle. I think it's a Remington 700 but there's no sight on it. He was reloading when I looked out just now."

She took my place beside the door and, lightning fast, looked out.

"There's a boy with a gun out there," she said, as if she'd discovered him.

"Yes."

"He's pointing the gun at the kitchen window again," she said in a stage whisper.

"All right."

I moved in a manner much more decisive than I felt, grabbed the door handle, and tore out onto the front porch before I could think better of it.

"Hey!" I yelled as loudly as I could. "What the hell are you doing?"

The boy was so startled that he took several steps backward, lost his footing in the snow, and fell down. I had been hoping for something like that effect.

I stomped down the steps, attempting to appear hulking.

"I said, 'What the *hell* are you doing?'" I snarled, bearing down on him.

I was only several steps off the porch, perhaps thirty feet away from him. He scrambled up, backing away. There was a mixture of rage and terror on his clear and rosy-cheeked face—Satan's cherub.

"Is that your new girlfriend?" he sneered. "If I see her here again, I won't miss. I'll shoot her in the head!"

With that he turned, jumped a little like a rabbit, and sprinted away faster than I could possibly have followed.

"That was impressive" were the words that came from behind me.

I turned around. Dr. Nelson was standing in the front doorway.

"Not my first bullets," I assured her. "I've been shot at lots of times. By grown men. You always hear that you should rush a gun and run from a knife. Especially if the gun is being wielded by a child of ten."

"Who was he?"

I headed up the steps. "So, you saw him."

"Of course I saw him." Her arms were folded in front of her and she was shivering.

The day was clear and cold; the snow made everything so bright that it was hard not to squint. The sky was blue and cloudless. There was no wind. For some reason I had the sensation, for a very brief moment, that the world had stopped turning, a kind of psychic vertigo. I closed my eyes and tried not to pass out.

"Fever?" Dr. Nelson said immediately.

I brushed past her through the doorway and into the house.

"I'm fine," I mumbled. "I'm a little dizzy."

"Oh, well, adrenaline is a weird drug," she told me. "*I'm* a little dizzy. Plus, I can't stop shaking."

I looked more closely. She was shivering from head to toe.

I smiled. "I've been shot at so many times in the past couple of years, I forget what it feels like for amateurs."

"I need to get warmer," she said calmly.

I went to the fireplace instantly, tossed on three more logs, poked the coals, and almost at once there was, if not a blaze, at least a warmer hearth.

"Lucinda made this fire," I guessed. "She always banks the coals this way. Makes it easier to get it going when you need to."

She nodded and sat down on the floor right in front of the fire.

"Are you sure you want to sit right there?" I asked her. "It's going to spark and pop a bit. Sometimes the embers fly out."

"You don't have a fireplace screen?" She was staring into the fire as if willing it to get hotter faster.

"No." I went into the kitchen. "I'm calling the sheriff's office. This is something he'll have to take a little more seriously."

"Yes" was all she said.

I dialed. The phone rang. Skidmore answered.

"All right, look," I began, "a ten-year-old boy shot out my kitchen window and then threatened to kill my visitor, Dr. Nelson."

"Fever?" he said.

"You have to come out here and see," I demanded. "I have no kitchen window!"

"Somebody shot out your whole kitchen window?"

"No, okay, he shot out one of the panes, but the second bullet busted some of the tiles over the sink. And Dr. Nelson is in mild shock."

"Very mild!" she hollered from the living room.

"Is that Ceri?" His voice betrayed genuine affection. I could actually hear that he was smiling.

"You know her?" I asked, not bothering to hide my surprise.

"Dr. Nelson has helped me several times over the years, Fever," he told me, as if it were something I should have known. "She's famous. She's been on television. Don't you think she looks a little like the young Emmylou Harris?"

"Who?" I asked.

"You can't be serious," he said loudly.

"What has she helped you with?" I asked very deliberately.

"Well, most recently she came to talk to us all about what was happening to you when you were in the coma," he said very directly. "Before that she helped us figure out some things about Truevine Deveroe, or, Truevine Carter now."

Truevine had been a shy young woman who'd lived in the more remote reaches of our community with a pack of wild brothers. Because she'd been strange, and beautiful, she'd been tormented by bullies of both genders—labeled a witch. Of course, it had been mostly teasing, but Truevine did have abilities that had been difficult to explain. She was now happily married to Able Carter and living in Athens, Georgia, with a baby daughter.

"What about Truevine?" I asked.

"I took her to the Rhine Center in Durham," Dr. Nelson answered. "Don't ask him anything more about her. Tell him about the boy with the gun!"

"Yes," I said instantly, "there was a boy with a gun. Dr. Nelson saw him. I'm definitely not imagining this."

"Damn, Fever," Skidmore said, laughing, "you're a pestilence. Every time I turn around, somebody wants to shoot you."

"Actually," I snapped, "I think the kid was trying to kill Dr. Nelson. He seems to think that she's my new girlfriend."

"Who was he?" Skidmore was instantly more serious.

"Wait," I objected, "when it's me that's getting shot, it's a joke, but when it's Dr. Nelson . . ."

"Fever," he interrupted, "did you know the boy?"

"No."

"Where is he now?"

"He ran away. I chased him and he ran away but he threatened to come back and shoot Dr. Nelson in the head."

There was a silent pause.

"You chased after some crazy boy who had a rifle?" Skidmore asked slowly.

"Yes."

"Lord." Skid sighed. "How was he dressed?"

"White," I answered, "like a snow-season hunting getup."

"Any other description?"

"I couldn't see much. The snow was really blinding. I couldn't tell hair color or anything, but I'd judge him to be between ten and twelve years old."

"Are you all right?" he said, the sound of his voice sweetening.

"I'm never going to match these tiles in the kitchen. They've been here since before the Flood."

"Yes," he said, "that's your biggest problem."

"My biggest problem is that a strange woman came into my home last night and no one will believe that it happened," I shot back. "Second, there's a psychiatrist in my house, shivering in my living room, who's going to catch on fire if she doesn't move away from the front of the fireplace. Third, I have to get something to cover the broken part of my kitchen window because it's cold in here already. Fourth . . ."

"Stop," he said. "Just what does Dr. Nelson have to say about the woman you saw last night?"

"Why do you want to know that?" I asked him.

"Fever." His voice was strained.

I lowered the receiver. "Dr. Nelson? The sheriff wants to know if I'm crazy or not."

"Jury's still out," she called affably.

"You heard?" I asked Skidmore. "So if the woman *was* here last night, then she and the boy today might be connected."

"I doubt it," he said, "but I am currently not ruling out any possibility."

"Well." I heaved a sigh. "That's a start."

"I'll be right over. You need me to bring something to cover the window?"

"No. Thanks."

"Right." He hung up.

"You took Truevine Deveroe to the Rhine Center?" I asked Dr. Nelson, hanging up my phone and heading back into the living room.

"Not going to talk about that," she insisted.

"My parents took me there when I was little," I told her, sitting down on the sofa.

The fire had increased nicely, and was very hot. I still feared that my guest would catch fire, but she seemed content.

She turned to look at me. "You went there when it was still called the Foundation for Research on the Nature of Man. I already know this."

"Yes, it was still in that dilapidated old building," I continued, pretending not to care that she knew about my past, "on Buchanan Avenue."

She locked eyes with me. Her face was red from the heat. "Have you seen the new facility on Campus Walk?"

"No," I told her.

She turned back around. "You know the new place was the first building in the world built expressly for parapsychological research."

"Yes." I looked into her eyes.

"Why do you think your parents took you there?" she asked softly. "To the old building, I mean."

"They were afraid of me."

She turned back around and stared even more deeply into the fire. "They weren't afraid of you," she said gently, "they were afraid of the things you saw, the things you could do."

"They were afraid that they might have been responsible for my strangeness," I told her. "They felt guilty. I've always wondered how that affected their relationship."

She cleared her throat and began to stand up. "Well," she said, "this has been quite an afternoon for my little investigation."

"You're welcome," I said coldly.

She rubbed her eyes and took a seat in the chair across from me. She'd stopped shivering.

"So, are you psychic?" she asked casually.

"No idea," I told her. "I took lots of tests and did lots of things, most of which I don't remember very well. My parents never shared any of the 'findings' with me."

"Never?" She shook her head.

"Hints and allegations," I said, smiling. "But never any real information."

"You're not curious?" she asked, leaning forward.

"Very," I answered. "I guess I've always been a little reticent to— I don't really want to be any stranger than I already am."

"I can certainly understand that." She smiled.

"I have to cover the window in the kitchen." I stood.

I glanced out the picture window behind Dr. Nelson. I saw something moving in the shadows of the trees beyond the blinding yard. I thought it might be a deer, but it was black. I took a step around the coffee table trying to get a better look.

"What?" Dr. Nelson asked, turning around to look out the window. "Is he back?"

"No." I took a few quick steps to the window.

The shadows converged, and there was only a sense of movement, an innuendo, an inflection. But for some reason I wheeled around to face Dr. Nelson. I couldn't tell, at that moment, what had made me remember something important.

"I think I forgot to mention something to Skidmore and to Lucinda," I said, and I could hear that my voice sounded hollow. "Something that my visitor told me last night."

Dr. Nelson stood. "What is it? What did she say?"

I turned back around to see if I could make out a black form in the midst of black shadows, a tall woman in a dress and shawl. I couldn't be certain. My eyes were blinded by the white lawn.

"She told me," I answered Dr. Nelson, "that there was a child."

7

I spent the next twenty minutes taping a too-large square of quarter-inch plywood over the hole in my kitchen window, with duct tape. I knew I probably should have left everything alone until Skid could look at the scene, but it was cold.

Dr. Nelson made several attempts to amplify my notion that the boy who'd shot out my window might be the child my phantom wife had mentioned. When that failed, because I really hadn't known what to say, she'd made several phone calls. I gathered, though I did my best not to eavesdrop, that she was rearranging her schedule to spend more time with me. When she was finished, my work at the window was done and I called Lucinda to apprise her of the most recent events. I only succeeded in convincing her not to come back to my house after telling her three times that Dr. Nelson and I were all right and that Skidmore was on his way. She insisted that I hand the phone to Dr. Nelson, who confirmed that we were fine, and that there was no need for Lucinda to leave the hospital. After that Dr. Nelson and I sat at the kitchen table and waited for the sheriff to come.

"It's a nice kitchen," she said, taking it in. "Cozy."

"It is," I agreed. "And except for the espresso machine, it's exactly the same as it was when I was a child. Or *was,* until somebody shot holes in it."

"You think the boy who shot at us might be the child of the woman you saw last night?" she asked again.

"I don't know." I was staring at the wrecked tiles over the sink. "I'll have to retile the whole thing."

"You're concerned about finding the tiles to replace the ones—the tiles . . ." but she couldn't quite seem to discover the perfect way to finish her sentence, for some reason.

"Don't you feel a little weird about what Lucinda wants you to do?" I asked her. "I mean, especially after this—shooting event—doesn't it seem odd for you to be investigating me or examining me or whatever it is you'd call it?"

"I feel uncomfortable because you don't want me here," she said, "and because we're a little attracted to each other. But I actually do this sort of thing all the time. I think that the sheriff might have mentioned that I've worked with him before. In a very official capacity. Lucinda and I have known each other professionally for years. It's really a little remarkable that you and I have never met. I mean, I've certainly heard a lot about you in one way or another over the past several years."

I folded my arms. "We're a little attracted to each other?"

"Well, I'm a little attracted to you," she said plainly, "and I'm also a keen observer of human nature, as I may have mentioned, and I can tell how you feel about me."

"Do people usually find your observations annoying? I mean when they're transparent and you see through them, are they irritated?"

"It's about fifty-fifty," she answered cheerfully.

A car roared into the yard, going too fast for the snow. I craned my neck around the plywood and made out Skidmore's patrol car.

"Sheriff's here," I said.

"In the nick of time." She stood.

I could hear him slam the car door and stomp up the steps. I made it to the doorway just as he was barging in.

"You saw one boy?" he asked, a little out of breath.

"Hi," I said.

"One boy?" he asked again impatiently.

"Yes. Do you want some . . ."

"Because there were at least two sets of prints out there in the woods along the road, past your yard," he told me, taking off his hat.

"Two sets?" I nodded. "I thought I saw something else. I think it was the woman."

I closed the door.

Skid glanced at Dr. Nelson as she came into the living room.

"Did you see her?" Skid asked Dr. Nelson. "This woman?"

"No," she said, "just the boy. But the boy did ask Fever if I was his girlfriend, and said something about shooting me in the head."

"He told me," Skid said, nodding in my direction. "And neither of you recognized the boy?"

"Never saw him before in my life," I said.

Dr. Nelson shook her head.

"No better description than what you told me on the phone?" he asked.

"I only glanced at him for a second," Dr. Nelson said.

"He had a gun," I reminded Skidmore. "I looked at that more than I did at his face."

"He might have had blond hair," Dr. Nelson said.

"Really?" Skid asked me.

"I didn't notice," I answered. "What about the footprints?"

"Footprints in the snow," he said, shaking his head, "are the worst. They deteriorate almost as soon as they're made, especially when the sun's this strong. Plus, the two people met up and ran together, so that also tore up the prints."

"Doesn't this give a little credence to my story about the woman visiting my house last night?" I asked them both.

They both answered as one: "No."

"Why not?" I whined.

"Fever," Skidmore began, "you've been back home for, what? Eight, nine years now? In that time you have found countless dead bodies; dozens of people have tried to kill you. You've been nearly killed a half a dozen times, and legally dead twice. You've seen ghosts, witches, time travelers, racist murderers, and an albino dwarf! So some wild boy shooting up your house a couple of days before Christmas? That's just another ordinary day in your life. As for seeing this woman last night, I've come to take nearly everything you *ever* say with about a half a pound of salt."

"Add to that," Dr. Nelson chimed in, "the fact that you're currently under a psychiatrist's care, so all of your perceptions are called into question."

"*That* should have happened a long time ago," Skid agreed.

"I am not currently under a psychiatrist's care!" I protested.

"Like it or not," Dr. Nelson said, "I am a psychiatrist, and you are a legally verifiable patient of mine. Lucinda Foxe hired me. I've been paid; I have a contract. Sorry. Lucinda should have told you that."

I stared at both of them for a second, unable to decide how I felt about what she'd said.

"Lucinda *hired* you?" I asked, a bit weakly.

"She should have told you," Dr. Nelson repeated softly. "Or I should have. I don't like to use the word *hired,* but I'm assigned to your case, officially as a follow-up to your hospital care from earlier this year. I'm to 'assess your competency.'"

"Did you know about this?" I asked Skidmore.

He nodded. "Lucinda and I talked about it. It was her suggestion, but I helped her to make the decision awhile back. It was already kind of in the works at the hospital anyway. I'm a little surprised you didn't know that."

I looked back at Dr. Nelson. "You're not just here to talk with me as a favor to Lucinda."

"Look," Dr. Nelson said, not unsympathetically, "I tried to explain to you that Lucinda has some guilt about your condition. She thinks she might have caused some sort of brain damage when she packed you in ice and snow last year to keep you alive. Or to keep you from being completely dead. Apparently you were dead when she got here after you'd been shot. So, no, it's not just a favor to Lucinda. It's much more complicated than that, and it's not just Lucinda. The hospital administration has legal questions about Lucinda's actions, and there are possible charges pending against her. The hospital lawyers are worried about possible litigation from you. It was all beginning to die down, of course, because it didn't look like you were going to sue the hospital, and you and Lucinda are about to get married. Lucinda's probationary period was over. Things were just about back to normal. Then you had this episode last night."

"It wasn't an *episode*," I insisted, but a good deal of the fire had gone from my convictions.

"Fever," she said sweetly, "you're a strange man, and you're in an even stranger place right now, mentally and emotionally speaking. You probably can't see how very, very odd it is that you called your fiancée in the middle of the night to tell her that your wife was in your living room. I mean, as I understand it, this isn't even *your* ordinary weirdness—which has, as I have learned, a fairly wide latitude."

"But," I began.

"There's something quite troubling going on with you," she assured me, "and I can probably help."

"But what about this boy, this shooting?" I asked them both.

"This incident with the boy?" she answered. "It's what I like to call *ancillary madness*. When someone like you gets this far into trouble, you become a magnet for all kinds of strange things. Not just you. It happens to lots of people, really. In your case, though, I think it may have been going on with you for quite some time.

Even before your coma. You're a kind of psychic magnet for bizarre events. But the condition has clearly gotten worse since you were in your coma—or, really, since you died. And there we have it. That's primarily what interests me. That's why I'm here."

"I don't understand," I told her, feeling a rising anxiety, like a giant horse about to leap out of my chest.

"I think you died," she answered solidly. "I think that when *that* happened, a certain kind of psychic energy attached itself to you, and you brought it back with you. It acts like a magnet for— for all kinds of things. To make matters worse, or to exaggerate the effects of this energy: I think you're stuck, right now, between life and death. You see and experience things—and they're all real to you—but the rest of us can't see them, or know them, or understand them."

"That's why you think you're here?" I asked. "To help with that?"

I glanced at Skidmore. He looked almost as upset as I felt.

"It's not exactly what I told Lucinda," she went on, "or the hospital, or the sheriff, here—but, yes. That's why I'm here. To pull you out of the doorway because you're stuck between life and death."

I swallowed hard, staring into her eyes. She sounded insane to me, and I knew that Skidmore had already decided she was in worse shape than I.

The problem was, I agreed with her. I believed every single syllable of what she'd said. And I was terrified.

8

In 1927, Joseph Rhine and his wife Louisa came to Duke University with the idea of investigating, in a scholarly way, psychic phenomena. By 1935 these investigations had produced enough evidence to warrant the establishment of the Duke Parapsychology Laboratory. Naturally, this work met with great skepticism in the academic world. In 1965, close to retirement and fearing that colleagues might discontinue his life's work, Rhine moved his laboratory off campus. He created an organization called the Foundation for Research on the Nature of Man, which was supported by, among others, the founder of Xerox. In 2002 a new building was constructed expressly to house the Rhine Center and its work. It was built in western Durham, close to the Duke Medical Center.

My parents had taken me to the old building when I was eleven years old or so. I'd made the mistake of telling my mother that I'd seen an angel. When questioned about it, I did further damage to my credibility with both of my parents by telling them that I saw other people in the house all the time, shadow people. Some were like laundry on a line, waving in a gentle breeze. Some were like the steam from a teakettle. Some were like ordinary people who came into the house, sat down, smiled, and talked with me.

This had been enough to send my mother into a frenzy of accusations: I was lying, or, alternately, I'd been put up to the whole thing by my father in an effort to drive my mother out of her mind. Both suggestions were ironic, I'd thought at the time, since my mother and the truth rarely existed in the same county at the same time. If anything, it would be my mother who drove my father mad.

Ultimately it had been my father's suggestion that I go to a place in North Carolina about which he'd heard, a center where some people took seriously the idea that an eleven-year-old boy might not be crazy if he saw things that other people didn't see.

I don't remember much about my experience at the Center. I was asked a lot of questions, hypnotized, given several tests. I do remember speaking with a woman who was very calm, very reassuring. I remember that she made me feel better, but I don't remember what she said or did to accomplish that.

We came back home, my parents and I, without discussing, even for a second, what had happened in North Carolina. They never spoke of it again unless I asked them about it, which I rarely did. And when I saw strange things in my room or the yard or, later, at the university, I absorbed them. I thought of it as nothing more than a phenomenon like any other: there's a tree, there's a friend, there's a transparent Viking.

Surreal as this often made my world, the world itself more than rose to meet the challenge. Advertising, world events, news coverage—everyday television—all seemed inspired by Fellini or Dali or Hieronymus Bosch more than by any so-called normal human being. Cows painted billboards, banks needed money, and wars were televised live. A little madness seemed an essential quality for survival in a world like that.

Furthermore, I believed that if people couldn't see the things I saw, they just weren't paying attention.

So, folded into ordinary existence, these so-called paranormal phenomena of my life went along quite happily hand in hand with everything else.

Most of the time.

"Fever?"

Skidmore's voice snapped me out of my trancelike thoughts and memories, and there I was, in my kitchen, with Dr. Nelson, who feared I was quite disturbed, and Sheriff Needle, who was certain I was out of my mind.

"Sorry," I said, "what were we talking about?"

Dr. Nelson and Skidmore exchanged a glance.

"Doesn't matter," Skidmore mumbled. "Point is: I got to go look for that boy who shot up your house."

He stood, scraping his chair on the kitchen floor.

"I'm going with you," I said immediately.

"No you're not," he fired back. "You're staying right here."

"Skid, look," I began, "this kid, he shot into the house to scare Dr. Nelson. I don't know why, but that's what his motive seemed to be."

I turned to Dr. Nelson.

"Well," she said, and shrugged, "he's right. The kid threatened me, not Dr. Devilin."

"So I'm not really at risk from him." That was my argument, admittedly thin.

"No," the sheriff said, shaking his head vehemently, "you're not going to go out there in those woods to wander around and get shot by some aggravated child!"

"I have a little something at stake here," I told him. "I want to prove to everyone that the woman I saw last night is real, and that the aggravated child is her son. It seems obvious to me, and I want to make it obvious to everyone else."

"By sloshing through the snow after a boy with a gun," Skid retorted reasonably. "That's what you think is best."

"I want to find him so that I can ask him about his mother. Yes, Sheriff, that's what I want to do. And then I want to bring the mother here and get Dr. Nelson to use her voodoo to help that woman, who is significantly more deranged than I am. And then I want almost everyone to go away so that I can have a nice quiet rest until, maybe, spring."

A moment of silence ensued before Dr. Nelson said, quietly, "Voodoo?"

"I can't just sit here in the house and wait for something to happen to me," I said very deliberately. "I have to do something. Anything. I can't just sit here."

Skidmore was about to say something when Dr. Nelson beat him to it. "You want to define the parameters of your *dasein*, not the other way around."

"Exactly," I said, and looked at Skidmore.

He stared. "I don't know what that means. Not at all. But if I have learned anything over the long course of our friendship, it would be that you'll do what you want no matter what I say. I can tell you 'no' all day long, and it won't do a bit of good if you've already got 'yes' in your head."

"Yes," I said.

"Okay then," he said haplessly. "Get your coat on. You stick with me, though. No going off on your own and I mean it."

Dr. Nelson scrambled. "I'm not staying here by myself."

"Maybe you should just go home," I suggested, sounding a little colder than I'd meant to.

"No," she said, not the least bit offended. "You have to find out what you have to find out, and I need answers to my own questions. So, I stay. Or, I mean, I go into the woods with you."

"Ceri," Skidmore said, "I may not have told you this before, but I only understand about half of what you say. Ever."

She smiled. "Me too," she said.

I headed for the living room and my coat. "It's been at least a half an hour since the boy was here," I said. "We should really get moving."

"Even though the footprints are not good for much in the way of forensics," Skidmore told us, moving toward the front door, "they will give us a fairly obvious path to follow."

Dr. Nelson pulled her coat around her and followed Skidmore out the door, and I was close behind. Down the front porch and into the snow, the three of us made our way fairly easily for a while.

Beyond what might be referred to as my front yard there was a road. Other than that, the woods were more or less what they had been for thousands of years, and they were thick with a rather remarkable variety of larger trees, black walnuts, scarlet oaks, white pines, hickories, ashes, maples. The underbrush was nearly impassable with Mountain-laurel, but other shrubs impeded progress: rusty blackhaw, littlehip hawthorn, and Red Buckeye. Beautyberry stood out here and there, mostly purple, against the snow. And the trail of footprints slogged through the worst and most difficult parts of the mountainside, weaving incoherently to and fro. Within twenty minutes, I was winded.

"These footprints don't seem to have an aim or pattern," I said, white ghosts of frozen breath surrounding my face.

The day was lovely, really. The sun high and white, the sky a thick blue glass through which a crescent moon and, I imagined, several planets could be seen.

"They're going in a circle, more or less," Skidmore panted.

"There are definitely two sets of prints," Dr. Nelson said. "Look."

We'd come to rest in a small clearing, about five square feet of open space beside an ancient pine. It appeared to be a place where our quarry had also rested for a moment. Two sets of prints were indeed visible: a larger pair of women's boots and a smaller, child's shoes.

I looked around. "You're right, I think," I said to Skid. "We are going in a circle. If we keep going this way, we'll head past my house and down the mountain."

"How can you tell?" Dr. Nelson asked, trying to get her bearings.

"I grew up in these woods. I spent more time here than I did in that house. I've stopped in this same place, by this same tree, a hundred times before."

"Of course," she said quickly. "Sorry."

I looked at her profile. She was wearing an odd sort of secret smile. The sunlight made her hair seem made of the same snow that was on the tree limbs, and her face was alabaster and roses.

"Was that part of your examination of my faculties?" I asked her.

She started to say something, then obviously thought better of it, and settled on, "Yes."

"Okay," Skid said, and launched off into the maze of laurels.

I followed him; Dr. Nelson followed me.

In no time we were headed downward. The slope was slight, but the progress was easier. Skid got a little ahead of me, and when I hurried to catch up I heard Dr. Nelson whisper.

"Fever," she said.

I could barely hear her. I turned around. She was holding several strands of black thread that had caught on one of the laurel branches.

"Didn't you say that your visitor last night was dressed in black?" she asked me, still whispering.

I nodded.

"And the boy was in white today," she went on, "I saw that."

I turned back around to call out to the sheriff, but Dr. Nelson touched my arm.

"Wait," she said.

She pointed to the ground. At first I couldn't see what she was pointing to, but after a second it was obvious that something was wrong with the pattern of snow just below the laurel branch.

I knelt. It was impossible for me to be certain, but it appeared as if there was only one set of prints, the boy's prints, in the snow from that point on. It was as if the woman had simply vanished.

I looked up.

"I don't see two sets of prints from here on," I said softly.

"Right," she agreed.

"Skidmore!" I called out.

My voice was much louder than I'd thought it would be. I could hear animals scrambling in trees and several irate crows complained.

"I wish you hadn't done that," Dr. Nelson said, shaking her head.

"Why?" I asked, getting to my feet.

Skid appeared through the dense branches a second later.

"What is it?" I couldn't tell if he was concerned or irritated.

"Dr. Nelson discovered something important." I pointed.

She held up the branch from which the black threads hung.

"What is that?" he asked, coming closer.

"I think they're threads from the clothing worn by my imaginary visitor from last night," I told him. "And there's more."

"After this point," Dr. Nelson said, "there's only one set of prints. The boy's."

Skid's head snapped back, he scowled, and then began to examine the snow around us.

"Damn it," he muttered, "we walked all over these prints. Hang on. Stay right here."

He took off again and vanished down the slope. I imagined he was going to the place where he'd stopped when I'd called out, to see if there were one or two sets of prints.

I turned to Dr. Nelson. "Why did you say you wished I hadn't called out?" I asked her.

"Because it might not just be the sheriff who heard you," she said. "Anyone could have heard you."

I instantly saw her point: if the people we were pursuing had been anywhere on the mountainside, they would have heard my voice. I'd alerted them to our presence.

"You know," I told her, "considering that it isn't exactly your field, you're doing fairly well at this investigation."

She nodded. "I'll tell you what I believe. I believe that if you can do anything well, anything at all, you can do everything well. If you can make a really good loaf of bread, and you need to repair your car, all you have to do is fix the car the way you'd make the bread. Even if you don't know a spark plug from a toadstool, you'll be able to figure it out."

I glared. "Now you're just deliberately goading me," I said.

"What do you mean?" She seemed genuinely surprised by my reaction to her comments.

"You know very well what I mean," I snapped. "That's my story. What you just said. That's what I tell people. It comes from a— it's a Taoist story about a tea master and a swordsman. They're traveling together and night comes. The swordsman is tired. A gang of robbers comes at them. The swordsman says, 'I'm too tired to fight them, you do it.' And the tea master says, 'No, I make tea. They have swords.' And the swordsman says, 'Take my sword and fight the fight exactly the same way as you would make the tea.' The tea master understands, takes up the sword, and stands in the road to face the robbers. They see him, know that he'd already won because he's a master, and take off in the other direction."

"Yes." Her smile was an impossible combination of delicacy and aggression. "That is a good story."

"So you admit that you're— I don't know what you're doing," I stammered, "but stop it."

Before she could respond, Skidmore reappeared. "One set of prints. Damn."

He was breathing hard, and was now clearly irritated. He came to a halt in front of the laurel branch with the black threads attached.

He stared at the threads for a moment, then at the ground,

then looked all around. But the underbrush was so thick, even in winter, that people could have been standing within fifty feet of us and we wouldn't have seen them.

The sheriff sighed very heavily. "If I had a deputy here," he complained, "one of us would look around these parts and the other one would keep going after the footprints in the snow."

"Good," Dr. Nelson said immediately, "then I propose that you go after the boy with the gun and Fever and I wander around here looking for the phantom woman in black."

She and I looked at Skidmore.

"God Almighty piss damn and *piss*," he whispered.

"I know I've mentioned this before," I told him, smiling, "but your language has gotten a lot worse since you became sheriff. When we were boys, you would never curse."

"That's cursing?" Dr. Nelson asked me, disingenuously. "That's not cursing. I've heard patients . . ."

"Fine!" Skidmore growled. "You two look around here. I'll go down the mountain. Either of you have a watch?"

Dr. Nelson held up her arm to reveal a very expensive piece of jewelry that looked spectacular and also told time.

"No matter *what*," he insisted, "we meet back at Fever's house in exactly half an hour from now. Right?"

"Half an hour's not long enough to—" I began.

"Half an hour!" he stormed.

"Right," Dr. Nelson said immediately.

With another monstrous sigh, Skidmore was gone.

9

For an instant there was silence again. No birds, no wind, not even the sound of my own breathing. That silence, combined with the white snow and the limbs, the occasional evergreen and the chiseled air, all seemed to conspire to give the landscape a floating, dreamlike aspect.

Then Dr. Nelson turned to me. "Is he always that grouchy?"

"He didn't used to be," I told her, "but I've given him a lot to worry about, and being sheriff around here is surprisingly difficult."

"Really?" She looked around. "It seems so peaceful."

"So does a corpse, if you don't know what's eating at it from the inside," I said, relishing the image just a little too much.

"Lovely." She shook her head.

"So I'm going to start here and make a spiral," I said, beginning to walk around the laurel tree with the black threads attached.

"What?" she asked.

"I'm going to make a spiral," I repeated. "It's the most efficient way to proceed in searching for anything from a single point."

She only thought about it for a second before she agreed and came to my side.

I stopped. "What are you doing?"

"Making a spiral," she told me.

"No," I corrected her. "I'm making a spiral. It's a one-person enterprise."

"Then what am I doing?" she asked without a trace of ire.

"You're staying here at the center of the spiral to examine the bush and the threads and the snow more carefully," I answered, "to see what we've missed. You're the one who spotted the threads. And that was just while you were walking by. Who knows what you might see if you take the time to examine the scene more thoroughly."

She looked down at the snowy ground underneath the laurel. "The place where her footprints stop does look odd."

"There you are," I said, and resumed my ever-widening circular patrol.

"You actually are good at this," she said.

"Again"—I sighed—"not my first time."

She nodded, but it was clear that she was already lost in concentration, staring at the base of the shrub.

Good, I thought, now she'll leave me alone.

I made my way more-or-less spirally around and around the spot where she was, but it wasn't easy. I had to dodge other laurel branches in the thicket and work my way around sudden dips rendered unperceivable by the snow.

The woods were quiet. Soft snow and windless cold seemed to muffle sound, although the air was clear. Or was it that things were silent on purpose? Was there something in the woods, something close by, that hushed the birds and squirrels, even the wind?

I glanced up occasionally to make certain I was still maintaining a relatively concentric pattern, but most of my concentration was on the snow at my feet, the branches through which I fought, the occasional sudden movement out of the corner of my eye. As

I got farther and farther away, I lost sight of Dr. Nelson's rust-colored jacket altogether.

Then, without warning, I came upon a flock of crows, twenty feet away from me. I was just beginning to wonder why my clumsy stumbling and heavy breathing hadn't already frightened them away when I saw the blood.

Black crows, white snow, and red blood surrounded an unidentifiable carcass. It was large, and freshly dead. There was steam rising up from its flayed abdomen.

I froze. A single crow looked in my direction. The rest continued their grisly work. The staring crow seemed to assess me, then blinked, and went back to its gnawing.

I craned my neck, trying to see what it was they were eating. My heart was hammering in my ears and my breathing, already labored, threatened me with hyperventilation. I didn't want to imagine that the crows had come across a dead body, a human body, but the thing in the snow was the right size and approximate shape to be a human being.

Just as suddenly as I had stopped, my wits returned and I rushed the bloody scene. The crows scattered at once, raising an ear-shattering alarm. Their cries seemed to crack the cold air, and their wings, momentarily, blotted out the sun.

I stared down at the dead thing. It was a young deer. The birds had done damage, but the obvious bullet wound across the top of the head was likely what killed the deer. The animal seemed too young to be legally killed, but I wasn't very knowledgeable about hunting regulations. I did know it was illegal to kill the animal and just leave it like this.

I knelt down. The steam from the carcass was beginning to wane. The wound on the head, however, was dried and even crusted a bit. I surmised that the animal had been shot, wounded, and had run away from its assailant. It survived for a while, but eventually came to rest in the snow, where the crows had found it. It hadn't been dead for long.

There was a sudden snap behind me and a voice whispered, "He didn't mean to do that."

I whirled around, still crouching, to see the woman in black, my phantom bride.

I stood quickly. "The boy did this?" I demanded.

"He didn't mean to." Her face was stricken. She was clearly disturbed by the sight. "He was trying to get us some food. We haven't eaten in some time."

"Look," I said harshly, taking a step toward her, "I can't have a little boy running around these woods with a rifle shooting up my house and leaving deer to die. And I can't have people thinking that I'm crazier than I actually am. So you're coming with me."

I took another step and she took off running.

She raced up the slope, and I did my best to keep up. But she was astonishingly nimble, and I was already winded.

"Why won't you forgive me?" she called out, an anguished sound.

"I'll forgive you if you come back down to my house with me," I panted, barely aware of what I was saying.

She stopped. She was, perhaps, thirty or forty feet away from me, partly hidden by bare limbs and holly boughs.

"You will?" she said weakly.

I stopped, too, though in truth I might not have been able to go on much farther no matter what.

"Yes," I gasped. "I'll forgive you."

"I'm jealous of her, you know," she said. Her voice was like the creaking of tree branches and the moaning of the wind. "I don't have any right to be, but I'm jealous of that woman in your house."

I stared at her. The face was contorted by a certain kind of madness, a dizzying array of wants and needs and fears.

"I don't know who you mean," I said, and it was true.

"The one with the white, white hair, like Noah's dove," she sobbed.

"No," I said instantly. "That's Dr. Nelson. She's not a person that— she's not someone who should cause you any disturbance, she's a— she's a doctor who's trying to help me. I was in the hospital for a long time earlier this year."

"Dr. Nelson?" was all she would say for a moment.

I inched toward her, trying not to be too obvious about my intention to lay hands on her.

"And the other one," she said, looking away, obviously thinking. "She wore a nurse's costume once or twice."

"Yes, exactly," I told her. "I'm under medical care."

She turned her full attention on me and I stopped moving.

"But I can help you better than they can," she said, taking a few tentative steps my way. "I have medicine—potions that can make you well. I think you know that. Or you remember it, I mean."

"Well, yes, of course I remember," I lied. "And I could certainly use your help."

"Yes," she said, her voice suddenly filled with benevolence. "You need my help."

She kept coming my way. I thought it best, then, to stay put, waiting.

"Naturally"—she continued in her more loving vein—"I'm more concerned that you forgive your nephew. That's a bond, the bond between the two of you, that I hated breaking. I wouldn't have done it for the world. I want to heal that too. You must forgive him most of all."

"My nephew?" I asked before I could think better.

She stopped coming toward me and I instantly wished I hadn't asked the question, but as I actually had no nephew, the words had come out of my mouth without much help from my conscious brain.

She cast her head downward. "Why do you delight in taunting me? I know I deserve it, but you were never cruel. Not until now."

"Yes," I said, instantly. "My nephew. You're right. I should forgive him, too."

There, I determined, that's it. Say whatever it is she wants to hear until you get her back to the house where *anybody* else can see her. Sort out the rest after that.

But she shook her head. "You'll never truly forgive him, I know that. I had hopes, once, that the two of you would reconcile, and he could return to us. But that will never happen now. He's dying. Away, off in a foreign land."

There was such an overwhelming sadness in her voice that it was impossible for me to remain objective. I experienced a very odd sensation, possibly brought on by the shock of seeing the deer. I was moved by this woman's pain in an almost cellular way. It was clear that she was insane, but I began to wonder if Dr. Nelson might help her. That thought began to be nearly as important to me as proving to other people that the woman existed. Even at that moment, it seemed a strange transition for me.

"Listen," I told her softly, "you should come back to my house with me. You should rest. You're obviously tired and hungry."

"We both are," she said, not looking at me.

"Yes," I agreed, "you both are—you and your son."

It was a risk, but it seemed obvious that the boy was her son, or a person she thought was her son.

"We've been staying here, in these woods." She cast her eyes all around, taking in a grand sweep of the hillside. "I don't know how long. You lose track of time in winter. The days are so short and the nights are filled with such troubling dreams: howling cold and bitter recollection. Ice and regret, that's winter."

"You've been living in the woods all winter so far?" I asked, not really believing her.

"He didn't mean to leave the deer," she said suddenly, as if some gear or cog in her mind had slipped and her thoughts had gone to a previous point in our discourse.

"We frightened him," I said, trying to use my most soothing tones. "We didn't mean to, but our voices—"

"I heard *your* voice," she interrupted. "And the woman. Who was the third?"

"That was the— that was my boyhood friend," I responded, changing my answer in mid-thought. No point in saying the word *sheriff* to this woman. No telling how she'd react. "He's helping me, too."

"Yes, there, you see," she sighed, "you have so many of your people willing to help you. Why can't you forgive Tristan?"

"Tristan," I repeated. "Tristan Newcomb?"

"It's not our fault that we fell in love. You know that. You know what happened. It's been told over and over again down through the long years."

"No, I'm sorry—Tristan Newcomb? The man who owned the Ten Show, the traveling carnival that employed my parents? Is that who you're talking about?"

"Tristan," she repeated more emphatically. "Your nephew."

"No," I told her, "Tristan Newcomb is most certainly not my— there were rumors that he was my father, but I'm certain now that it was just gossip. He and I—Tristan and I—how do you even know about him? He's certainly old enough to be your father, and, in fact, died, I believe, when you were around nine or ten, unless I'm guessing your age completely incorrectly. I'm sorry, but— what are you talking about?"

She smiled and looked at me with great benevolence, but it was not a look that I found comforting.

"Oh—you're confused," she said very sweetly. "I see that now. Your great jealousy has led to madness, of a sort, but that's not incurable. You— I think you're confusing dreams and reality. I know because I do that sometimes. People I meet in dreams seem real; people I know in my waking hours are phantasms, really. Sometimes they don't even have corporeal substance."

Realizing that my plan to say whatever she wanted to hear had gone hideously awry, I thought to salvage something by asking questions, a lesson learned from field research. Ask specific questions. Let the informant talk about herself. No telling what information might come out.

"I am confused," I began. "That's very true. For example, I don't understand what you mean when you say you've been living in these woods most of the winter. Where? Someone's house?"

"No." She was still drifting, very slowly, my way.

Her movement was disconcerting because her dress or skirt came all the way to the ground and it was impossible to see her feet moving in the snow. She seemed to be gliding down toward me.

"Where then?" I pressed. "I'm worried about you. Is it warm enough? Is it protected?"

"We found a cave down the mountain from your house," she answered, and seemed greatly amused by the thought. "Isn't that just perfect? There's even a kind of crystal formation in the center of one part. We've made it quite habitable, really."

"A cave," I repeated, not believing her for a second. "Good."

I knew every inch of this part of the mountain, and while it was true that there were small caves here and there, certainly none of them could be made remotely "habitable" in the dead of winter.

"And we've been able to find enough food," she went on, "what with one thing and another."

She was still floating toward me, only, perhaps, ten feet away.

"Hunting?" I asked, mostly to keep her talking.

"He didn't mean to leave the deer," she said again, her voice hollow, her eyes staring past me into another reality.

"We frightened him," I assured her. "Our voices."

And just at that moment, a sudden shout frightened us both.

"Fever!" Dr. Nelson called. "Where the hell are you?"

My ghostly wife began to run back up the slope.

"No," I called after her. "Wait!"

"What?" Dr. Nelson shouted.

"Quiet!" I yelled down at her.

"What?" she called again.

By that time the woman in black was twenty feet away from me, and disappearing into the undergrowth. I barely had time to catch sight of something strange. Her cloak dragged heavily in the snow behind her. A closer, quick examination of the hem revealed that it had been knotted all along its edge with small stones. The stones weighted the cloak down just enough to drag a small amount of snow after the hem. This had the very significant effect of completely erasing her footprints. Behind her, where she had just run, the snow did not exhibit a single sign of her passing, no trace at all. A second later, she, likewise, vanished altogether into a twist of branches, darkness, and the odd, dizzy patterns there.

At that exact moment I heard Dr. Nelson right behind me.

"What the hell are you doing?" she demanded. "I thought we were going to—"

I spun around. "Tell me that you saw her."

She stopped dead still. "What?"

"Tell me that you saw the woman, just up there." I stared into her eyes.

She stared back, and then glanced behind me for the merest of seconds.

"Fever," she said firmly, "there's no one there."

"Actually," I said, my voice a little high pitched, "there is someone there. She's just past that loblolly pine. If we hurry—"

"We're going back to your house now," she said, and I heard the iron in her voice. "It's already been a half an hour and we have to meet Skidmore, so come on."

"It hasn't been a half an hour," I told her.

She held up her expensive watch. I was forced to reevaluate my statement.

She took a hold of the fabric on the forearm of my jacket and pulled. "You think you saw your phantom bride again, but you didn't. Let's just get that out of the way right now. And I've got news. On further examination of the threads that I found on the branch down there? I think they came from Skidmore's sweater. I think he's wearing a black sweater underneath his police coat."

She tugged once more on my forearm.

"She was right here!" I told her, pulling my arm out of her grasp.

She sighed. "Really? Where, exactly?"

I turned and pointed.

She took a few steps in that direction. "And her footprints? You don't see footprints here, too, do you?"

"No," I said quickly, "she doesn't leave any footprints."

The instant I said it I wished that I hadn't. Dr. Nelson looked deeply into my eyes, as if she were looking to find something hidden in my pupils.

"Well, you're not having an episode, I don't think," she mumbled. "And you seem too awake and coherent for a fugue state performance, so, I'm not sure what's going on."

I started to try to explain about the stones on the cloak and how they could erase footprints in the snow, but as I was piecing it together in my mind, it sounded almost as crazy as saying that she didn't have footprints. So I decided to stick with something that I hoped would be completely verifiable by any so-called sane observer.

"All right," I said, chin up, "but there's something over here that might be interesting, although it's a little disgusting. I think the boy with the rifle shot a deer recently, then heard us and ran off. He left the deer, it died, and crows got at it."

She frowned. "You think you saw an animal carcass."

"Yes." I started off in the direction of the deer.

"And you think that it has something to do with the boy who shot at us?" She took a few tentative steps after me.

"Yes." I didn't look back. "Come on, you have to give me this one. If it's there, then you see at least one weird thing that I see. And if it's not, then you can give me shock treatments or whatever it is you people do."

She followed along behind me. I could hear her feet sloshing in the snow.

It didn't take long to find the deer. Crows had already returned. They had gathered around the food, heads bowed, like priests at a silent table. Though, as I got closer, I began to hear the liquid noises of their ravening.

"Jesus," she whispered, behind me.

I still didn't turn around to look at her. For some reason it was hard to take my eyes from the macabre feast. It seemed, at that moment, to have significance beyond the actual phenomenon. It seemed to mean that everything living off of death and blood had surrounded the innocent.

"I'm having a genuine Yeats moment," I whispered to Dr. Nelson over my shoulder.

"What?" she whispered back.

"I look at this," I explained to her, "and 'things fall apart; the center cannot hold.'"

"You're— what?" she said a little louder, coming up to me.

I motioned my head toward the grotesque avian banquet. "'The blood-dimmed tide is loosed, and everywhere. The ceremony of innocence is drowned.'"

It only took her a moment to understand.

"Yeats," she said. "'The Second Coming.' That's what you're thinking of?"

I nodded. "'The best lack all conviction,'" I said.

"'While the worst are full of passionate intensity,'" she went on. "I know the poem."

"Do you know why I'm having this feeling, then?" I asked, a little off kilter.

"No," she said, more steadily. "Do you?"

"Well," I said, a bit more animatedly, "look."

We both stared at the spectacle for a moment.

"And you think the boy shot this deer?" she said finally.

I nodded. "Come here."

I started toward the blood circle, stomping a bit as I went. The crows complained, and some were reluctant, but all of them flew from the carcass when I clapped my hands twice.

Then I wished that I hadn't clapped my hands, because they were really cold and it really hurt.

I knelt beside the head of the deer and blew warm air onto my palms.

Dr. Nelson moved a little slowly, but she came to where I was kneeling and looked down.

"Here," I pointed briefly, "is the bullet wound. You can see that it's dried, as opposed to these more fresh wounds everywhere else."

She leaned over a little. Her face was slightly contorted, and I was momentarily afraid she might be sick. She straightened up very quickly, turned away, and took a few steps down the slope.

"What makes you think it was the boy who shot this animal?" she said thickly, not looking my way.

"Nobody around here hunts on my property. Some people are afraid of me, which is nice, but mostly they avoid this land because they know I'd object. And there are plenty of places that are better for hunting anyway. Add to that: this animal is very young and I think there must be some kind of lower age limit in general, which is something that a sort of wild boy wouldn't know or wouldn't care about, but most of the hunters around here take very seriously."

"Okay," she said, but she sounded unconvinced.

I stood up and headed her way.

"And finally," I said, "the wound on the deer's head looks very much like it might have been caused by a Remington 700, the kind of rifle the boy used to shoot at us."

She turned to stare at me. Her face still betrayed a trace of uneasiness. "How in the world would you know that?"

"I may have mentioned that I've been shot at lots of times since I returned home. After it happened a few too many times, I started doing what any good quasi-academic would: I did the research."

The truth was that I had only guessed about the bullet wound in the deer's head. I might have been greatly exaggerating my powers of observation in order to convince Dr. Nelson that I wasn't crazy. Or I might have been doing it to impress her. Either way, my behavior was confusingly uncharacteristic.

"All right," she said, but it was impossible to tell what she was thinking. "But if we don't head down the hill right now, we'll be late for our meeting with the sheriff, who doesn't seem to be in the mood for any shenanigans from the likes of us."

"*Shenanigans?*" I repeated. "Is this really the word that you want to use?"

We began to walk down the slope.

"I like that word," she insisted. "It's funny."

"It's hilarious," I agreed, "but I'm telling you right now, most people would *not* want to be diagnosed by a doctor who uses it."

"Oh," she said breezily. "Well. Point taken."

10

Back in my living room, fire stoked, shoes off, feet up, all three of us were slumped down in our seats close to the hearth.

Skid had, indeed, arrived at my house before Dr. Nelson and I, but only by a few moments, so his ire was somewhat dampened. He'd announced that he had important news, but would say nothing more without hot coffee and a warmer fire.

"So," I said, sipping from my espresso cup, "what's the big news?"

"You're not going to believe it," he told me, gulping from his coffee mug. "I didn't."

He shook his head and stared into the fire.

"Are you going to tell us, or do we have to guess?" I asked impatiently.

"Not— can't be more than five hundred yards below your house, after the slope starts to get steep? After your backyard ends? There's a big old cave down there."

I sat up a little. "A cave?"

"I mean a big one," he went on, a little excited. "It looked to me like it'd been all covered up by vines and shrubs for a hundred years, but somebody found it. Somebody opened it up. Because, well, there's furniture down there. And supplies, and a fire pit and two sleeping bags."

"That's not possible." I sat all the way up and set my cup down on the table.

"I know," said Skid, clearly amazed himself.

"I mean," I went on, "I've been— you and I have both been over every inch of this part of the mountain. For all our lives. How could it be that we never found a cave that big?"

"I *know*!" he repeated, only louder. "It was weird. I marked it off with yellow tape, so I can find it again. I called Melissa to get out here. We'll go down together and search the place completely quick as she gets here with some better flashlights and some better equipment. Maybe it's just some tramp living down there for the winter, but it's fairly organized. That boy could be living down there. I asked Melissa to check on any missing persons or runaways before she comes up. You all see anything?"

Dr. Nelson just looked at me.

I held my breath for a second, not certain if I should say what was on my mind or not. Then, a bit reluctantly, I let it fly.

"I saw the woman again in the woods, just now." I sighed. "She— actually she told me that she and her son were living in a cave. Down below my house."

Skid's eyes shot to Dr. Nelson. She shook her head.

"I didn't see her," she reported, "but I did lose sight of Dr. Devilin for at least five minutes, and in that time . . ."

"No," Skid said to me, now also sitting up, irksome mood returned. "No. See, if you'd told me right away that you'd seen the woman, and that she'd mentioned the cave, *before* I told you I found one, that might have made me think twice. But when you wait until *after* I tell you about it, I don't believe you even a little bit. You understand that, right?"

He stood up to punctuate his dismissal.

"What are you doing now?" I asked, a little haplessly.

"I'm going to examine the cave," he said, as if he'd told me a dozen times already. "No matter what, it's odd, and it constitutes, at the very least, a criminal trespass of your property, so Melissa and I are going to go over it pretty good. Maybe we'll get lucky and the vagrant who's trying to live there will show up. Happens."

At that moment we heard a car pull up in my yard. A quick glance revealed Deputy Melissa Mathews, chestnut hair up in a tight bun, hat under her arm, climbing out of her patrol car.

I was always glad to see Melissa. She was lovely, kind, braver than most human beings I'd ever met, and, also, she'd saved my life. A recent bout with cancer had left her thinner than she ought to have been, but the disease was in complete remission, and she looked quite strong as she strode confidently toward my porch.

Skid was at the door before she knocked, pulling up his boots, one arm of his coat on and the other dragging the floor.

Melissa stood in the doorway, smiling sweetly.

"Hey," she chirped.

I stood. "Melissa, this is Dr. Nelson."

But I was prevented from finishing the more lengthy explanation of Dr. Nelson's presence.

"Ceri," Melissa said, stepping around Skidmore and coming into the living room.

Melissa and Dr. Nelson embraced briefly, and smiled at each other.

"Melissa, you look fantastic," Dr. Nelson said.

Melissa blushed. "Too skinny."

Melissa was the shyest person I had ever met. Scores of young men buzzed around her all the time, but she seemed oblivious to their advances. She loved her job and had been a deputy for a good number of years. In that time she'd been in danger of losing her life at least five times.

Melissa patted Dr. Nelson's arm lightly. "You take care of Dr. Devilin, hear?"

"Will do," Dr. Nelson replied.

"Let's go," Skid mumbled, heading out the door.

Melissa smiled my way. "You take care of Dr. Nelson, too, right? We can't have her get all shot up."

"Agreed." I smiled back at Melissa.

Without further ado, she was out the door behind Skid.

Dr. Nelson immediately sat down again, this time on the floor, close to the fire as she had before.

"Now then," she said, all business, "what is it you're not telling me?"

I stared at her as if I'd never seen her before in my life.

"What are you talking about?" I complained.

"I have a spectacularly strong sense that you're not telling me something." She sat cross-legged, hands folded in her lap, staring into the flames.

I rolled my head to loosen my neck. My neck crackled like popped corn.

"Look." I sighed, collapsing onto the sofa. "I'm sorry I *ever* mentioned that my parents took me to the Rhine Center when I was little. I don't think I really— I don't believe in this psychic— in the— not in the way that you do, at least."

"Well," she answered archly, "at least you've honed your thoughts on the subject into a nice coherent argument."

"You don't have a sense that I'm not telling you something," I snapped back. "You just want to get me talking so that you can diagnose me."

"Well, that's always a possibility," she admitted, still staring into the flames, "but in this case, there *is* something you're not telling me."

I started to answer in two or three different ways before I gave up and admitted it. "Yes, all right, there is something I'm not telling you, but it's something that the woman told me and you don't think there was a woman so I'm naturally loathe to exaggerate your already looming suspicions that I've gone around the bend."

That made her look at me. Her gaze bore into my eyes.

"Brother, that ship has sailed; you *live* around the bend," she said without a trace of humor. "You just have to know that most people *don't*."

"You think I've lost my mind."

"I do."

I hadn't expected her to be so— blunt. I was momentarily knocked back on my heels.

"You do?" I finally managed to ask.

She turned back around and stared, once again, into the flames. "Not all of it. But you lost a part of it when you died. I'm going to help you find it."

"Then I'll be all right, you think," I said.

"Depends on your definition of 'all right,'" she told me. "You don't have much hope of being what most people would call normal, but you never had much hope of that."

"Or desire for it," I chimed in.

"Right," she sang out, "but we can get you back on an even keel. So. Whether she's real or not—and you have to believe me when I say that I haven't made up my mind about that yet—you have to tell me what the woman in the woods said to you."

I settled back. I was a bit self-conscious that my feet were closer to her than my head, owing to the way I was laying on the couch. I wondered why I would think a thing like that.

The fire popped. She sat silent and motionless. I took a deep breath.

"She started in the same vein as before, I think," I said softly, "apologizing to me for something she'd done, and wanting me to forgive her. Then, very oddly, she brought up a person from my distant past, or, my family's distant past. She wanted me to forgive a man named Tristan Newcomb."

"Who's that?"

"He was a modestly famous sideshow attraction whose family,

the Newcomb family, owned most of the land in these mountains. Tristan bought a traveling show called the Ten Show that employed my parents. That's how they met, in fact, my parents, in the traveling show."

"What did they do?" her voice was a little hypnotic.

"My father was, or became, a well-known magician. My mother was a snake charmer who became his assistant. She was also well known, but primarily for her prodigious promiscuity."

"Go on."

"It was often rumored that my mother'd had an affair with Tristan Newcomb, and that Tristan was my biological father."

"And was he?" she asked. "Was this Tristan Newcomb your father?"

"No."

"You're certain."

"Nearly one hundred percent," I assured her.

"Why are you so certain?"

"Because Tristan Newcomb was a little person. He'd made his fame as 'The Newcomb Dwarf.' And I don't carry any of the genetic properties generally associated with dwarfism, not achondroplasia; not growth hormone deficiency."

"All right, but there are a few other causes . . ."

"He wasn't my father," I interrupted. "He was, however, by all reports and from the very few childhood memories I have of him, a genuinely kind person."

"So maybe the woman in the woods wants you to forgive him owing to the rumors about him and your mother?" she suggested.

"How would she even know him? I mean, I think she was claiming to have been in love with him, but he died when I was a child, and as far as I can tell, the woman in the woods is younger than I am. Although it's hard to know for certain."

"She said very specifically that she wanted you to forgive Tristan Newcomb," Dr. Nelson pressed.

"Her exact words were, 'Why can't you forgive Tristan?'" I insisted.

"Hm." Dr. Nelson shifted a little in front of the fire. "Fascinating."

"What is it?" I asked.

"Okay," she told me, "I'm just tossing this out there, but is it possible— I mean try to look at this, for a moment, like the academic that you used to be, and try to be objective in some way. But is it possible that this woman is somehow a manifestation of your mother when she was young, and she's asking you to forgive her?"

"God," I moaned loudly. "Way too Freudian—too Freudian by half!"

"Just throwing it out there."

"Well," I said, sitting up a little, gaining strength, "here are my several responses in no particular order: I quit being an academic because I didn't like it; I think it's impossible for me to be objective about my own life, by definition; and I'm not really so much a Freudian as I am a Jungian. And, add to that, *the woman is real!* She's not a manifestation of anything. She's a walking, talking time bomb. Eventually she's going to explode, and we're in her broadcast radius. That's what I'm worried about—not my mother, not my past, not my academic career."

She appeared to be unaffected by my vehemence. "Just tossing it out there," she repeated.

"You'll at least admit that the boy is real," I prompted.

"I'll admit that I saw him," she answered. "Whether or not that makes him real is really a trickier ticket."

"Oh, for God's sake," I growled.

"Why did you stop?" she shot back. "Why did you stop your so-called academic career?"

I settled back onto the sofa. "How much do you know about it?"

"You were the head of your own folklore program," she said, "and then you quit and came back up to Blue Mountain, which was, as far as I've been able to determine from my investigations, the only place on earth that you *didn't* want to be."

"Well." I folded my arms across my chest and stared up at the ceiling. "In the first place, the university shut down my program, because it was the general belief that folklore was an increasingly irrelevant course of study at the beginning of this new century. I could have continued teaching a few folklore courses and mythological literature in the English Department."

"But you didn't," she said, "or, I mean, you chose not to."

"I chose not to because I disagreed with the concept," I said. "My contention was that folklore and mythology are foundational aspects of our culture. To ignore them is to ignore the basis of all societies, all psychologies, all religions."

"So, instead of staying and fighting for that proposition," she said, "you chose to quit your job and come back to the home you had escaped—and I use that word deliberately. You hated growing up here."

"I did not hate growing up here," I corrected her. "I hated aspects of my life here, most of them having to do with my parents, specifically my mother."

"And here we are back to your mother again," she said, a little amused. "I'm not making these things up, then."

"No," I objected, "that's not— this is very irritating, your constant— I also hated being so strange in this community. I thought that I would fit in better in a more urban environment, and I thought that my more intellectual observations would go down easier in an academic environment."

"And how did that work out?"

I closed my eyes for a second. "Sometimes—some parts of it—it was great."

"So you left here, bound for college, when you were . . . ?"

"I left home when I was sixteen, the year I graduated high school."

"And you shot away from Blue Mountain like a cannonball," she said, "that's the way you've described it before."

"Yes." I closed my eyes. "Skidmore was the only one there to say good-bye. He shook my hand and told me he'd never see me again. And I agreed with him. I was very glad to think it was true. I knew I would miss him, but the rest of the place? I sloughed it off like a snake sheds old skin. I jumped onto that train out of town, threw open the window; let the air blow away all the caked remnants of hearth and home. That moment might have been the happiest I'd ever known."

"Nice bit of melancholy," she said, still amused, "but let's return to your real reasons for leaving the halls of the academy."

"All right," I acquiesced. "I believe the phrase I may have used in the past is: 'hellish pit of flesh-eating vipers.' It not only captures my perception of the university, but has the added delight of alliterative consonation."

"I don't think that *consonation* is a word," she insisted.

"But you see what I mean," I responded. "The *sh* sounds, the *v* and *f* and *p* sounds."

"Oh, it's a nice turn of the phrase," she admitted, "and very sort of poetic—in an academic sense."

"Oh, look who's talking," I snapped. "You don't have a doctorate? You don't run a department?"

"Not anymore." She sighed, and it was a singularly satisfied sound.

"But the point is," I began.

"But the point is," she interrupted, "that you came back here. You didn't stay in the city, you didn't move to Wales or France; you didn't travel the world. You came back to Blue Mountain."

"But you're interpreting it as a psychological response," I objected, "whereas it was almost exclusively an economic necessity.

My parents had left me this house, a small bit of money, which, as it turned out, was not so small, and in the intervening years I— look, coming back to Blue Mountain was, at the time I left the university, the path of least resistance. I was a little depressed and it was Occam's answer, the simplest, the most essential. But since that time I've— life here hasn't exactly been boring. My old college professor tried to kill me here, a witch saved my life, I met an albino hit man and the ghost of a preacher; I lived through a coma and a surreal, Jungian exploration of my recent ancestors. *And,* I got engaged."

She turned away from the fire, leaned her elbows on the coffee table, and faced me.

"See, this is exactly my point," she said. "You're a spook magnet. That's why all these odd things have happened to you up here over the course of the last eight years or so."

"Christ." I sighed.

"No, I mean it," she insisted. "Here's how I think it works. All bodies, all human bodies, and maybe all living things—they all have an electromagnetic field. It's what you read on an EKG and an EEG machine."

"I'm familiar," I assured her.

"And each of these fields," she went on, "has a specific signature, a wavelength, a pattern—a personality. Yours, believe me, is particularly magnetic, or attractive to the more bizarre elements, people, and phenomena that surround you. That's why you can't sleep. That's why so many strange things have happened to you since you came home. You have to at least admit that a lot of strange things have happened to you since you came home."

I didn't want to answer her.

"Fever," she continued, her voice lowered, "I've done the research. The first day you came back from the city to this house, there was a dead body on your front porch. And as recently as last night, one of two strange things happened," she said. "Either you hallucinated a manifestation of your young mother, or a stranger who thinks she's married to you appeared in your house. I mean, either way—come on."

I sat up. I tried not to think about all the things I'd seen in my house that had not, actually, been there in the strictest physical sense. I tried not to think about all the people who'd tried to kill me, all the people who'd been killed, all the unexplainably twisted events that had, indeed, swirled around me, a maelstrom of dark matter, a turning, an ever-increasing gyre expanding around a center that wouldn't hold.

But trying not to think about something is exactly the same as thinking about it too much: eventually the walls collapse, the mind gives in, and there they are, the events you were hoping to solve—or avoid—sloshing in a pool all around you, a dark pool.

"And— and you think there's something you can do to help that situation?" I asked as calmly as I could manage.

She brought to bear, somehow, the most intense concentration I'd ever felt from another human being, and I was her entire object.

"I did it for myself," she whispered harshly. "I know the way out."

11

Night had arrived by the time Lucinda knocked on my door. Dr. Nelson and I had spent the entire afternoon arguing, wrangling, laughing, complaining, and, in general, getting acquainted. We had settled into a much more comfortable, albeit wary, approach to each other.

Lucinda came crashing through the front door carrying two bags of groceries. "What's those squad cars still doing in your yard?" she demanded. "I thought Skid would be gone by now. What's going on?"

I got up and took one of the grocery bags.

"Come on in," I said, "and I'll tell you. Everything's fine."

"Everything's fine," Dr. Nelson repeated.

Lucinda looked at me, then at Dr. Nelson, and seemed to notice right away that we'd gotten very comfortable.

"Good," she said, absently kissing my cheek, still agitated. "You'uns getting on better, at least. That's good."

For some reason I'd never understood, Lucinda laid on her mountain accent more thickly around urban company. When Dr. Andrews, my rugby-playing Shakespeare scholar friend from the university I'd abandoned, came to visit, she dialed up the quaint phraseology as far as it would go. It was curious to me that she was doing the same thing with Dr. Nelson.

"He still won't use my first name," Dr. Nelson complained.

Lucinda went into the kitchen and set her bag down on the counter before she noticed the damaged tiles.

"What the hell!" she said suddenly. "This is where they shot up your kitchen?"

"Yes," I said quickly, coming into the kitchen and setting my bag down.

But when she turned to face me, she noticed the plywood over the window and interrupted my explanation.

"Look at that window!" she roared.

"That's what I was trying to tell you earlier on the phone," I said, taking hold of her shoulders. "A boy, a young boy, shot a hunting rifle through the window and into the kitchen earlier."

"But that was hours ago," she raved.

"Well, see, I called Skidmore," I said, deliberately calm, "and he came over, and then we went out—Dr. Nelson and Skidmore and I—and now Skidmore and Melissa may have found the place where the boy is hiding out—"

But again she interrupted me. "Hiding out?"

"There— there's a cave," I stammered.

Dr. Nelson swept into the kitchen and began talking. Her words were lightning fast and preternaturally calm. "A boy shot at me through this window. We called Skidmore. The three of us searched the woods. Fever saw the strange woman again. Skidmore and Melissa are currently examining a cave down the slope behind this house because that may be where the boy and the woman are staying. They should be back any minute now. Everything's under control."

Somehow the way Dr. Nelson had spoken seemed to calm Lucinda. I felt it too. It was almost as if we'd been hypnotized, just a bit—if there was such a thing as a *dash* of hypnosis.

"Now," Dr. Nelson continued, a little slower, "let's sit down at the kitchen table and have a cup of tea or a drink or something.

Skidmore and Melissa will be back soon, and we'll figure every-thing out."

Lucinda blinked. "Fever," she complained, but that was all she said.

"Tea?" I suggested.

"Actually," Dr. Nelson said, "I wouldn't mind something stron-ger."

Lucinda sat down. "Tell the truth? Me too. I had a really hard day."

I started to say something, because it was so unusual for Lu-cinda to have liquor except on special occasions, and never on a weeknight. But I looked at her profile, and I could tell that she had something on her mind.

"I do have some superior apple brandy," I suggested. "It's made from a three-hundred-year-old recipe by a family that lives within five miles of this house. This particular vintage has been aged in oak for five years, corked, and set aside in a cave for another ten. It is the equal of any Boulard or du Pays d'Auge Normandy Calva-dos, and the best I have ever tasted anywhere in the world."

"Glowing reference," Dr. Nelson said, smiling. "I'll start with five glasses and see where that gets me."

"It is good," Lucinda said softly.

I went immediately to the cupboard over the refrigerator and pulled down one of the bottles. The top of the bottle had been wound around with brown twine, and the cork was firmly in the bottle.

I fished in a drawer, found a knife and a corkscrew, cut the twine, popped the cork, and set the bottle and the cork on the table. The vapors rose everywhere around us, and promised unearthly delights.

I pulled three brandy snifters from a relatively unused shelf and set one down in front of each of us. After a moment, I poured the copper-colored nectar.

The first taste was cinnamon, then vanilla, and finally, baked apples with a hint of sweet caramel. All three of us closed our eyes as we swallowed the first sip.

Lucinda smiled. "Tastes like Christmas."

"Well, Christmas is right around the corner." I nodded.

"God in heaven." Dr. Nelson sighed.

We each finished a first glass, and a second. On the third round, when all three of us seemed much more relaxed, Dr. Nelson launched into what she must have thought would be a surefire way to engage me.

"Did you ever dwell, for any length of time in your academic studies, on the Arthurian cycle?" she asked, staring into her snifter. "My father, God bless him, was a fanatic."

"I taught a course called the Literature of Folklore," I said. "The stories are much more wide-ranging than most people imagine. I'm sure you were curious, at some point in your life, about your name, if that's what you're getting at. Of course the stories that involve your namesake are a bit tangential."

"King Arthur?" Lucinda asked. "The round table? That's folklore?"

Since the bulk of my own studies had focused almost exclusively on Appalachian material folk culture, songs, and stories, I rarely talked about the wider scope of my interests. With Lucinda, it had simply never come up.

"Folktales, folk culture, oral traditions," I began, "are the basis of all history and culture. Long before most human beings could write things down, or read anything that had been written, we told one another stories. Some were about our families; some were about important events. Some were told to explain things, like the origin of the world, or the beginning of our race. Every culture on the planet, for example, has a specific creation myth, a sort of Garden of Eden story, an explanation of how men and women were made. Some of the bigger or more important stories like

Gilgamesh or Beowulf or King Arthur—it's almost impossible to separate what might have been historical description from a larger or more general moral or educational purpose. Joseph Campbell describes his Hero with a Thousand Faces in such a way as to make it understood that the hero character is universal, something common to all cultures and all people. And the beauty of these stories to me is that they're told over and over again. There are elements of the King Arthur saga in twentieth-century American politics. You know, for example, that the early Kennedy years were often referred to as Camelot."

Lucinda grinned at Dr. Nelson. "He likes you," she said. "He only talks like that, like a college professor, around people he likes."

"No," I protested, "I was just trying to say . . ."

"My first name, Ceridwen," said Dr. Nelson, to Lucinda, "figures into the Arthurian cycle, which is what he's trying to get at."

"Exactly," I said, glaring at Lucinda.

Lucinda continued to grin and shoved my shoulder. "You like her. Go on. Admit it."

I looked down at the table. "Ceridwen," I said very deliberately, "is a name from Welsh medieval legend. She was an enchantress. She and her husband lived in Bala Lake in North Wales. She owned the cauldron of poetic inspiration. Some writers give that name to the Lady of the Lake in the Arthur stories, but that name is also given as Vivian, Elaine, or many variants of those names."

Dr. Nelson stared at me with an overwhelming intensity. "But it's not my name you're really trying to figure out, is it?"

I looked up. "What?"

"You're trying to remember the name of the mystery woman," she said, very clinically, I thought.

"No I'm not," I snapped. "I don't even— what makes you— why are you saying that? Damn it. Now I *am* trying to remember her name. What are you doing?"

She shrugged. "Sometimes it works," she said. "You make a kind of sudden, shock statement, see where it gets you. Sometimes it throws the conscious mind off guard just enough so that your deeper response tells you something."

I scowled. "How did that work out in this case?"

"Just seemed to confuse you more." She smiled. "Sometimes that happens, too. Sorry."

"Are you just— do you actually have a degree in psychiatry or something, or are you just guessing at what to do next?" I shook my head and glared at Lucinda. This was her fault, really.

Dr. Nelson only smiled bigger. "Why can't it be both?" she asked.

I kept my gaze locked on Lucinda. "What good is this doing?" I asked her. "Do you think this is helping me? Because it's not. It's irritating."

"It's irritating because it's not you that's in charge of it," Lucinda mumbled.

"It's irritating," Dr. Nelson chimed in, "because I'm a stranger in your home and you think that I'm trying to prove you're crazy. Anybody would be irritated by that."

"You're not trying to prove that I'm crazy," I admitted. "I know that. You're trying to see how crazy I am. It's really just a question of degree, right?"

"Right," she said instantly.

Lucinda poured herself another snifter of apple brandy. "All right," she said, "I think I'm calmed down enough to hear a little bit more about what's going on, or do I have to wait for the sheriff to come back and get him to tell me?"

"A boy shot at me with a rifle," Dr. Nelson said matter-of-factly, "and broke the window in the kitchen, also cracked up some tiles. We called the sheriff."

"You already told me that," Lucinda complained.

"When the sheriff got here," Dr. Nelson went on, as if she hadn't been interrupted, "the three of us went out into the woods to look for the boy. We found footprints, two sets, followed them until one disappeared, then Skidmore . . ."

"Wait," Lucinda held up her glass. "Wait. One set of footprints disappeared?"

"Yes," Dr. Nelson breezed along. "So Skidmore followed the boy's prints and Dr. Devilin and I tried to see what had happened to the second set of prints. Dr. Devilin believes that he met his mysterious bride for a moment, then, but she ran off when I came up the hill to where he was."

"Wait," Lucinda said again, more exasperated than before, "wait. He saw that woman again?"

"I did," I confirmed grimly. "And then Dr. Nelson yelled out, and she ran away."

"I see," Lucinda said. Then she took a very deep gulp from her glass. "And Skidmore is somewhere down the mountain, with Melissa, looking for the boy and the woman in some cave that wasn't there before today."

"What makes you say that?" Dr. Nelson asked, cocking her head in Lucinda's direction.

"I never knew there was a cave down there," she said. "And Fever never knew it was there either, I could tell by the way he mentioned it."

"All right, well, then," Dr. Nelson concluded, "that brings us to this moment, when I'm trying to get Dr. Devilin to remember the name of this strange woman."

"She told you her name?" Lucinda asked.

"She did," I said, rubbing my eyes, "I just can't— I can't quite remember it. It wasn't a common name."

"Fever," Lucinda said, setting down her glass a bit clumsily, "you know I love you, but you surely are one for trouble. I mean, getting shot at's a common thing with you. I've come to live with that, and with the dead people dropping all around you. But when you start making up an imaginary wife, I have to try and get you some help.

You understand that, right? You need to listen to Ceri, and be nicer to her, and do what she says. She's the doctor. I'm— I'm tired."

I looked at her. She had closed her eyes. Her face was a little flushed and her lips were dry. I suddenly, quite suddenly realized the effect that my odd life might be having on her. I hadn't really ever thought about it before.

"I can tell, most of the time, if I really think about it," I began softly, "the effect that events in my life are having on me; but it's harder to gauge how those same events might affect the people around me, the people who care about me. I hadn't ever really considered that before now, before right now. I'm sorry."

I put my hand on Lucinda's.

She let out a sigh that I thought might break the kitchen table in two.

"I had a patient a few years ago," Dr. Nelson said, not looking at either of us, "a commercial shrimper from Charleston. He'd fallen overboard and nearly been eaten by a shark. All his co-workers saw the shark and were yelling and screaming and genu-inely afraid—imagining everything that might happen to their friend. But the man who had fallen into the water was only think-ing about one thing. He was only swimming for the boat. His in-surance required that he see a therapist, but it turned out that he'd been less traumatized by the event than the rest of the crew."

Lucinda and I stared at Dr. Nelson as if she'd been speaking in tongues.

"The point is," Dr. Nelson went on, "that Lucinda might be more troubled by these events in your life, Dr. Devilin, than you are."

"Yes," I said, "I'm beginning to understand that possibility."

Lucinda opened her eyes. "I'll be fine."

But her voice lacked all conviction.

Loud stomping on my porch prevented further emotional ex-ploration. Seconds later, and without knocking, Skidmore came into my house, Melissa immediately behind him.

"Nobody," he declared. "Nobody down in that cave now."

"Oh, but there's been people there all right," Melissa said.

They both looked cold as they came into the kitchen, faces red, eyes blinking.

"Hey, Lucinda," Skidmore said, taking a seat at the kitchen table. "What are we drinking?"

He stared at the half-empty bottle of apple brandy.

Melissa stayed in the doorway between the kitchen and the living room. "I'm going to run on back with the prints and all, right?" she suggested.

"Okay," Skidmore said absently.

"You found fingerprints?" I asked

"Plenty," Melissa said enthusiastically.

I stood. "That's great! How many? I mean, how many people's prints, can you tell?"

"Hard to tell," Skid answered, "but more than one."

"That's great," I said again. "You'll find out who the kid and the woman are!"

"Maybe," Skid said. "What are we *drinking*?"

"You want you some apple brandy?" Lucinda asked, getting up and going to get another glass.

"So I'll go ahead?" Melissa asked again.

"Would you like a little something to warm you up?" Dr. Nelson asked Melissa. "Before you go?"

"Well," she answered hesitantly.

"You're on duty," Skid growled.

"Right," she answered quickly.

Without another word, she was gone.

"Aren't you on duty too?" I asked him.

"Let me see." He looked at his watch. "It's just— wait, three seconds to— okay, I'm off. Pour."

"Oh, that's nice," I complained. "You just sit here and drink while Melissa does all the work."

Lucinda poured a healthy glass. Skidmore drank it all down in one shot.

I looked at Dr. Nelson. "Do you see the effect you have on my friends? Lucinda never drinks during the week, and I don't think I've ever seen our sheriff, here, knock one back like that. I hope you're happy."

She smiled. "I'm pretty happy."

Skidmore blew out his breath, unaccustomed as he was to the single-shot-drinking mode. "I wanted to get Melissa out of the room. I didn't want her to hear what I'm about to say, or to see what I'm about to show you. Not just yet. She gets upset about stuff like this."

All eyes turned his way.

"Stuff like what?" I asked.

"Fever," he continued, not looking at anyone, "I found something in the cave down there that I think you should see right away. Melissa don't know I got it. Have you a look."

He reached into his coat pocket and slapped something down onto the kitchen tabletop. It was an older, three-by-five photograph. I squinted, and then my head snapped back. Lucinda covered her mouth with her hand. Dr. Nelson, at last, stopped smiling.

The photograph was a picture of me, much younger, with my arm around a young woman.

"Is this, by any chance, the woman who came into your house last night?" Skidmore asked quietly, tapping his finger on the photo.

For a second I couldn't breathe, and then I couldn't remember words—any words. At last I was able to nod and say, "That's the woman exactly, the woman from last night."

"Uh-huh," Skid said, barely audible. "Turn it over."

I did. On the back, in neat block printing, was written:

 # 173, Dr. F Devilin with Issie Raynerd (1972–1999)

12

We all stared at the writing for a moment before Dr. Nelson spoke up.

"So, are we to infer," she asked, "from these parenthetical dates, that Issie Raynerd passed away over a decade ago?"

"That's what it looks like," Lucinda said softly.

"Well then, Dr. Devilin," Dr. Nelson continued, "if that is the case, you'd have to admit that she probably wasn't here in your house last night—as you originally supposed."

"But," I said back to her, "it's not just my— my *supposition* that she was here last night. You found threads from her black dress caught on a branch of mountain laurel just up the hill."

"We discussed that, remember?" Dr. Nelson reached into the front pocket of her jeans. "I had the foresight to bring them with me."

She set four or five strands of black thread on the table beside the photograph.

"And you still think these came from this woman's dress?" Skid asked.

"They did," I said, only a bit belligerently.

"I didn't think about it, really, but you should have a look at this." Skid opened his coat and untucked his scarf. "Couldn't be from this?"

The scarf was black, and frayed, and the loose threads on it looked exactly like the threads on the table.

"Jesus," I whispered, sitting back.

"Fever," Skid said firmly, "you're going to have to come to grips with the fact that you're not right in the head. I mean, more than usual."

"I'm sorry, sweetheart," Lucinda added, "but he's right."

I shook my head. "But you both saw two sets of footprints in the snow," I said, "and then you saw that one of them was gone."

"Maybe," Skid said.

"I'm more interested," Dr. Nelson said, in a somewhat affected manner, "in the fact that we have before us a photograph of you with your arm around this woman. You said that she claimed to be your wife but you'd never seen before. So that's not quite accurate."

"Yes," said Lucinda, eyes locked on me, "what about that?"

"Well," I offered, "it's absolutely possible that she was a student of mine. This is about how I looked—I mean the way I look in this photograph is about how I looked when I first started at the university. I taught a lot of big lecture classes then, a hundred and twenty, even a hundred and fifty students. They knew me but I didn't know them. It happened a lot: I'd be walking down the hall and some student would say hello as if I ought to know who they were, and I developed a very convincing way of answering back that seemed genuine when, in fact, I was only confused."

"But," Lucinda pressed, "you have your arm around her. You're smiling."

"You do look like you know her," Dr. Nelson said.

"Hold on," I responded. "What's the implication here? That I knew her, that I know her now, and I'm lying to all three of you? Lucinda, have I ever lied to you?"

"Not that I know of," she answered, uncertainly.

"This can't be," I complained, volume growing. "You can't tell me that I imagined the woman, and then in the next breath tell me I'm trying to hide my secret marriage to her."

"We're just trying to make sense of it," Skidmore ventured.

Dr. Nelson turned the photograph back over. "Have a good look at her face now," she suggested. "And try to concentrate on the name *Issie*. It's a very unusual name, and you said that you couldn't remember it."

"And I suppose that's suspicious too?" I snapped.

"A little," Dr. Nelson fired right back.

"Christ!" I said, throwing up my arms.

"Just look at the picture," Dr. Nelson encouraged.

I didn't really want to, but I acquiesced. As would be the propensity for most people, I looked at myself first. My hair was longer. I looked so much younger. I'd never felt that I'd gained much weight over the years, but the younger man in the photo was thin. Very thin. And he was smiling—using facial muscles that I rarely used in my current life, I realized.

Then I looked at the woman. She did seem vaguely familiar, but that was all. It was like looking at a high school yearbook picture of someone I had barely known. Twenty years later, who could remember the tangential acquaintances of adolescence? Maybe she'd been my student.

I cleared my throat. "I don't know how to say this, what I'm about to say, without sounding—I don't know, something. But in my first years at the university, I was a relatively popular professor. A lot of students liked me. I was eager to make them love folklore studies as much as I did, and I was very enthusiastic about the course work. And, in those days, I would often play music or tell stories in class. I'll admit I was a bit of a performer, and probably more interested in my own appeal than in the actual teaching."

"It was more important to you that the students like you than it was for them to learn anything," Dr. Nelson suggested.

"It wasn't quite that bad," I said, "but, yes, it was very important to me that I was the most popular professor. In fact, that was my initial association with Andrews. He was my rival in that regard, and better looking. Initially we met to size each other up. It was luck, really, that we ended up liking each other as much as we did—as much as we do."

"Yes, about Dr. Andrews," Dr. Nelson began. "Shakespeare scholar, your best pal at the university—but, sorry, has there ever been any suggestion that the two of you might have had a more intimate relationship?"

"Oh, for God's sake," I snarled.

Lucinda giggled, and Skid laughed out loud.

"Okay," said Dr. Nelson right away, seeing the reaction she got from all of us, "that's out. It is my job to ask questions like that, you understand. So. No intimate relationship. But you are close, you and Dr. Andrews."

"Yes," I said. "He's the one person, really, from the university— what should I say?"

"He's your only real friend from your city days," Lucinda ventured.

"All right," I agreed.

"I was just thinking, then," Dr. Nelson went on, "that you might consider giving him a call to see if *he* remembers this person, Issie Raynerd."

I blinked. "Actually, that's a great idea. His memory has always been better than mine. Especially where attractive women are concerned."

"Absolutely," Skidmore said. "Call him."

"Something better would be for you to scan this photo," Dr. Nelson suggested, "e-mail it to Andrews, and *then* call him. Right?"

"Excellent," I agreed. "I'll scan both sides."

I grabbed the photo and dashed upstairs in a flash.

The office was spare but extremely efficient. The desk sat against the wall facing out the window. The vista was spectacular, no matter what time of year. Besides the desk, which was an oak antique, something from my great-grandfather, only a tall filing cabinet and two floor-to-ceiling bookshelves occupied the room.

I went to the desk, scanned the photo in an instant, and attached it to a quick e-mail to Andrews: "Sorry no time for small talk. Very important that you look at the attached photo and tell me if you know, or at least recall, this woman. E-mail or call immediately. Fate of world hangs in balance. FD."

No point in underestimating the importance of the missive.

I hit SEND before I realized I hadn't scanned the back of the photo. I sat for a second trying to decide if I should send another e-mail, thought better of it, sat for a moment to see if he'd respond, and when he didn't, scurried back downstairs.

"We should hear from him soon," I called from the bottom of the stairs. "He checks his e-mail obsessively."

I appeared in the kitchen doorway to see all three people at the kitchen table looking at me with a mixture of patience and concern. I found it extremely irritating.

"Stop it," I said instantly.

"Stop what?" Skidmore asked, very genuinely.

"You know what," I said, coming into the room. "Stop looking at me as if I were a problem patient."

"Ceri was just telling us her theory," Lucinda said, a bit stiltedly, "that you're a kind of magnet for odd things."

"She says you've always been that way," Skid added. "And without a doubt, I'd have to agree."

I glared at Dr. Nelson. "Really? You have to scare my oldest friend and my fiancée with that? Is that remotely professional?"

"Yes." That was all she said.

"No, I mean—" but I trailed off. Because what I meant was that Skidmore and Lucinda weren't equipped to deal with the concepts that Dr. Nelson was scattering around my house like evil seeds.

That made me realize that I considered myself the intellectual superior of my oldest friend and my fiancée. That realization was very disturbing, because no matter how I tried, I couldn't seem to chastise myself for that feeling of superiority.

Instead, I began to have a very uneasy sensation of alienation. I sat down at the table and my mind began to seesaw. I watched myself, as if from above, a third-person observer. But I not only saw my present self, I could see my entire life, the way some people describe seeing themselves on an operating table when they've been pronounced dead. I saw myself at age nine, when boys at school began to make fun of me. I saw my teenaged years, when I was absolutely convinced that everyone in the world knew something that I didn't know, some key element to the general process of living. I saw my first year at college, younger than anyone in any of my classes, certain that everyone was smarter, more attractive, better read, from a much better family, and, in general, superior to me in every way.

When had that deflated self-perception reversed itself? When had I started thinking that I was smarter, more perceptive, and more capable than anyone I knew?

I was shaken from this pestilence by Lucinda's voice.

"Fever?" she whispered. "Are you all right?"

I looked around at them, all three, as if I'd never seen them before.

"No," I answered weakly. "I don't think I am all right. Something— something's going on."

Lucinda started to stand, but Dr. Nelson placed her hand on Lucinda's arm.

"He's going through a transitional moment," Dr. Nelson said.

"He's been presented, by circumstances and by me, with a lot of distressing information. He may be making some discoveries, or coming to some conclusions about— something."

I blinked. "I can't make up my mind if you're really good at what you do," I said to Dr. Nelson, "or you're a complete charlatan. What kind of a diagnostic comment is 'He may be making discoveries about *something?*' "

"A vague one," she answered proudly. "One that's almost impossible to prove or disprove. The cornerstone of side-show mentalists and psychiatric professionals."

I laughed in spite of myself.

"What were you thinking about?" Lucinda asked, much less amused. "Your face was so strange."

I wondered how honest I should be. I had, alas, just been touting my veracity, insisting to Lucinda that I'd never lied to her.

"I was thinking," I told them all, "about an unusual reversal in my life."

"Go on," Dr. Nelson said, mostly to irritate me with another one of her vague impersonations of an analyst.

"When I was younger, I felt inferior to everyone," I said quickly, "but at the moment I'm fairly convinced that there aren't many people in the world more perceptive or more intelligent than I am. It's a kind of dizzying feeling."

"Oh," said Lucinda, and she sat back, greatly relieved. "Well, Fever, you *are* smarter than anybody else. Everybody knows that."

"Why do you think I tolerate your rude behavior?" Skidmore added, grinning. "Somebody's got to be the brains of the outfit. Lucinda's the caring, beautiful one; I'm the one who's brave and strong. And good-looking. You're the scarecrow."

"Scarecrow?" I asked.

"*Wizard of Oz,*" Lucinda whispered, as if she were helping me to cheat on a test. "The Scarecrow wants a brain?"

"Oh, for God's sake." I shook my head.

"You felt guilty saying that," Dr. Nelson told me, more seriously. "I mean you felt guilty saying that you were smarter than everyone else."

"No," I said, but I didn't look her in the eye.

"Oh, if there's one thing I'm *really* good at recognizing, it's guilt," she said. "And I think it's sweet."

"Sweet?" I sighed. "I'm really sorry I said anything."

But I felt better. It felt better to say it out loud.

Thank God the phone rang at just that moment, because it changed the subject.

I sprang up, expecting to hear Andrews on the other end.

"Andrews," I said into the phone excitedly, "do you know her?"

"Um, it's me, Dr. Devilin. Melissa Mathews? Is the sheriff still there?"

"Ah," I said, contritely, "yes. He's here."

I held out the phone.

"Who is it?" Lucinda asked.

"Sorry," I said, "it's Melissa."

Skidmore leaned forward and raked his chair backward, standing up, obviously a little in his cups. The apple brandy had done its work quickly.

He took the phone from my hand and started talking before he got the receiver to his mouth. "You did the prints already?"

He listened for a second and then turned around, eyes wide, to face the rest of us.

"Don't get out of the car," he said sternly, "hit the flashing lights, lock the doors, and sit tight. I'll be right there."

He hung up and started for the front door.

"Melissa ran off the road and hit a tree," he called out.

We followed him.

"She swerved to avoid hitting a boy," he said, pulling open the front door. "There was a child with a hunting rifle standing in the road with his back to the car, staring down the mountain. She hit the tree and he ran off."

"I'm coming with you," I said, reaching for my coat.

"No you're not," he snapped harshly. "The three of you are staying in this house and locking all the doors. There's a crazy boy with a rifle out there!"

I nodded. "She'll be all right, Skid."

He took in a breath, and then loped away, toward his squad car. The engine roared seconds later, all his lights were on, and he squealed and skidded away.

We stood for a second in the living room.

I rubbed my face. "God, what a day."

"Seriously," Lucinda agreed. "I'm beat down to the ground. I really have to get some sleep. I'm supposed to take a midnight shift."

"No," I objected immediately. "Call in. Get somebody else."

She smiled at me. "I'm in charge, sweetheart," she said wearily. "There isn't anybody else."

I realized, once again, how self-centered I'd been for a long while. Lucinda's world at the hospital was increasingly difficult. The economics of the hospital were currently its guiding dictum. Costs were going up, public health care and the health insurance industry were in a shambles, and callous administrators were slashing budgets and wreaking havoc nearly every day. I found it hard to fathom how Lucinda could ever concentrate on actually caring for a sick person. But she did. She knew every patient's name, knew their family members, details about their lives, spent extra time with them, always smiling, always warm. In fact, she was the caring, beautiful one of the group—or of any group I'd ever known.

I took several steps in her direction, sidled up to her, and kissed her temple. "Truer words were never spoken: there isn't anybody else like you."

She smiled, and I was momentarily filled with appreciation for everything in the universe.

Which sensation was instantly shattered by the sound of snoring.

Dr. Nelson had fallen asleep on my sofa.

13

Lucinda managed to get a few hours sleep before midnight. I woke up when she got out of bed, but only for a second. Moonlight slanted in through the window and seemed to be reflected from her spirit, out to the moon, and back to my bed, covering me like a sheet. I thought of John Donne: "Here lies a she sun, and a he moon there; She gives the best light to his sphere." I tried to wake up enough to tell her that, to quote the poetry to her, but Nepenthe overtook me, and I forgot how to speak, and she was gone.

When I woke up again, the unruly sun had invaded, invoking, this time, Emily Dickinson: "There's a certain slant of light, on winter afternoons, that oppresses, like the weight of cathedral tunes." I was very unhappy to be in bed alone.

I sat up, rubbed my eyes, and was suddenly, delightfully, accosted by the smell of bacon. I had heard or read that the smell of bacon was one of the few universally appealing sensations to the male of the species. Loath as I might have been to participate in a stereotype, I actually jumped out of bed, pulled on my pants and boots, and charged downstairs in my T-shirt, expecting to find Lucinda in the kitchen.

Instead, there was Dr. Nelson, chirping some unrecognizable

tune and turning bacon in the cast-iron skillet with a pair of silver tongs.

"Good morning!" she sang out, not turning to look at me.

"Bacon," I said.

"No," she corrected, "this is *Benton's* bacon, best in the world. I couldn't believe it when I saw it in your refrigerator."

"I don't drive to Tennessee *just* to get it," I said, coming to the stove, "but it would be worth it if I did."

"Yes."

She removed the finished delight from the skillet and laid the pieces gently on a paper towel, then blotted them with another paper towel.

"I also made eggs Florentine," she told me.

She stooped to open the oven door. Sure enough, there were two ramekins bubbling at the top. She used the tongs to pull them out and set them on the tiles beside the stove.

"Eggs Florentine?" I whispered, as if something holy might be happening.

"Well"—she shrugged—"it's closer to lunchtime than breakfast, really—you slept late again. And you had spinach and cheese, and eggs, so I thought. You know. If we had some kind of fresh baguette or something, this would be the perfect morning meal. Late morning. Do you see what time it is?"

I didn't look at the kitchen clock. I couldn't take my eyes off the eggs Florentine. But I did manage to recall something essential.

"You're not going to believe this," I told her, "but two days ago a loaf of Poilâne sourdough came in the mail, from Paris."

She didn't bother to hide her disbelief. "How is that possible?"

"I have odd friends," I told her, "and two of them live in Paris. They overnight the bread to me about once every other month or so."

"Why?" she asked, still clearly not believing that I had the bread.

"Because I like the bread, and they like me," I answered, squinting.

I went to the refrigerator, pulled out a plain brown bag, and took out what was left of the loaf. It was golden and the crust was hard and it smelled like a wheat field in summer—in the south of France.

"Pop it into the oven, just like this, not on a baking sheet, not wrapped, for about ten minutes while the eggs cool, and bread of the gods is yours."

She stood immobile for an instant, in awe of the world's greatest bread.

"This may turn out to be the best breakfast on the planet," she said.

"Certainly the best in Blue Mountain," I amended.

She opened the oven, tossed in the half-loaf, and beamed. "You know, I wait in line at this bakery whenever I'm in Paris."

"Because you don't have two friends who live there and send it to you in the comfort of your own home," I told her.

"Exactly," she agreed.

"Now, a bit of espresso, I would think," I said absently.

"Make mine a double," she said. "I really passed out last night. Sorry."

"You hit the sofa," I said, smiling, "and you were gone."

"Somebody covered me with a very nice quilt."

"That was me," I told her, tending to the espresso machine. "And that quilt was made by a woman named June Cotage, a kind of second mother to me. She's gone now, but the quilt is here, and it reminds me of her. And now you've been touched by her, too."

"Thank you, June," she said sweetly. "I slept unusually well."

"I did too." I pulled down two espresso cups from the cupboard. "Unusually well, I mean. I could barely wake up when Lucinda left."

"She went to the hospital?"

I nodded and pushed the button on the machine. It growled and whirred and then gave me espresso, two cups.

We sat at the kitchen table in silence for a moment, then, drinking espresso and blinking.

"Look, I— I do have to say," I stammered, "that something you said last night. I mean— I actually am having some kind of— some sort of very real transition, or something. And as I reflect on that process, those personal realizations, I wonder if it's possible that you might, somehow— well, be helping me."

"Sweetly, if a bit hesitantly, put," she responded. "That was obviously a little difficult for you to say. But just to be clear: you're the one making those things happen, whatever they are—not me. I open a door, or, really, just point out that there *is* a door. You do the rest; you walk through the door; you make the discoveries."

I sighed. "Every time I speak with you like this," I said, shaking my head, "you revert—deliberately, it seems—to the clichés of your profession."

"Ah," she said, sipping her espresso, "now you're getting to something useful. Let me see if I can put this correctly: in folklore studies, one particular, elementary focus is on folk motifs, is that correct?"

"Well, yes, a study of archetypes is essential to the basic understanding of folklore in general. Frazer's *The Golden Bough*, the Aarne-Thompson classification system, certainly Joseph Campbell's work—all depend, to a certain extent, on a knowledge of universal motifs for— wait. I see what you're getting at. You think you're so clever."

"I do?" She took another sip. "And what am I getting at?"

"You think you're explaining to me, in terms I can really understand, the value of the stereotype."

"And did it work?"

I sat back. I exhaled. "Yes," I admitted.

"Then I guess I really *am* so clever."

I smiled. "I guess you are."

Moments later the bread was perfect—hard crust, warm crumb. We ate in silence, as if we were in church, at Eucharist, accepting, taking into our bodies and our spirits, the essence of all life.

And when it was done, I gave thanks.

"What did you do to the eggs, exactly?" I asked. "I can't believe how fantastic they were."

"It's the paprika and nutmeg in the béchamel," she answered. "Plus, where did you get those eggs? They were amazing."

"Lucinda keeps chickens," I told her. "Aren't they good?"

"Who could have imagined that a visit to Blue Mountain would include a side trip to culinary heaven?"

I sighed. "Well, you're a few years too late for a truly spectacular, unique gastronomic experience. There used to be a place in town."

"Let me stop you," she interrupted. "I just had a very nice peak experience. I want to savor."

"Fair enough," I agreed.

And, anyway, how could I possibly have communicated the splendor of Miss Etta's cooking, the sweet creamed corn, the stewed-all-night beef, "white cloud" turnip-potato-butter mash, the golden chicken wings, the pickled beets, the carrots with handmade butter and homegrown tarragon? Miss Etta, like June Cotage, was gone, but never forgotten.

"Okay," Dr. Nelson said, "what do you say we bundle up and head down to the creepy cave where your demon lover lives?"

That made me laugh. "Right, my demon lover. I'm surprised to say this, but I really like the way you think. None of my other friends would ever suggest that kind of thing. I always have to be the one to offer the inappropriate and inadvisable course of action."

"I'll just skip the fact that you just said 'my *other* friends,'" she beamed, "and move right along to the 'let's get going' portion of the program."

"All right." I grinned. "Skidmore would hate this."

"Wait," she said, her usual smile gone. "Skidmore."

I knew what she meant. "Melissa. We should call to see if Melissa's all right."

I went immediately to the phone and dialed. Skid answered on the first ring.

"Sheriff," he said expectantly.

"Skid," I said back.

"Oh, I thought it was the— are you all right?"

"Yes," I answered quickly, "I was just checking to see if Melissa was all right."

"She's fine. The car's a little banged up, but we got it out of the ditch. Look, I was expecting another call. If you're all right and I'm all right, can I call you back in a while?"

"Of course," I said.

He hung up without another word.

"And?" Dr. Nelson wanted to know.

"Melissa's fine," I said, hanging up my phone, "but Skidmore seems preoccupied."

"Good," she said, getting up. "Let him be preoccupied, so we can go explore the cave."

14

The mountain sloped downward in back of my house. At a certain point, there was an astonishing panoramic view of the valley below, where the little town of Blue Mountain is nestled. That morning the images were stark: black tree limbs against the new-fallen snow; cold white sun against a colder blue sky. Dr. Nelson and I stepped and fell and waded and slipped our way downward for nearly a half an hour.

She was still in her rust-colored jacket. She'd pulled her hair back in some sort of ill-constructed braid, with no hat. I had donned a gray wool coat and a scarf. I had a wool hat in my pocket, but when I'd seen that she wasn't wearing one, I'd decided not to wear mine either, for some reason.

Neither of us spoke as we made our way down the mountain. It was hard going and we were both breathing heavily.

At last we came to a more level spot and stopped to rest for a moment.

"I'm suddenly worried that we won't find the damned thing," she whispered, "the cave."

"That's not an inconsequential concern, even though Skidmore marked it with tape," I agreed. "I think I've already said that I've explored every inch of this mountain, and I've never seen this cave."

"Skid said that it was overgrown," she ventured.

"I don't think you understand what I mean by 'every inch of this mountain,'" I told her.

"Well," she said, a little louder, "it didn't just appear overnight."

"No," I agreed.

"How will we know if we've gone too far down?" she asked.

"If we get to the bottom of the mountain," I said, "we've gone too far."

"Fine." And without another word, she was off, downward.

I followed. "Maybe we should fan out."

"I don't know," she objected. "The last time we did that, you had a strange interlude."

"I did *not* have a strange interlude," I protested. "But I see your point. We'll stay close enough to see each other at all times, right?"

"Right."

Another half an hour passed before I had to admit that we had probably passed the place where the cave was hidden.

"Hey?" I called out.

"Yes?" she answered.

"It didn't take Skid this long to get to the cave, do you think?" I said, walking toward her. "I'm pretty sure we should make our way back up. There was another place where the ground leveled off enough to handle a cave entrance back up about, I don't know, maybe eight hundred yards."

"We didn't see police tape," she objected. "Skidmore said he put up police tape. That's pretty noticeable, in all this snow."

"Right," I said, mostly to myself. "We should have seen that."

"Still"—she sighed—"I have to agree with you that we've probably passed it, somehow. Did it snow more last night? Could the entrance and the tape be covered with snow?"

"I don't think so," I said.

She shrugged and headed, slowly, back up the mountain.

I stood for a little longer. I wanted to take in the upward slant of the mountain in a sort of panoramic sweep. Everything looked different from that angle, and I thought perhaps I might see something new.

As Dr. Nelson trudged up the hill, I forced my eyes to move very slowly over every inch of the terrain. All the bare trees, the rock outcroppings, the dips, the level places—I tried to see them as if I had never looked at them before. Sometimes familiarity, I thought, can make things invisible. If you see something every day for years and years, you eventually take it for granted; you don't really notice it at all. Whereas new eyes might see it right away. Like the fabled purloined letter, I was looking for the obvious cave, hidden in plain sight.

Dr. Nelson was at least fifty feet away from me before I saw the granite boulders.

"Wait," I called out. "I think I might have something."

I began to make my way upward, toward her.

"What is it? Do you see the— did you find the cave?" She was gasping. The way down had been exhausting, the way up was excruciating.

"Not exactly," I said very softly, "but I did see something new, or new to me."

I pointed toward three giant boulders that we'd avoided on our way downward.

"Those rocks?" she asked. "They're new? They're not new."

"Sh," I told her, whispering. "The rocks aren't new. I've sat on those rocks, eaten and slept on them, stood on them to see farther—probably even jumped off them when I was very young. But I saw something new about them, just now."

I headed in the direction of the outcropping.

"What was it?" she asked, her voice lowered. "What did you see?"

"There's a space between the two biggest rocks that hasn't always been there," I said, grabbing on to a small tree to help me along, lungs bursting.

"What do you mean?"

"I mean there used to be something, a bush or a rock or a tree, in between these two boulders. I think it might have, until recently, covered up the cave."

"But," she began, barely audibly, "there's no police tape."

"Someone's taken it down, and covered up the opening," I said.

"What? What makes you think that?"

"Because the only reason I noticed the fissure between the rocks now," I told her, my voice at its lowest, "is because of the smoke."

"Smoke?" She craned her neck.

I stopped to join her in searching out the air. It was difficult to see, set against the snow and the gray of the rocks, but there was clearly a wisp of white smoke escaping between the two boulders. And once the eye defined that smoke, it was easier to see that there must be an opening that was somehow covered up, with only a tiny hole left through which the smoke could escape.

"What's covering the entrance?" she asked, barely making a sound.

"Can't tell," I answered. "Want to find out?"

She hesitated for only a second. "Okay."

Now that we both could see where we were headed, we moved slowly, trying very hard not to make a sound. Of course, it was a good bet that our voices had carried into the cave already, but I hoped that our current silence might afford us a modicum of surprise when we eventually entered there.

As we got closer, we slowed.

"You know," I said, my lips next to her ear, "this might be a bit foolhardy if, in fact, the boy with the gun is in there."

She nodded.

We stood for a second, uncertain what to do.

Then she put her face close to mine. "On the other hand, if your imaginary wife is in there, I'd really like to see her."

"Good," I said. "Right."

We were close enough now to see that someone had rigged a large square of canvas over the fissure. It was covered, or had been covered, with snow and twigs. Space had been left at the top, and it was through that space that small trails of smoke escaped.

We made it to the edge of the biggest boulder. There was a smaller rock by my left foot that held down a corner of the canvas. I leaned over, picked up the rock, and set it aside.

Hand on the canvas, I turned to look at Dr. Nelson. She was right behind me.

"Ready?" I asked.

She gave her head a single nod.

I took in a breath, held it, and tossed the canvas upward.

Instantly from inside the cave there were noises of surprise and scrambling.

"Issie?" I called, praying I would hear her voice answer me. "It's Fever. Fever Devilin. And Dr. Nelson, the doctor I was telling you about. The person who's helping me. Can we come in?"

Silence followed.

"Well?" Dr. Nelson whispered into my ear.

The canvas edge had folded back on itself and made an opening large enough to crawl through, but left little room for dignity or decorum. I peered in. The cave was dark, and now there wasn't a sound coming from its depths.

"I'm coming in," I announced loudly.

I hunched over and made my way through the opening on hands and knees. I could hear Dr. Nelson doing something similar behind me.

Once inside, I moved slowly. I could barely see. I raised a hand above my head to make certain there was room to stand, although the little bit of ambient light that came in told me there probably was. I got to my feet.

"Issie?" I called out.

Dr. Nelson managed to stand beside me.

My eyes were adjusting to the lack of light when a sudden shock of brightness blinded me again. Someone was shining a very powerful flashlight in our faces.

After a second a voice whispered, "It's all right, David."

A youthful grunt was followed by the cessation of light in my eyes. I was barely able to make out the fact that the boy we had seen before, still dressed in white hunting camouflage, was setting down an emergency road torch so that it was pointed upward. Light reflected from the ceiling. The boy picked up his firearm.

There was a taller, shadowy figure beside him. The orange glare from the flashlight illuminated the cave nicely, if a bit bizarrely, but I still couldn't make out who was standing beside the boy, though I had hope.

"What if they're not alone?" the boy asked his companion. "What if that sheriff is out there?"

The shadow moved toward some wooden crates and turned on another bright light.

I made a loud, involuntary gasping sound when I saw her. It caused the boy to twitch, and made the shadow-form smile. Because the shadow-form was Issie Raynerd.

I turned to Dr. Nelson. "*Now* do you see her?"

Dr. Nelson's enigmatic smile had returned. She nodded in the direction of the woman in black.

"You're Issie Raynerd," she said. "I've just seen a picture of you and Dr. Devilin. You look great."

"So you can see her?" I asked archly.

"I can," Dr. Nelson confirmed.

"So I'm not crazy."

"Jury's still out on that," she corrected. "But I see a woman standing over there that looks a whole lot like the woman in that photo."

"Give me my picture back," Issie said, moving toward us with alarming speed. "The sheriff took it. It's mine."

Her swift approach seemed to make the boy nervous, and he aimed his rifle directly at me.

"The picture's up in my house," I said quickly. "It's in my kitchen. It's fine. It's safe."

Dr. Nelson took a different tack. She thrust out her hand in friendship. "I'm Ceri Nelson," she said.

Issie stared at Dr. Nelson's hand.

"You think you can help him," Issie said, her eyes flickering, "but I'm the only one who can heal him. He doesn't know how sick he is. He's mad with his rage, and he'll do harm before he's better."

Dr. Nelson dropped her hand. "He needs all the help he can get, I'll grant you that. Why don't we work together?"

I could already see what Dr. Nelson was doing. I could hear it in her voice. She was using the same quasi-hypnotic voice on Issie that she had used on Lucinda in my kitchen, and before that, on me. But she was also encouraging Issie to think of her as a cohort, a colleague with a mutual cause. I found that to be clever.

"Work together?" Issie said weakly. "That— that would be nice. I haven't— I used to work with my mother sometimes, before. But she's— she's gone now."

"Well I'm here," said Dr. Nelson, holding out her hand again, "and I'd like to work with you."

This time Issie responded, but not to shake hands. She took Dr. Nelson's right hand in her left, holding hands. I saw Dr. Nelson exhale, just a little, and I had the impression that she was relieved, but I wasn't certain why.

"I don't trust them," David said suddenly.

"You can put your rifle down, David," Issie said. "Dr. Devilin won't hurt us, and Dr. Nelson is here to help."

The boy grumbled, obviously disagreeing, but he lowered his rifle, then set the safety and leaned it against a nearby cave wall.

I took a second, then, to survey the cave. It was larger than the interior of my house, and I couldn't believe I'd never explored it, or even known it was there. Someone, presumably Issie and David, had moved in boxes and crates, some chairs, lots of firewood, and three portable cots. These were arranged, it appeared, completely at random.

To one side of the entrance there was a large fire pit. It was still smoldering; some of the coals were orange and red. Smoke was sucked outward with remarkable efficiency through a small opening in the top of the canvas that covered the entrance to the cave. I couldn't tell how that was happening exactly, except that there also seemed to be air moving toward the opening from deeper inside the cave.

Beside the cots there were piles of clothing, and one of the wooden crates had been set up as a kind of dining table. The remains of a recent meal were in evidence.

"I can't tell you how happy I am to see you," Dr. Nelson chirped on. "I was beginning to be afraid that Fever had imagined you."

"Imagined me?" Issie stared into space for a moment. "I wonder sometimes if maybe he did."

Dr. Nelson and I looked at each other, and she shook her head, warning me, it seemed, not to comment on her strange observation.

"I can't understand how I never knew there was a cave here," I said, trying to sound casual. "Something this big, and so close— not five hundred yards from my house! How is that possible?"

"There was a big old rhododendron covering up the entrance,"

David volunteered, his voice only a little surly. "Nobody would ever a knowed this was here."

"No, but that's what I'm saying. How did *you* find it?"

"Ask her," he said, lifting his chin in the direction of Issie.

I turned to look at her.

"I knew about this place when I was little," she said dreamily. "Mother brought me here."

I shot a glance at Dr. Nelson.

But Dr. Nelson spoke quickly. "Issie, you said that you could heal Dr. Devilin. That's all I'm interested in. How can you do that? What can you do that would help him?"

"I have my mother's knowledge," Issie said, but her voice had gone a little high-pitched. "I know things. I have my mother's ways, her potions, and her poisons."

"She needs to rest," David growled, rushing to Issie's side. "She needs to lie down. This happens after she eats. She just needs a half a hour."

He moved toward us, nearly sideways, and took Issie by the arm.

"Wouldn't it be better if we went up to the house?" I suggested, stepping toward them both.

From nowhere the boy produced a vicious-looking blade, some sort of nightmare version of a hunting knife. It gleamed even in the dull light of the cave: it had been polished; it had been cared for. The point moved within inches of my Adam's apple, but not before I saw the serrated top.

I froze. There was no telling, I thought, what a wild boy that age would do.

Issie seemed dismayed at the presence of the knife but was unable or unwilling to say anything.

"Don't touch her," the boy snarled.

I took a step backward, very slowly.

Suddenly Dr. Nelson dropped, as if she were going to tie her shoe. Or as if she might be having some sort of fainting spell.

But instead of collapsing, she grabbed the boy's ankle, held it firmly, and simply stood up. The boy went backward, a terrible look of surprise on his face, and landed hard on his back, which knocked the wind out of him. The knife clattered to the stone floor and the boy began to grunt and gasp for breath.

Issie hugged herself at the elbows and swayed, looking around wildly, as if she didn't know where she was or what was happening. She began to moan.

Dr. Nelson took two steps, scooped up the hunting knife and tossed it behind her, in the direction of the cave entrance. Then she fell immediately to one knee and put her hand gently on the boy's chest, patting him.

"You just got the breath knocked out of you," she said gently. "You'll be all right in a second. Breathe slowly, all right?"

The boy blinked, then nodded.

"But if you threaten Dr. Devilin or me with that knife again," Dr. Nelson continued. "I'll stick it right here until it comes out your back through your spine. You understand that?"

The boy managed to nod.

Dr. Nelson looked up at me. "Let's get him to one of those cots," she said.

I nodded and moved toward her and the boy.

Issie continued to rock and moan, every once in a while singing bits and half phrases from ancient tunes.

Dr. Nelson and I easily managed to get the boy onto one of the cots. He was very thin, as it turned out, and couldn't have weighed more than fifty pounds, probably less. We set him down, and Dr. Nelson covered him with a blanket.

I turned to Issie.

"Listen," I began reasonably, not moving too close to her, "why don't you and David come back with us to the house. It's nice and warm, there's plenty to eat, and you could get a good rest."

"No"—she sighed, hopelessly—"I have to wait here. I have to stay here. He won't find me otherwise. I know he's trying to find me."

"Who's trying to find you?" Dr. Nelson asked softly, coming to stand beside me.

Issie stopped twitching and moaning for a second and looked at Dr. Nelson. Her face was a mask of impossible despair. "You don't know my story," she said, "and Fever, he's not right. I thought he was tormenting me, but he really doesn't remember some things. He's sick. I can see that now. I see that you're trying to help him, too. But it's no use. I'm the only one who can help him. You don't know our story."

Dr. Nelson nodded. "Then why don't you tell me," she said, her supernaturally mesmerizing tones dialed up to dizzying effect. It was clear that she was in a kind of extreme therapist mode.

The sound of Dr. Nelson's voice seemed to overtake Issie's state of mind. She opened her eyes all the way, her vision seemed to clear a bit, and she dropped her hands to her side.

"All right," she said to us, her voice eerily calm, "I'll tell you what happened. I'll tell you how I came to be the wife of a man I couldn't love, no matter how hard I tried. And then I'll tell you how I died, and how I'll die again."

15

"I first met Fever as a student," Issie said. "That's how it began."

The three of us were seated close to the fire coals. The two women were on folding chairs and I was perched a bit uncomfortably on the top of a heavy wooden box. The hem of Issie's dress was dangerously close to the embers, but she didn't seem to notice.

I started to ask her something, but Dr. Nelson, again, gave me a stern look.

"World mythology class, do you remember that much at least?" Issie asked me.

I nodded.

"I loved that class," she said dreamily. "Oh, there were more than a hundred people in the room, and everyone enjoyed the lectures and the stories and the songs, but no one liked it as much as I did."

Beside us I heard a scuffling. I turned to see that the boy was sitting up, still somewhat dazed.

"He tried not to show it," Issie continued, "but I think it was clear to one and all that I was Fever's favorite. He looked right at me when he sang 'Sweet William and Lady Margaret.' I love that song."

One of the coals popped and red sparks shot in every direction.

"But it wasn't until summer that the trouble began," she said.

"Fever went away. He went to Cornwall, that's in England. Didn't you go to Cornwall?"

She looked at me, waiting for a response.

I glanced briefly at Dr. Nelson, but clearly Issie was waiting for an answer.

"In fact," I said, "I finished my doctoral dissertation, or research for the dissertation, in Cornwall, but that was fifteen—more than fifteen years ago."

"Oh," she said, her face beaming for the first time since I'd encountered her, "you do remember. That's a good sign. Don't you think that's a good sign, Dr. Nelson?"

"I do," she said curtly. "Go on with your story."

"Well," Issie responded, "I wanted to go along. I thought I could be a research assistant or an intern—they had both at the school. But they said I wasn't a graduate student. I had just started. So, I went to Mother. She was against my going. She didn't want me to bother Fever. But I cried and cried, you know how young girls are. And she finally relented. She gave me the money for the trip, and some potions and powders to help me on the way, because I was prone to seasickness. I was prone to seasickness, but I could never fly, never, so we booked a ship's passage. She gave me medicines for the ocean voyage—and some special powders for another use when I got to Cornwall—but I'm not supposed to talk about that. You understand: everything might have been all right. It could all have worked out. But then she made a mistake, my mother. She insisted—she made *him* come along with me, to accompany me on the trip—like a chaperone. Wish to God that she hadn't and I mean that, Fever, with all my heart. You have to believe me. I wish to God that he'd never come with me."

"Who came with you?" Dr. Nelson asked softly. "Who was your chaperone?"

"Tristan," she whispered violently, as if the name had been ripped from her throat.

I took in a breath, about to explain to her in no uncertain terms that Tristan Newcomb would most likely have been dead by the time I was in Cornwall, but Issie forged ahead with her story.

"I didn't mean to, but we were both so sick," Issie moaned. "There came up a terrible storm on the sea. The waves were black and the ship— we thought the ship was like to capsize. I knew we were going to die. I was certain of it. But he said it was just a storm, and we should take the medicine and go to sleep. He said we'd feel better. It was his idea. I got the powders, and prayed and prayed. He was sick, but not as wild as I was. He tried to calm me down. He tried. But I was so afraid. And then it happened. I mixed the powders. I got the powders mixed up, I mean. I gave us the wrong one. I could barely open my eyes to concentrate. It wasn't my fault. It was his idea. I didn't mean to do it. We were so sick. I got confused."

Her voice had grown high-pitched again, and she was reeling, nearly hysterical.

From behind us I heard an all-too-familiar clacking sound. It sounded very much like the bolt of a rifle.

"Stop it!" the boy shouted. "Stop making her tell this story! She's going to have a spell!"

I turned to see the boy, on his feet, with the rifle pointed at us once more.

"Maybe I should have collected that gun when the boy was down for the count," I said out loud, to no one in particular.

"Shut up," the boy snarled. "Issie, you come over here. Right now."

Issie stood, a little in a trance.

"She wanted to tell us the story," Dr. Nelson ventured calmly. "We didn't ask her to do it."

"It makes her crazy," the boy said.

Issie looked me directly in the eye. "I'm not crazy," she said.

The look in those eyes was terrifying.

"Come on," the boy said to Issie. "Come on over here."

Issie nodded, still in a kind of trance, and moved, nearly floated toward the boy. I wasn't certain if I should say anything or try to stop her, because she did seem on the verge of collapse.

I looked at Dr. Nelson, but she had her eyes locked on Issie, a mix of strange fascination and crooked amusement on her face.

"I just wanted to tell them," Issie mumbled as she drew nearer to the boy.

"Sh," he said, a little impatiently. "They don't know."

"They don't?" she asked, completely lost.

"No," the boy snapped. "Now, tell them to get along."

"What?" she said, looking around the room, once again as if she had no idea where she was.

"Tell them two to clear out!"

"Oh," she answered immediately. "Dr. Devilin, Dr. Nelson—you should leave now."

Dr. Nelson folded her arms in front of her. "We could leave, but I'm not sure how that would help you. The sheriff knows you're here. And now that you've accosted us, he'll have more than a simple trespassing charge against you. I mean, you can't really stay here, you know that, right?"

"We stayed here for near a month before anybody knew," the boy sneered. "You don't know everything."

"Well, I know this," Dr. Nelson went on. "Now that the sheriff knows you're here, he'll cart you off to jail."

"If he can find us."

The boy took a hold of Issie's black cloak and pulled her gently toward him with one hand, keeping the other hand on his gun.

"I'm not going anywhere," Issie said, "until Fever tells me that he doesn't hate me. Until he forgives Tristan."

"I don't mean to go far away," the boy whispered, "just go hiding, like we done before."

"Oh." Issie looked over her shoulder, toward the back of the cave. That's when I realized that the slight breeze I had felt at the entrance to the cave, and the unusual drawing of smoke outward, probably meant that the cave had another entrance—that it wasn't a cave at all, really, but a tunnel.

Issie started walking, or rambling, toward the inner reaches of the cave. The boy picked up one of the road torches, then moved to turn the other one off. He turned, very suddenly, away from us, and darkness descended. All I could see was the deeper recesses of the cave where the flashlight pointed as Issie and David moved away from the entrance and downward into the deeper part of the labyrinth.

"Don't follow us," David called out, his voice echoing. "I don't mind if I shoot you and leave you for dead. I think you know that."

"He won't mean to kill you, Fever," Issie called out, her voice only a little more stable, "but he might do it by accident. Like the deer. In the woods."

In my mind's eye the deer appeared, sleeping in its pool of blood.

"You can't run around down here forever," Dr. Nelson called out reasonably.

"Yes I can!" the boy shouted. "I was *born* in a cave!"

"No, but this is— you're being shortsighted." Dr. Nelson took a few steps in their direction. "Issie?"

But the cave obviously took a turn to the left and farther downward because the last of the light disappeared in those directions. Except for the red coals in the fire pit and a small stream of clearer light from the hole in the canvas, illumination had vanished.

"Come on," Dr. Nelson said, heading toward the back of the cave.

"Wait," I said instantly, taking a single step in her direction. "Wait a second. You get twenty feet back there and it's going to be impossible to see. Impossible."

I could barely make out her silhouette. She paused. Then she strode deliberately toward one of the boxes and picked up another flashlight.

"Unless we use this," she said, and turned on the light.

"Well," I admitted, "yes, that would make a difference."

I moved toward her, and she took off at a fair pace. I caught up with her just as the cave began to slope a little downward. Twenty more steps and the pathway took a fairly sharp turn to the left.

The problem was that with our own torch illuminated, it was impossible to see the bouncing glow from David's flashlight. And if we turned our light off, it was impossible to see at all.

We tried, a few times, stopping dead still and turning off our flashlight, but to no avail. Every time we did, there was no sign of the other light; we were only plunged into impossible darkness. And that darkness was remarkably oppressive. It only took a few seconds of total deprivation to make the eyes and the mind play tricks. And any sound in the stone midnight was amplified beyond reality. The slow intake of breath was cannon fire. The slightest shifting of a toe was an avalanche.

When we came to a place where the cave split into three separate passages, we stopped for good.

"At this point I have to tell you," I said to Dr. Nelson, "that if we continue down any one of these halls, the news story will be a sad one. First there will be alarm; a massive hunt. But that will be followed by the great sorrow of never finding our bodies. Eventually, as the years roll on, there will only be the occasional remembrance of friends and acquaintances—maybe at Christmas—to say that we'd ever been on this earth."

"Nice," Dr. Nelson chided. "But I agree, alas. It would be insane to go any farther."

"And a plethora of insanity already abounds, abroad in the land," I intoned.

"Indeed," she said, heading back the way we'd come.

We walked for a moment in silence, neither one of us wanting to admit the fear that we might already be a bit lost in the caves.

Luckily, seconds later, the cave turned to our right and I could just make out a bit of crimson on the ceiling, painted there from the red coals of the fire pit. It was beautiful.

Unwilling to acknowledge her own relief at the sight of the entrance, Dr. Nelson chose, instead, to continue with her therapy games.

"What is it that she wants you to forgive, Fever?" she asked me.

"Hold on," I said as we made our way past the cots and the wooden crates. "Just a second. Let's not skip over the very important, 'You were right, Dr. Devilin. There *is* a strange crazed woman in black.'"

"You want me to say that?" she asked.

"Yes. And then I want you to say, 'She's not a figment of your imagination. She's real. I was wrong, and you're not crazy, Dr. Devilin.' Go on. Say it."

She stopped several feet shy of the entrance and cocked her head. "Here's what I'm willing to say. I saw a woman. I saw a boy. I touched the woman, too, and I was greatly relieved to find her entirely corporeal."

"I wondered what that sigh of relief was about when she took your hand," I said, grinning. "You were afraid that she might be— what, a ghost?"

"Laugh all you want to," she told me. "I've seen people who looked more real than she does, and they were actually thin as air."

"What?"

"But as to that woman's being real?" she went on, ignoring my quizzical expostulation. "I haven't made up my mind about that. Just like I haven't made up my mind about whether or not you're crazy."

Then she headed for the entrance once more.

"Now you're just saying that," I whined, following her. "You're just trying to irritate me."

"Is it working?" She thrust the canvas outward. Snow fell around her and a rush of colder air stung my face.

"Beyond all measure," I responded. "You're one of the most irritating people I've ever met—and I think once you get to know my other friends, you'll be very insulted by that concept."

I could only see the side of her face, but I could tell she was grinning, as the expression goes, ear to ear. She stepped out of the cave; I followed.

The sky had clouded over a bit, a circumstance not unusual for the mountain. Clear weather could turn ugly in thirty seconds. As we trudged up the hillside toward my house, it looked as if it might snow again.

"I have to say," I told Dr. Nelson, "that I'm a bit uncomfortable with the idea that there are strange creatures crawling around in the caves underneath the house where I live. Part of me wants to tie some piece of twine to the mouth of the cave so I can find my way out, and then forge on into the darkness."

She slowed a bit, then turned around and looked back down toward the cave entrance. "Tie something to the mouth of the cave," she repeated. "Like Theseus and Ariadne on Minos?"

"Exactly!" I said.

"Really?" she went on. "What clearer metaphor for your subconscious could there be than that? You're afraid of the things that are hidden in the depths of your psyche—you're Theseus looking for his Minotaur."

That startled me. "You know, this is a little remarkable, but all during my time in and out of the coma, I was thinking about Minotaurs—seriously. I saw them in the clouds."

"Really." She stared at me.

I sighed. "I am a deeply troubled person."

"Amen." And she resumed her ascent toward my home, and away from the hollow labyrinth.

16

Dr. Nelson and I had decided to warm up in front of the fire with a bit of apple brandy. It had been her idea, but I couldn't have agreed more. My only addition was to include the last of the bread and a bit of Comté cheese. We'd taken off our coats and shoes, stoked the fire, poured the drink, and settled in the living room to ponder and discuss. She had sprawled on the sofa; I had slouched into one of the big chairs facing the sofa. We had decided not to call Skidmore to tell him about our adventure. He'd find out soon enough that his police tape was gone and the visitors had come back to the cave.

"You know," Dr. Nelson concluded, after a lengthy discourse on a particularly Jungian interpretation of mythic images, "Jung's biographer said that Jung never let any of these mythic figures from his dreams leave his thoughts until they had told him why they'd appeared in the first place."

I slumped a little. "You mean that I have to get Issie to tell me why she's here."

"I mean," she said, "that we both have to understand her reasons for appearing to you at all. I believe that you called her; you brought her here."

"You think I rang this woman up and *asked* her to visit me?" I demanded.

"Not on the telephone," she snapped. "I mean that your bio-electric magnet drew her here."

"Oh, for God's sake," I muttered.

"Just the way you've attracted so many— *so* many other odd people and events in your life." And with that, she polished off her second apple brandy.

"You realize that I don't, for one second, buy into your bizarre *magnet* theory."

"All right," she said, but she said it in such a way as to let me know that she knew better. "Tell me about Cornwall, then—your time in Cornwall. Did this woman visit you?"

"No."

"But you were there for your doctoral research."

"To investigate the Crick Stone," I nodded, "a very unusual, prehistoric grouping of rocks, several miles north of Madron."

"What, like Stonehenge?"

"Not entirely," I told her, setting my empty glass on the coffee table between us. "One of the stones has a huge hole in it, man-made. The formation is also called Mên-an-tol, which means, in Cornish, 'the hole stone.' It's basically three granite rocks, two upright narrow ones stuck one end in the ground on either side of the hole stone, so that, from a certain angle, it looks like the number 101."

"And there are various interpretations as to what the use or meaning might have been."

"Yes," I agreed, "it might have been the entrance to a tomb at one time, though there's no evidence of that. Or, like Stonehenge, some scholars think it could have been an ancient calendar."

"But that's not why you were there." She folded her hands and closed her eyes.

"No," I said. "I was interested in other stories."

"What other stories?"

"Variously?" I answered. "That the ring had a fairy guardian who could cure any malady, that any woman who went back and forth through the stone would become pregnant with an other-worldly child, or, conversely, that if your baby had been stolen by fairies and replaced with a changeling, you could pass the change-ling through the stone and get your real child back."

"Fascinating."

"But I found most interesting," I continued, "stories that in-sisted these stones were an entrance to another world, another reality."

She opened her eyes. "That's what you were there to investi-gate?"

"Yes."

"And?"

"I spent a month," I began, "gathering every bit of local in-formation I could find, in addition to the research I'd already done—several years' worth, on and off. The idea was that if you could properly walk around and through the three stones, just right, you would, on your last pass through the hole, step into another world."

"You walked in a hidden pattern around the stones?" She sat forward. "Like an invisible labyrinth."

"I—I guess so," I admitted. "If you insist on being a one-note tune."

"So?" she goaded.

"What?"

"So did you find the pattern?" She wanted to know. "Did you go into another reality?"

"No." I smiled indulgently. "I was doing research for my doc-torate, not writing a science fiction screenplay."

"You didn't even try?" she said.

"Of course not," I answered, exasperated. "I would have felt—it would have been ridiculous. Why are you asking me that?"

"Well, if I'd gone all the way to Cornwall to see a portal to another world," she said, "I would have at least given it a whirl. Damn."

"You're ruining a perfectly good intellectual discussion, you realize," I told her.

"And you didn't see this woman, Issie, at all when you were there," she said in a deliberate attempt to change the direction of the conversation.

"I did not. And aren't you going to say anything more about the fact that she's real?"

"The photograph already proved that she was sort of real," she said. "What else did you want me to say?"

"I've already told you what to say," I goaded.

"You were right," she sighed laboriously, "and I was wrong: the girl is real and you're not crazy—at least not on that account. Happy?"

"Delirious."

"Wait. The photo." She sat up. "You sent it to Dr. Andrews. You should check your e-mail or your answering machine or something, in case he got back with you, right?"

I stood and went immediately over to the answering machine, and surely enough, the red light was blinking. I pressed the button.

"Fever!" said Andrews's voice instantly. "Jesus. That's Issie Raynerd in that photo with you. You don't remember her? She was a student of yours. And mine. She was in my medieval literature course and your world mythology. How do I remember that? Anyway, that's who she is. Pretty as a picture, crazy as a loon. She scared everybody. Even I thought twice about dating her. I think it was partly the name. I mean, what cruel mother names her child *Issie*? I never did date her, in fact, because she only had eyes for you. How in the hell do you not remember her? Anyway, she died about ten years ago. That was the rumor, anyway. Why do you ask? And why on earth do you have that picture after all this time? Anyway, I'm in the middle of grading final exams and turning in final grades and committee work and departmental changes and— look, all is madness. But maybe I could come up and visit after Christmas. By the way, there's some shrink nosing around, asking questions about you. Dr. Nelson is her name, very pretty. I told her nothing. Your secret is safe with me. Just kidding. That was for Lucinda, in case you're listening to this with her. Hi, Lucinda! All right."

That was the end of the message.

Dr. Nelson had come into the kitchen and listened to the message with me.

"I guess that confirms it," she said softly. "She's real, she was a student of yours, and she died."

"And apparently there's some shrink nosing around asking questions about me."

"Andrews is a relatively bold fancier of women, wouldn't you say?" she asked, heading back into the living room.

"He made a pass at you," I assumed.

"Several, but that's not what I'm asking. He remembered this woman. You didn't. That tells us something about both of you, doesn't it?"

"Does it?" I asked.

"For one thing," she said, settling back down onto the sofa, "it tells us that after all this time he still remembers that a young woman liked you better than she liked him."

"Andrews and I— haven't I already said that in my early days at the university I was really more interested in having students like me than I was in— well, in anything else. He and I were in a kind of friendly competition. He felt secure in his pursuit of les femmes because it was his supposition that the English accent is the elixir of love for most American students. Whereas I was, if I

may encroach onto your territory, compensating for a pathological shyness and a nearly complete lack of any social grace in
my attempts to interest women."

"He was cocky, you were scared," she said, as if it were obvious. "Got it."

I sat back down in my chair. "I *was* scared, as a matter of fact.
My upbringing was so very bizarre that it did nothing to prepare
me for any genuine sort of human intercourse, if I may use that
word."

"A lesser man would just have said *interaction*." She smirked.

"At any rate, I eventually settled down—not certain why. And
Andrews won in the Casanova arena."

"Hm," she said, making it clear that she was unconvinced
about something that I'd said.

"I have to confess," I told her, a bit more reflectively, "that try
as I might, I still don't actually remember this woman, Issie. And
by the way, I agree with Andrews. It's a terrible name."

"It's probably not her *name* name," Dr. Nelson said. "Don't you
think it's short for something?"

"Oh," I admitted. "Probably so. Isadora, maybe?"

"Maybe," she responded. "But wouldn't that be *Izzie*?"

"Did anyone ever call Isadora Duncan *Izzie*?"

"Not that I know of." She laughed.

"Why can't I remember her?" I asked, surprised to hear the
question coming out of my mouth.

"Yes," she said slowly, "that is the question. You're— I mean,
excuse my language, but you're repressing."

"I'm not repressing," I said instantly. "And are you actually
required to use every psychological cliché in the world?"

"The reason they're clichés is that they're most often true," she
said slyly. "If you weren't repressing, you'd have taken a moment
to consider the possibility. But since you shot right back with your
'I'm not repressing'—know what that means?"

"I'm repressing?" I answered, eyebrows raised.

"But why?" She sat up.

I stared into the fire. "I'm repressing. I probably am. I hate saying that. I actually have a pretty good memory. I mean, I don't remember every student, but someone like that, especially if she was that crazy even back then, you'd think it would at least ring a bell."

"And if Dr. Andrews's memory of her is that she was—what did he say, pretty as a picture, crazy as a loon?"

What happened then would be difficult to describe. I had another feeling of being dizzy, the way I'd had when the boy had shot into my house, the same as I'd had when Dr. Nelson's hypnotizing tones had affected me.

I saw the living room shift. A kind of vague, golden light seemed to come from behind everything, making the room almost two-dimensional. I had a vague humming in my ears, an almost musical sound.

It only lasted for a second or two, but Dr. Nelson noticed it.

"What just happened to you?" she asked.

I shook my head. I couldn't tell her what had happened, because I didn't know.

"But I was afraid of the stone formation in Cornwall." I closed my eyes. "I wanted with every fiber of my being to try the various patterns that local people had talked about. I wanted to walk around the stones and step through the portal and find another reality. When I was there, by myself, I wanted it more than anything I've ever wanted—before or since."

"But you were afraid," she said softly. "Why?"

"Because I knew I wouldn't come back."

"Right," she said.

"Because I knew that I'd already gone through other portals like that one," I told her, almost silently, "without ever finding my way back."

"Yes," she encouraged, "but there's more to it. What happened in Cornwall?"

"What do you mean?"

"You know what I mean," she said. "Something happened."

"No," I answered, more strongly than before. "I did my research, I took a little time off to visit some . . . some other places, and I came back to the university. That's all."

"What other places did you visit?"

"Just, it was just a— look it was kind of personal."

"Embarrassing?"

"No," I said quickly, and a little defensively, "I went to Ireland to see the place where my— I had an ancestor, sort of the founder of the Devilin clan, who was born in Wales but went to Ireland for work when he was young. He was apprenticed to a silversmith, fell in love with a woman who didn't love him, and killed a man."

"Oh," she said, sitting up, "I have to hear about this."

"His name was Conner Briarwood," I said, with a small portion of melancholy. "He narrowly avoided being hanged for murder, and was set free on something like a technicality. He changed his last name to Devilin, and escaped to America. He came to these hills, married, had children and grandchildren—lived a good life."

"There's more," she said.

"Yes." I sighed. "After he was dead I found a trunk of his. In it there were hundreds of pages of his story. But it was the same short story, written over and over again, obsessively. Every one with only slight variations. It was clear to me that he was trying, desperately, to make the ending come out differently. But it never did. In the end the woman still didn't love him, and the murdered man's life would not be restored. The discovery of that trunk was at least partially responsible for my interest in folklore, because it engendered a keen, strange longing to find answers in the past. And, of course, I realized when I read those pages, that I would never have any hope of being normal. I knew then that it wasn't just my parents. I had historical genetic trouble."

"And?" she insisted.

"And what?" I said, genuinely not knowing what she was after.

"It's obvious." She leaned forward. "There you were in Wales trying to figure out a way into a different reality, and there's the ghost of your ancestor who also wanted to manage some kind of metaphysical chicanery to make his own reality come out differently. But something happened that we're still not talking about. Something happened in Wales, or in Ireland. It triggered something or set something off in you—maybe made you go to Ireland to see where your ancestor had killed a man. How did you get there?"

"Get where? To Ireland?" I thought for a second. "Small boat."

"Interesting," she said.

"Look," I said, standing, "I don't know where this is getting us. The problem is not what happened in Wales years ago, the problem is that there is a crazy woman and a boy with a gun crawling around in a cave under my house right now!"

I began to pace, something I never did.

"I hope you're listening to yourself," Dr. Nelson said, settling back onto the sofa. "Your entire intellectual career is based on things that happened in the past, long ago. That's what you think is important. Well, me too. What happened in your past is important because it made you what you are now—a sleep-deprived, pacing product of too much hallucination and not enough acceptance of who and what you really are."

"Who and what I really am?" I snarled. "And just what would that be?"

"A man who needs to excavate the caves underneath his house," she said calmly.

"Oh really," I sneered.

"I just want you to observe," she continued, very softly, "that you're up on your feet, snarling and sneering at me, for absolutely no immediate reason. I would have to surmise that we're getting closer to what it is that actually happened in Wales."

"Nothing happened in Wales!" I exploded.

She sat silently. It was exactly the right thing to do. It made my outburst stand alone in the room, as unattractive and unwarranted as it was: an obvious sign that something was wrong.

My shoulders sagged. The fire popped. Dr. Nelson smiled.

"I guess something happened in Wales," I said weakly.

"I guess it did."

"Is that why I can't remember this woman, Issie?"

She shrugged good-naturedly. "Could be."

"And you think it's more important to find out about that," I said, returning to my chair, "than it is to capture Issie and Wild Child and turn them over to a zoo."

"I think that the two go hand in hand," she told me, "and I think that's just the start. You have a lot of work to do."

"Work?"

"The things that have taken years to make you strange," she said, "can't be undone in a few days."

"Oh," I said. "That work."

"So tell me about Ireland."

I slumped down in the chair. "I'd done the research about that, too. I didn't know the name of the town where my ancestor Conner Briarwood had been, but I knew that the silversmith with whom he apprenticed was named Jamison, and that Jamison silver pieces were valued quite highly in the antiques marketplace. So finding that he'd worked in the fishing village of Dunmore East was no trouble. At a certain time in history, there had been a relatively large harbor in the village, and that enabled easy commerce for Jamison. I knew from previous research that along a walk from Dunmore East to Ballymacaw, by a brook underneath a hazel tree, was the place where my kin had killed a man with a dagger or a rapier or some such. I can't explain why, but I had been seized with an irrational obsession to see the spot where it happened. I tried for several days to deny the impulse, but in the end I chartered a small boat and crossed the Celtic Sea. It was a choppy voyage, but not entirely unpleasant. The village is very lovely."

"Did you find the place you were looking for?"

"I did." I closed my eyes, picturing it. "I found the hazel; the small brook. The sun was out, and very warm, lovely. I tried to imagine Molly, that was the woman's name, the woman that Conner loved. He discovered her underneath the tree with another man, and the other man was making advances that appeared unwanted. Conner was enraged, and took out his rapier and dagger. They fought, this other man and Conner. All the while this Molly was screaming, trying to stop the fight. In the end the other man was dead and Molly, at last, explained that she had recently married him, or was about to marry him. Conner had killed the man she actually loved."

I opened my eyes.

"That's where your family tree took a turn," she said.

"Yes," I admitted. "That had to be part of my obsession, the fact that without that event, Conner would most likely have gone back to Scotland, or stayed in Ireland, and I wouldn't exist. But every family tree is filled with odd twists and turns. It wasn't just that."

"No," said Dr. Nelson firmly. "It wasn't just that."

"I was overwhelmed by a sense of betrayal." I heard those words come out of my mouth as I was saying them, as if someone else were talking.

"Betrayal," she said. "That's fascinating."

I rubbed my eyes. "All right. Enough of this. I mean, I can't do this any more right now, this sentimental journey. I realize that we actually should have called Skidmore as soon as we got back to tell him about our adventure. And I'm absolutely dying for you to confirm to him, and to Lucinda, that my demon bride does, most assuredly exist. In the flesh. In the cave."

"All right," she agreed instantly. "Let's call now."

She stood. I was only a little taken aback, and stood, too.

"Good," I said, a little uncertainly, thanks to her sudden change of direction.

"But didn't you find it interesting," she added, walking toward the kitchen, "that Issie talked about a choppy sea, and seasickness, on her journey to visit you in Wales? What was all that—about taking the wrong medicine or something?"

"That was odd," I agreed, going to the phone. "Very odd. No idea what she was talking about."

Into the kitchen, I dialed the telephone. Skidmore picked up almost instantly.

"Sheriff." His voice was unusually cold.

"Skid, it's Fever," I began. "Look, don't be mad, but Dr. Nelson and I went down to the cave where this woman and the boy—"

"Damn it, Fever," he snapped. "This is not—"

"Your police tape was gone, the cave was covered up again, we barely found it, the woman and the boy were in there, and Dr. Nelson was with me the entire time." The words spilled forth, a torrent from a broken dam. "She saw everything."

Skidmore was silent.

Then: "Put her on."

I handed the phone to Dr. Nelson.

"Sheriff," she said calmly, "the woman who visited Fever the other night is real. I saw her. And the boy. They've been living in the cave. And the cave has at least one other entrance."

She listened, and as she did, her perennial smile disappeared.

"Oh." She looked at the kitchen floor. "You're absolutely sure about that?"

She listened for another second, and then handed the phone back to me.

"Fever?" he asked.

"I'm here."

"We did manage to get some print evidence from the cave. That's what I was waiting for when you called awhile ago. The boy? He's been missing from Central State Hospital in Milledgeville for several months. Considered armed and dangerous. And he's not a boy. He's thirty."

I think my face must have flinched. Dr. Nelson nodded, as if agreeing with whatever surprise I was registering.

"That can't be right," I said slowly. "I mean—he's not thirty. You have erroneous information."

"Prints are a perfect match," he said flatly. "Fever, his name is David Newcomb."

"What?" I gaped at Dr. Nelson. "David Newcomb?"

"Wait," she said, "Newcomb? As in the Newcombs who kind of owned this town? Skidmore didn't tell me that."

I nodded, but Skidmore kept talking.

"It's unclear why he was in the mental hospital, exactly," the sheriff told me curtly, "but he may have killed as many as seven people. And he was only in the hospital for less than a week, far as I can tell—I'm still in the process of acquiring information about him. He seems to have committed himself, for some reason, and then broken out a short while later."

"But, what about the woman?"

"The other prints didn't get any match in the database," he answered. "And there's no one in the database at all by the name of Issie Raynerd. But since there *was* another set of prints in the cave, I'm prepared to listen to what Dr. Nelson has to say about the woman you encountered there. Which, let me just say this again: *don't go down there anymore!*"

"Right," I answered immediately. "Exactly."

I could tell how angry he was. I just didn't know why. I'd gone places he'd told me not to go, and done things he'd told me not to do, dozens of times. Ordinarily he just would have thought I was—maybe *incorrigible* would be the word. But this was obviously different. He was genuinely upset.

"Is there something you're not telling me, Skid?" I asked quietly.

More silence ensued.

"I don't know how much of this I can tell you right now," he said finally, sighing.

"Because it's confidential—what? Police business. In the past you've never hesitated—"

"Because I don't know your state of mind," he told me bluntly. "Because I don't know how much you can take. Sorry."

I would have to admit to being significantly deflated by that pronouncement. It must have shown, once again, on my face, because Dr. Nelson put her hand on my arm.

"What?" she whispered.

"Look, *Sheriff*," I said, a bit tersely, "you thought I was crazy because I imagined a woman in my home. Now it turns out she was here. So, I was right and you were wrong. How does that make me so delicate that you can't tell me everything about this situation—a situation that obviously involves me in ways I don't even yet know?"

"You died and came back to life," he began, his voice rising inappropriately, "stayed in a coma for three months, hallucinated for weeks after that, and now you're under the care of a very serious psychiatrist. I don't see how that makes you entirely *stable*."

By the end of his short tirade I had to hold the phone away from my ear because he was shouting so loudly. Dr. Nelson heard.

"I'm not that serious a psychiatrist," she sang out.

"You listen to me, Dr. Devilin!" the sheriff growled. "I'm telling you to stay put in your house until I get there. Melissa and me, we're coming back with dogs and guns and people—state troopers, maybe FBI. We're going to find this David Newcomb. He's a very, very bad person. I haven't told you everything and I'm not going to. But you stay away from him and you make Ceri do the same. Do you hear me? I can't have either one of you get dead. Not at Christmas time!"

He slammed down the phone.

"Hey, that's right," Dr. Nelson chirped. "It's only a couple of days until Christmas."

I gaped for a moment. "I have to sit down."

I reached out for a kitchen chair and sat, unsteadily, facing the plywood window covering.

Dr. Nelson took a seat beside me.

We sat for a while, staring out the remaining windowpanes. Snow clouds were low in the sky, a charcoal smudge covering up the sun.

"What does this mean?" I asked at last. "Another Newcomb dwarf, a phantom bride, and a psychiatrist with a mythological name—all visit my house at Christmas. Three twisted Magi. Something is genuinely wrong with my life. I mean, maybe I *am* some kind of magnet for weirdness."

"The first step," she said, mock-heroically, "is admitting you have a problem."

"Please shut up," I mumbled. "I'm having a significant feeling of— I feel very strange. There's something going on in the caves beneath my home. And, actually, I mean that in any metaphorical sense you care to imagine."

She put her hand on my shoulder then. It was warm and oddly comforting. "Want to call Lucinda now? Tell her you're not as crazy as she thinks?"

"Good," I agreed. "Yes. Set her mind at ease—a bit."

But I didn't get up. I was momentarily drained of all energy. I couldn't understand why for a moment.

"Is it possible," I asked Dr. Nelson, "that I'm exhausted by the weight of hiding something in my mind? I mean, this repression thing—could it be that it takes up more energy than just letting it all out?"

"Absolutely," she said, sitting back and folding her arms. "It's the most tiring thing in the world, trying to hide something that you actually want to expose. Ambivalence. It's the heaviest thing in the world. It's the heaviest substance known to humankind. It's the main thing that causes trouble in any interaction. It makes you crazy."

"It makes you Hamlet."

"It stalls your process of actualization," she concluded. "It makes you unable to be who you really are."

"Yes." I nodded.

"You're tired."

"Very," I told her.

"So call Lucinda. You'll feel better; she'll feel better—all's right with the world."

I only took another second to consider before I agreed.

17

Sometime in the next hour Skidmore and Melissa Mathews appeared. Skidmore was still terse and perfunctory in his conversation, and he avoided eye contact. Melissa was nearly stuttering she was so nervous. They both had rifles, flak jackets, and extra pistols on their gun belts. Their collective image was surreally filmic. They were more heavily armed and armored than I had ever seen either one of them. Skidmore all but threatened me with life in prison if I so much as stepped out of my house onto the porch.

"Lock the doors. Do you still have that hunting rifle I gave you?" He was staring off to the side of the house.

"Somewhere," I answered vaguely. It had been a Christmas present when we'd both been in high school—his one and only attempt to normalize me for our small-town environment.

"Find it," he snapped, and then stepped backward down the steps and off the porch.

"We've called the State Patrol," Melissa whispered, as if she were afraid that Skid might hear. "They're sending someone. He just didn't want to wait. This man, this Newcomb? He's a very, very bad man."

I had never seen Melissa frightened; her anxiety gave me pause. If she was afraid of David Newcomb, that was genuinely cause for concern.

Skid sniffed and looked in Dr. Nelson's direction. "You saw this woman, this so-called Issie Raynerd."

"Yes." Dr. Nelson was uncharacteristically curt.

"Call Lucinda," Skid commanded us both.

"I did," I answered, irritated by his manner. "I talked with her shortly before you arrived. She was relieved to hear that I'm not *quite* as disturbed as she might have feared."

"Good," he said, still not looking at me. "When's she coming over?"

"Well, there's something strange. She accepted my commentary and was happy to hear it, but when I suggested that she come right over to talk about it, she begged off. Long day at the hospital, she said, and sleep was what she needed."

"Oh." That seemed to surprise him.

"I understood, of course," I assured him. "She hasn't slept much lately."

Still, upon reflection as the sun was going down, it seemed very strange to me that she'd reacted so mildly to the fact that I hadn't imagined or hallucinated the strange woman. That Issie was actually real, albeit difficult to explain.

Without much more ado, Skidmore and Melissa trudged off down the hill and Dr. Nelson and I locked ourselves into my house. I spent awhile in relative silence putting together a nice duck cassoulet made with dried white beans that Lucinda had grown and a duck that Skidmore had brought me. It was very satisfying: onions, garlic, of course, but more Benton's bacon, that was the real secret.

Dr. Nelson and I finished up the last of the meal, and I poured her the last of a very nice Côtes du Rhône. Despite the food and wine, I would have confessed to feeling a bit sorry for myself.

"I mean," I complained, slumping down in my kitchen chair, "everyone's up in arms when they think I've made up some succubus from beyond, but when said *animus mundi* turns out to be a very real woman, where's the commensurate relief, or affirmation? It's almost as if my friends *want* me to be out of my mind."

Dr. Nelson leaned forward. "Maybe they do."

That sobered me a little. "They do?"

"Maybe they're more comfortable with your role as resident crazy. Seriously. Every village needs a shaman."

"I'm the *shaman*? Not really."

She laughed. "Not really. But the thing about any close-knit social interaction—"

Alas, she was not to finish that sentence.

Melissa Mathew's voice, like a slash in the entire fabric of the night, tore through our heads and shook us both out of our wine stupor. She was screaming as if she were being murdered.

Dr. Nelson got up so quickly that her chair toppled. I scrambled over it and we both were at my front door in time to see Melissa, wild-eyed and covered with scratches and blood, careening up my front steps.

"Hurry, God Almighty," she gasped, "they got Skidmore! You'uns got to help him!"

Then she tripped over the top step and stumbled into me, nearly knocking me over.

"What the hell is going on?" I demanded, holding her in my arms.

"That crazy woman and the little man shot Skidmore and dragged him off down in the cave," she gasped hysterically. "I chased after them, but I got all lost—and I got scared, tell the truth. Them people's not right. And Skid's all tore up. And the damn state patrol ain't never show up!"

I don't know how or why, but an eerie calm overtook me. I took Melissa by the shoulders, stood her up straight, and locked eyes with her.

"Call the state patrol again now," I said softly. "Tell them what's happened. Wait for them here. I'll go get Skidmore."

She saw that I meant to do what I'd said, and nodded, a little trancelike.

"You're not going down there by yourself," Dr. Nelson said firmly.

"You're not going with me," I assured her.

"Oh, yes I am," she told me in no uncertain terms. "Who kicked that man's ass once already, you or me?"

"David? You didn't kick his ass, you surprised him. He's on to you now. He'll just shoot you in the head the next time you try to mess with him. That is, in fact, what he's already promised to do."

"Look," she began.

"I'm the one he *doesn't* want to shoot," I interrupted, "because I'm Issie's husband, and he's her protector. Obviously."

"Yeah," she snapped, "he was her love child son a couple of hours ago. You don't actually know what he is. Except an escapee from a mental institution."

"I don't care."

I let go of Melissa's shoulders, stepped inside to get my heavy coat, and was back out, heading down the steps, before Melissa finally responded.

"Dr. Devilin, you can't go down there by yourself," she said as if I were an idiot. "That little man's got a big gun and he shoots real good. I'm a call the state troopers, all right. But you wait right here 'til they come, and I mean it."

"Okay." I nodded.

She took another second to exchange looks with Dr. Nelson, then headed in toward my kitchen phone.

The second she left the porch, I continued putting on my coat and heading into the yard.

"Damn it, Fever," Dr. Nelson whispered.

But she disappeared inside in a flash, grabbed her coat from its place by the door, and followed me.

We'd only taken a few steps before I slowed just a little.

"Damn. I should have thought to get flashlights. It'll be dark in those caves. I always keep several right by the door."

From out of her coat pocket Dr. Nelson produced not one but two flashlights.

"They were sitting there by the door," she said. "Seemed like the right thing to do to pick them up."

I took one from her. We made our way down with relative ease, trying to be as quiet as we could. As we approached the large rocks where the cave opening was nestled, Dr. Nelson took my arm and put her lips to my ear.

"Do you have anything like a plan?" she whispered.

I shook my head.

"Do we just barge in and hope for the best?" she asked, skeptically, so softly that I could barely hear her.

"I'll just look inside to see if they're, you know, right there," I whispered back. "If they are, we'll announce ourselves and enter as if we've been invited. If they're not there, we'll slip in and see what's what then."

She nodded without comment on the insanity of my proposal.

We inched our way down the rest of the slope to the rocks, only skidding and sliding a little in the snow. We ended up right at the mouth of the cave, the canvas curtain pulled tightly down to the ground and covered, at the hem, with snow.

I moved as silently as I could manage, and pulled the canvas ever-so-slightly to one side. The fire pit was burning brightly, and Issie was lying on one of the cots with her back to me. I didn't see anyone else, but I couldn't pull the canvas far enough to get a good look at the entire interior. Someone might have been sitting close to the fire, or at one of the makeshift tables.

I turned back to Dr. Nelson and whispered, "Issie's right there. Don't know about anyone else."

Dr. Nelson held out her hand with a flourish, as if she were inviting me into a nineteenth-century parlor.

I shrugged, took a breath, and called out, "Hey, Issie? It's Fever. Can I come in?"

She nearly jumped out of the cot. There was shuffling elsewhere, enough to indicate that someone else was, indeed, in the cave with her.

A second later David snapped the canvas back, gun first, and lowered his face.

"Dr. Devilin," he simmered. "Here to see Issie, or your friend the sheriff?"

"Skidmore!" Dr. Nelson called out.

David's arm shot forward and the barrel of his rifle poked me hard enough in the stomach that it tore my coat and brought me to my knees.

"You'd best tell her to shut up," he seethed.

"Do you have the sheriff in there?" Dr. Nelson demanded.

David pointed the rifle directly at her head, and then called out over his shoulder, "Sheriff? You in there?"

"Fever," Skidmore groaned. "Get away, get away from here!"

"They can't," David answered matter-of-factly.

He motioned with his gun for us to step into the cave. Dr. Nelson helped me to my feet, and we stepped inside.

Issie was wildly distraught. Upon closer examination in better light, it appeared that she might have been clawing her forearms with her own fingernails. Thin tracks of blood raked her skin, and her eyes were rimmed in rouge. She looked more like a ghost than ever.

But that wasn't the sight that burned my brain to a cinder.

Skidmore's body was covered in blood, tied to one of the cots with baling wire that bit into his arms and legs so severely that it cut into his clothes and his skin. He was blindfolded with more wire, strands wrapped thirty or forty times around and around his head and eye sockets, a demon's halo.

Dr. Nelson took in a sharp breath, just short of gasping. I felt the pit of my stomach churn.

"If there is any permanent damage to Skidmore Needle," I said, my voice cold as iron, "I'll kill you in a way so painful that even you can't imagine it."

"Not if I kill you first," he said, smiling.

"Oh yes," I kept on. "Even if you kill me first. Especially if you kill me first. I've been dead several times, and I don't mind it at all. I'll absolutely come after you then, and there won't be anything in this world you can do."

"Hush!" Dr. Nelson barked.

The sound of her voice echoed in the cave, and it was a genuinely supernatural sound, not a human voice at all. The persuasive hypnotic tones I'd heard her use before were amplified by a factor of a hundred. Issie froze dead as a statue, I lost most of my muscle control, and David recoiled in horror, dropping his gun.

In the split second after her eerie shout, she snatched up the rifle, thrust it to me, and flew to Skidmore's side. My mind was clearing just as I saw David recover. Issie collapsed onto her cot.

I checked the rifle. The safety was off and the bolt had been set. All I needed to do was pull the trigger. I took a few quick steps in David's direction and the gun was nearly resting on his chest.

"I can't get this wire undone," Dr. Nelson said, her voice desperate, close to hysteria. "God."

"David," I said, barely controlling my urge to fire the rifle, "do you have wire cutters?"

He grinned maniacally. "Somewhere or another."

"Get them."

"No," he said. "I don't think I will."

"These wires are so tight around his head," Dr. Nelson said, trying to collect herself, "it's going to be very difficult to cut them off him without really hurting Skidmore."

"Don't care," Skid said weakly. "Get this off my head. 'Bout to pass out."

"Do you think," I said to Dr. Nelson, inching my way around David to get to the cot where Skid was lying, "that you might hold this gun on David?"

"What?" She looked up at me, suddenly lost.

"I understand what David has done," I said. "It's actually a variation of an Inquisition technique. He's twisted the wire somewhere, maybe under Skidmore's head, so that it would tighten slowly. If you'll hold the gun on David, I'll find the twist and undo it."

"Oh." She stood.

I looked David dead in the eye. "I want you to remember that Dr. Nelson is the one who kicked the snot out of you a little earlier in the day. She might not mean to kill you with this rifle, but she's not as used to guns as you are. She might slip."

I handed the gun to Dr. Nelson. David maintained his manic grin.

I knelt beside the cot.

"Skid?" I said softly. "I'm going to try to raise your head up. It's probably going to hurt because the rest of the wire around your arms and legs is very tight, but getting this thing off your head is the first priority, right?"

"Right," he whispered, out of breath.

I cradled his neck, which made him wince. I raised up his head a half an inch and he screamed so forcefully that he began to cough. Each cough brought spasms of twitching pain.

But as he was quaking, I managed to ease my hand behind his head. I found a small knot of wire and began to twist it counter clockwise with my thumb and finger. The sharp ends of the bailing wire cut me like thorns, but I could see that the wire was loosening, ever so slightly, around Skidmore's head.

He was still gasping and began crying, heaving, wrenching.

Slowly, slowly, the bloody blindfold unwound. I have no idea how long it took. Time was meaningless. But finally the wire was lax enough for me to slide it away from his eyes, over the ridge of his eyebrows, ripping a little of the flesh of his forehead, but getting it off. I tossed it into the fire.

Skidmore passed out.

I shot up, snatched the rifle from Dr. Nelson, and jumped forward, jamming the barrel into David's Adam's apple. It drew blood and I was glad.

David's face, at last, lost its grin and he clawed at the air as he fell backward, gurgling. At that moment I actually hoped that I'd opened up his esophagus.

"Fever!" Dr. Nelson snapped.

"Find wire cutters," I managed to say to her in an animal voice.

The sound of those words frightened me, and made Dr. Nelson step back from me.

"Cut those wires off Skidmore *now*." My voice was still not human.

Issie began to whimper.

Dr. Nelson took a few deep breaths, and then, very suddenly, began to look around the cave. Under one of the cots she found a tool kit. In it, she found electrician's cutters, and used them to snap the baling wire, one strand at a time, first around Skid's arms and chest, then around his hands and waist, down to his thighs, and finally his ankles. Skid remained unconscious. David remained on the floor.

Issie, however, sat up.

"I knew you wouldn't let us be," she said, sobbing.

"Let you be?" I exploded. "Let you torture my best friend?"

"Not that," she answered, shaking her head in horror at the sight of Skidmore's blood-soaked body. "Not that. I knew you'd never understand. I hoped against hope, but it's always the same.

The story is always the same, no matter how many times I tell it, the ending is always the ending, and Tristan is dead."

Dr. Nelson shot up and came to my side, her hand on my arm.

"We have to get Skidmore to a hospital," she said. "I don't care what happens to these two at the moment. I care about you, and I care about Skidmore. Leave them. Help me get Skidmore out of this place."

"Leave them?" I asked, a little too wildly.

"Fever," she said desperately.

I stared down at David. He was up on one elbow, his eyes heavy-lidded, as if he were groggy or drugged. I kicked his foot to wake him up so that he would see what was coming his way. His eyes widened. Lightning fast I took the rifle by the barrel. I raised it high above my head and let out a primal bellowing anguish, a prehistoric rage. David saw what was coming, brought his arm up reflexively, shrieking with terror. I brought the gun down on the rock floor right next to him so violently that the gunstock splintered into a hundred pieces, the metal bent, and a gunshot exploded. The bullet nicked my right ear ever so slightly. I didn't care.

David was still screaming when I threw down the wreckage of the gun, now useless.

Issie was up. She flew toward David, or so I thought. I was astonished to find that she flew into my arms, sobbing and clutching, her face buried in my chest.

"Fever, take me, too. Take the sheriff and let me help you and take me, too. I don't want to be here in this cave a second longer. Not with him. He's not Tristan. Please take me with you!"

Skidmore groaned then, and Dr. Nelson and I both looked. David took advantage of our momentary distraction to skitter like a spider into the shadows and then run into the depths of the cave.

I tossed Issie aside and started after him, but Dr. Nelson caught me by the arm. I nearly dragged her along with me before my mind cleared a little and realized that we really did need to get Skidmore out of the cave and into an ambulance.

I whirled, strode to Issie, grabbed her elbows, and shook her. "How did this happen?" I demanded. "What did you do?"

"David did it! David did it!" she squealed.

"Tell me what happened!" I raved.

"The—the sheriff, the sheriff," she stammered, "he and the woman, they came in. No warning. David shot. Then he ran. Down the caves. The sheriff chased him. I sat down. The woman came at me. She meant to do me harm, Fever. She meant to do me harm. I took out my penknife. I cut her good. I would have cut her up, all up, but there were more gunshots, and she took off down the caves. Next thing I know, there's David dragging the sheriff by his boots. Sheriff's dead, I thought. I thought, David and me, we get the body onto the cot. But the sheriff wakes up, so David, that's when David got the wire and all. And I sat down. I was very, very tired."

Then she started laughing, her shoulders shaking.

"David's not Tristan."

"What happened to Melissa?" I snapped.

"The woman? The sheriff's woman? I don't know. She never came back."

"Fever," Dr. Nelson said urgently, "we have to get Skidmore out of here."

I glared at Issie another moment, and then nodded once. "Right. You're right. The rest of this can wait."

I let go of Issie and headed toward the cot where Skidmore lay groaning before I heard the first siren.

Sound on the mountaintop is tricky—sometimes you can hear an owl that's five miles away but you can't hear someone step onto your front porch. My mother always told me, when I was quite young, that the trees and the rocks and the air all conspired at night, and if they liked a sound, they allowed it to pass, but if they didn't, even if it were a cannonball or dynamite, they wouldn't let it be heard at all.

I thought of that because it sounded as if the sirens were already up to my house, but they could very well have still been on the highway, not even yet to the gravel and dirt road that wound its way up the steep slopes to my front door.

Dr. Nelson heard the sirens, too.

"Police," Issie whispered desperately.

"And ambulance," Dr. Nelson said. "Maybe we should just wait here for them?"

I was suddenly plunged into doubt. The force that had maintained me, protected me from fear and common sense, while charging into the cave of the lunatics—that power was gone. I was more or less myself again, and uncertain about how to proceed. If we moved Skidmore, we might do more harm. If we stayed, David might come back and kill us all. Then I realized that Skidmore was probably shot, and my head snapped in his direction.

"Skid, can you hear me," I said, trying to seem calm. "Are you shot? Did David shoot you?"

I knelt beside the cot.

"He did," Skid affirmed. "But he got me in the jacket."

He managed to point to a place in his flak jacket close to his heart, and I could see that it was ripped and exploded.

"The jacket," Skidmore gasped, "it keeps the bullet from going into you? But it surely does hurt like hell when the bullet hits. Like being stung by a five-hundred-pound bee. Knocked me down. That little bastard hit me in the head with a rock and dragged me back into here before he started with this wire mess. He did it fast too, like he's had practice. Fast. Damn. I hurt all over. Where's Melissa?"

"She's safe," I said instantly. "I think she must have found another entrance to this cave—she found her way out without coming back through here. She's up at the house, called the state, they're here now, on their way down."

He managed to smile, his eyes still closed. "She— she told you not to leave the house."

"She did." I only took an instant more to reflect.

Dr. Nelson looked at me. "That's important," she said. "There's always another way out."

I was amazed at her ability to keep up with analysis even in such a situation, but I couldn't think about that then.

"We'll have to ask her how she did that," Skid said.

The sirens were obviously closer, and may have come to a standstill, ostensibly in my yard. I turned to Issie.

"So, are you coming with me up to my house so that we can all talk?" I asked.

She glanced toward the cave's entrance and began to shiver. "No."

"Look," Dr. Nelson told Issie reasonably, "you really need to sleep in a nice bed and clean up and calm down. I'm a doctor. I know these things."

"I'm not going back to that hospital again," Issie gasped. "David can tell you all about that. I can't go back to a place like that. I'm the reason he got in there, to help me get out. You have to understand that."

"I don't understand at all," I began, "but if you'll just come up to my house, you can explain it to me."

"No," Issie said, slowly backing away from me. "They won't listen. They'll just take me. That's what David says. They'll just take me and him away. Away from you, Fever. Fever. That's a funny name for you."

She took a few more steps away from Dr. Nelson and me. Then, almost as if she were able to vanish from sight, she turned, an odd pirouette, and dashed suddenly into the shadows at the back of the cave. I took one step toward her when a barrage of men and guns and flashlights and shouting assaulted me as the entire canvas that covered the cave's entrance collapsed inward and perhaps a dozen state troopers stormed in.

Everyone was shouting, pointing guns, telling me and Dr. Nelson to get on the floor, to freeze, to put our hands up, to put our hands behind our heads, not to move.

I stood very still, blinking in the harsh light of their torches.

Finally Melissa Mathews tore through the phalanx of burly men and stood in front of me.

"This is Dr. Devilin, you morons! He's the one that's just saved the sheriff, can't you'uns see that? Can't you'uns see the sheriff lying here on this cot?" And she jabbed the air with her index finger in the direction of the semiconscious Skidmore.

Skidmore mumbled, "I'm okay. I'm all right. Put those goddamned guns away. The bad guys are gone."

Melissa twisted herself in the direction of the now-silent state workers. "Morons," she repeated.

Then she jumped a little to the left and somehow appeared at Skidmore's cot. He was up on one elbow, blinking like me.

"Any chance you'uns can quit pointing those flashlights into my eyes? I've had a rough night."

Slowly the torches were lowered.

Someone said, "You okay, Skid?"

I tried to imagine what the scene must have looked like to them. Cots and barrels and crates everywhere, a blood-soaked sheriff, two strange academics, and a roaring fire pit.

"The alleged perpetrators," Skidmore managed to say, sitting up, "are a dwarf and a very pale thin woman dressed in black." Then he inclined his head in the direction of Dr. Nelson and me. "These two people saved my life. Now. If you want to chase off into the caves and see can you catch the man that did this to me, it's back that way."

Melissa pointed toward the back of the cave.

"Where's them ambulance men?" Melissa said harshly. "Get them in here now!"

There was a general bustle, and two men in hospital jackets stepped forward. They went immediately to Skid, began talking to him softly, dabbing something on his broken skin, and readying an emergency litter, ostensibly something to carry him up the hill and into the ambulance—though I imagined that Skid would object to that.

"Which one of you is Dr. Nelson?" one of the state troopers asked.

Dr. Nelson raised her hand but remained mute, for some reason.

"I'm Dr. Devilin," I felt compelled to say.

"Hey, Dev," another state trooper said. "You might not remember me, but I worked on that case up here when them two girls got killed by that train? In that nice orange Volkswagen? That was back— five years ago, I reckon."

I squinted to see the man. His face seemed familiar, but I didn't know him.

"Hi," I said.

"Hi," he answered back with a decidedly adolescent grin. "Let's get you and Dr. Nelson out of here and back up to your house. How 'bout that?"

"Good," Dr. Nelson responded, and headed toward the crowded cave's entrance.

"I'm worried about Skid," I said to no one in particular.

"I got it," Melissa said. "You go on up to the house."

I nodded.

Some of the troopers had begun to head toward the back of the cave, which prompted me to ask Melissa an important question. I stepped over to the cot and leaned over close to her ear.

"You found another way out of here," I said softly.

"Yes," she told me, distracted by what was going on with Skidmore.

"How?" I wanted to know.

"Oh." She took her eyes off Skid for a second and looked at me. "Well. You feel the draft over by the fire pit, that makes the smoke go out?"

"Yes."

"You feel that on your face and you follow the feel," she said simply. "Had to lead to the other entrance. Even when the cave splits in three. " She shrugged and returned her attention to the sheriff.

I straightened back up. "Yes," I said, more to myself than to her. "But where did it come out?"

"Down the way from your front door," she muttered. "Remember when my car ran off the road because I almost hit the boy? The one we thought was a boy?"

I nodded.

"Close to there," she continued. "You want to find it, just look for where my patrol car messed up the dirt road and the side brush."

"Right." I touched her shoulder and headed out of the cave.

I caught up with Dr. Nelson as we both cleared the cave, out into the colder air.

"You're a little more tight-lipped than usual," I whispered to her.

"I don't think you completely heard what Issie said," she whispered back. "Wait for just a second."

We walked upward in silence, and the sound from the cave faded quickly as we ascended the mountain.

After we were a hundred yards or so from the cave, Dr. Nelson began.

"Issie said, or at least indicated, that she'd been in the state mental hospital with David. That he'd somehow gotten himself into the hospital to help her, to get her out."

"Oh." I slowed down. "Right. She did say that."

"But Skidmore found David's fingerprints in the whatever database he searched, and not hers."

"Yes, but the other prints were only partials."

"And lots of people think Issie is dead," Dr. Nelson went on, squinting.

"Some people may think she's dead," I corrected cautiously.

"Okay, but the point is," Dr. Nelson said, "I need to find Issie, find out why she was in the state mental hospital. I'm beginning to have some very weird intuitions."

That stopped me. "Intuitions? About what?"

She stopped too and looked at me. "Can't put my finger on it. Can't put it into words. But you feel it, too, I know you do."

"I feel a weird intuition about this woman?" I rubbed my face. "I feel something. But mostly it's— well it is weird. And there is, I would have to say, a modicum of fear involved."

"She scares you."

"She scares the hell out of me," I said right away. "Doesn't she scare you?"

"No," Dr. Nelson said, looking down. "No, because I know who she is, or what she is."

"You do?" I asked. "What is she?"

"Well, she's not a ghost, but she's not a real person, either. She's stuck. A little like you. A little like me. That's why we both have some odd feelings about her—based on the takes-one-to-know-one school of analysis."

"I don't know what you're talking about," I confessed.

She took a second to consider, and then seemed to give up. "Yeah," she said, beginning to walk upward toward my house again. "Neither do I."

We walked a few more steps in the snow before an eerie cold clapped itself around my head and shoulders.

"Still," I said, suddenly feeling the muscles in my thighs

complain from all the hill-walking effort, "I can't escape the sensation that something—something just on the edge of my consciousness, just outside my view—is waiting in the shadows. Waiting for me to put together bits and pieces of something so obvious that I'm missing or not seeing because of a— some kind of blind spot, maybe. Something. It's right there, in the corner of my eye."

She nodded.

The lights from my house came into view then, almost as if it had just appeared. There were also flashing lights from squad cars and the ambulance. The yard was lit in red and blue and the warm buttery white from my windows, and I thought, "What an odd set of decorations I have for Christmas this year."

18

The house was warm, and the coals in the fireplace were cheery. My first thought was that we'd regroup and then head back out right away to find the other entrance to the cave. But that seemed increasingly unlikely as muscle fatigue and the general horror of the scene in the cave sank into our bones. Every time I blinked I felt my hand under Skidmore's sweaty neck, twisting bailing wire. My thumb and finger were cut deeply and needed tending. Dr. Nelson was unusually quiet. I didn't even think to offer her more of the apple brandy to drink, to take the edge off. I was suddenly so exhausted that I could barely move. She was shivering again. She sat down on the floor in front of the fire. I drifted upstairs to wash the blood off my hands and put antiseptic on the wounds. I don't know how much silent time passed before I found myself walking down the stairs again.

"You're right," she said, hearing my shuffling approach, not looking back.

"About what?" I mumbled, limbs nearly numb.

"There's something about this woman that we're missing. Something just out of reach or sight. Intuition only gets you so far, in my experience. After that, you just have to do the work."

"The work?" I asked, collapsing into my chair.

"Brain work, Mortimer," she sneered.

"Now I'm *Mortimer*?"

"Something obvious, hidden in plain sight," she went on, ignoring my objection to the newest of my appellations.

"Well, yes," I agreed, only a bit reluctantly, "like the cave entrance. I've been over that same stretch of hillside thousands of times. After a while, you can't see certain things. The obvious becomes invisible."

"Right." She nodded, still staring into the fire. "But the situation is complicated by the fact that even though you obviously knew this woman, you didn't remember her when she came to your door."

"Complicated because something happened to make me suppress the memory, something gave me situational or, I don't know, specific amnesia. Right?"

"Um," she hedged.

"Right?" I insisted again.

"The possibility remains that you've suffered more brain damage from your coma than was originally thought," she said bluntly. "It's entirely likely that you don't remember, now, lots of things in your past like that."

"No it's not," I snapped.

But the thought made me very uncomfortable. What if there were lots of things I would never remember? What if part of my mind was gone? How would I ever know it?

"Let's start with what we know now," Dr. Nelson went on. "What are the basic facts? Her name is Issie Raynerd—a very difficult name."

"Difficult?"

"The sound of it, as Dr. Andrews said, is icky."

"I don't think Andrews used the word *icky*."

"And the last name," she began. "There's something wrong with it."

"I know," I said.

"You know what?"

"I know," I told her reluctantly, "that if you pronounce her last name with the accent on the second syllable instead of the first, the way everyone does now—*and* you make the *e* an *a*—you get a trickster figure from French folklore: the fox."

She turned to look at me. "You do?"

"Ray*nard* the fox," I assured her.

"You've known this all along?"

"Yes, but I didn't mention it because it seemed— it seemed too paranoid."

"So what does it mean?" Dr. Nelson twisted around to face me, her back to the fire.

I sat forward, coming to conflicting conclusions.

"Either it means nothing and I *am* paranoid," I concluded calmly, "or this person has deliberately created a name for herself to— to flaunt my own discipline in my face."

"Why would she do that?" Dr. Nelson leaned forward, too.

"Because she's trying to confuse me and taunt me simultaneously. The way a trickster would."

"Again," Dr. Nelson said, "why?"

"Two reasons. Two I can think of at the moment. First: it's her nature. A trickster willfully disobeys or ignores traditionally accepted rules of normal behavior. Sometimes it's all in fun, sometimes the fun ends in blood."

I glanced around the house until I found the spot where Lucinda had hung mistletoe and pointed at it, tacked over the entrance to the kitchen.

"Why do we kiss under mistletoe?" I continued, pointing to the healthy sprig over the kitchen entrance.

Dr. Nelson glanced and then looked at me again. "Don't know."

"Loki, the trickster figure of Norse mythology, was jealous of another god, Baldr, whom everyone loved. Baldr was kind and loving and generous. Loki was cold and cunning and mean. So near the winter solstice, he challenged Thor to an archery match and Thor accepted. Then Loki told Baldr that he wanted to change his ways, and wanted Baldr to help him. Baldr agreed. Loki set the meeting place behind a stack of hay. Then Loki put the archery target on the other side of the haystack and taunted Thor until Thor was angry and shot his arrow with a greater force than usual. The arrow went through the target, through the hay, and into Baldr's heart. The most beloved of all the gods was instantly killed, by Thor, the son of Odin."

"Christ," Dr. Nelson whispered softly.

"When Odin, father of the gods, discovered Loki's 'trick,'" I went on, "Loki was banished to the underworld for a thousand years. And then Odin laid a curse on the tree from which the fatal arrow had been made, the mistletoe tree. Odin's curse was that mistletoe would no longer be a tree, but a poisonous parasite on other trees. Thor interceded, however, and told Odin that it wasn't fitting to completely ignore the great love all the gods bore for Baldr. So Odin added to his curse the invective that whenever human beings stood beneath the mistletoe, they would be compelled to kiss. We kiss under mistletoe in remembrance of a forgotten god whose love was the source of great compassion, and great treachery—like all love."

She stared, for a moment, at the mistletoe in the entranceway. "That's quite a story," she said.

"That's what a trickster is," I affirmed.

"You're afraid of Issie."

"Down to my marrow," I agreed in no uncertain terms. "And while some of my fear is a result of current events, I am slowly being taken over by a much more primal dread. I'm afraid that something big happened to me in Wales. Something big happened to Issie Raynerd. I'm afraid that I can't remember her, exactly, because something so traumatic happened to one or both of us that I drove her into— well, I mean, Christ, that I drove her into *the caves underneath my home*! Both figuratively and literally."

Dr. Nelson nodded. "Yeah. That's a big fear all right," she said, more to herself than to me. "Because it can threaten everything. That's why you're itchy when I press you about being a spook magnet. I thought you were just averse to the idea because your mind is closed about the subject, but in fact you may actually be a little too enthusiastic about it. It may be one of your biggest unconscious fears, maybe even a root fear."

I glared appropriately. "You're talking to yourself, I don't know what you're saying, and you referred to me as 'itchy.' Stop it."

She ignored me. "I love that you told me this story about the mistletoe," she went on, "because it completely reveals— I mean, of all the stories you could have told me about tricksters—coyote, rabbit, the briar patch story—you chose that one, one of the bloodiest, one about love and treachery. Man."

I think I blinked. "You know about coyote and rabbit tricksters?"

"Of course," she said.

"You were just seeing where I'd go," I said tersely, "because you're still *examining* me."

"Yes."

"And you knew about the mistletoe," I continued.

"No," she admitted, "that was new to me. Great story. But also great in what it reveals about your current state of mind."

"And what it reveals about Issie Raynerd, if I'm correct," I said pointedly.

She sighed. "Actually, I believe you might be right. I think there's something of the trickster mythology at work here. I'm just not certain that it's Issie."

"Who else would it be?"

"You said there were two reasons she might be doing this," Dr.

Nelson said, clearly not interested in answering my question. "The first, you said, was that it's just in her nature, her trickster nature. What's the other one?"

"Ah, well," I responded, "the second reason would be that she has a plan, like Loki. She wants to confuse me so that she can get something that she wants. Her trickster nature is, then, a magician's tool: misdirection. She wants me to think that she's not real, or out of her mind, or too troubled to deal with. That way I won't notice when she actually pulls off the *trick* of the magic trick."

Dr. Nelson sat back. "That's really scary."

"Which is why I'm scared. Because it's scary."

Dr. Nelson held her breath for a moment, and then gave out with the grandest and, quite possibly, most dramatic sigh I'd ever heard.

"Look. Fever." She bit her lip. "Don't you think it's about time you stopped using folklore and mythology to explain things in your life? Don't you think it's time to actually look at reality? I mean, square in the eye."

I let her accusation sink into the molecules of air that surrounded us both, just so there would be no uncertainty regarding their import. I folded my arms. I set my jaw. I took in a slow, long breath.

"First," I began, "let us imagine that I had said to you, 'Look, Ceri, isn't it about time you stopped using psychology to explain everything?' Let that take hold of you for a second."

To her credit, it appeared as if she might be doing just that.

"Next," I continued, "folklore and mythology *are* reality. A million years before the Viennese mama's boy invented your so-called science, human beings told each other stories to explain— well, to explain everything. Myth is at the foundation of *everything*: art, literature, medicine, government—even psychology. In fact, the prime function of mythology is to reconcile the conscious with the unconscious mind. Of course, I paraphrase Joseph Campbell."

She folded her arms in front of her. "Of course you do."

"And finally, I will bet you anything you care to wager that in the end, some great strain or strand of mythology runs through this entire matter. Anything."

"It is tempting to take advantage of you in your obviously deluded condition."

"Money?" I suggested.

"All right, if you insist, but not money," she said, throwing her hands in the air. "If some *major* bit of mythology has *important* bearing on anything *central* to this situation, I will provide you with an entirely clean certificate of sanity, suitable for framing, that you can show to all and sundry, signed by me, a licensed and highly regarded psychiatric professional. You can show it to anyone who says you're nuts."

"Thus completely invalidating your professional standing," I goaded. "I like it."

"But if you lose," she went on.

"Which I will not."

"But if you do," she insisted, "you will come with me to the Rhine Center and get a battery of tests that will prove to one and all that you are, in fact, a certifiable spook magnet, esquire."

I was, in spite of myself, greatly amused by her overwhelmingly jolly tone.

"Do you ever take anything seriously?" I asked.

"Try not to," she told me, smiling her smile—not exactly the Mona Lisa, but still guarding secrets. "I don't see the point."

I nodded. "Sometimes— sometimes I don't either."

At that point we both became aware that the ambulance and squad cars were leaving. Their lights moved weirdly outside my windows, and the sound of the engines rumbled and then began to fade down the road. It seemed odd that neither of us had the impulse to go outside, check on Skid or Melissa, ask what was happening. But then, Dr. Nelson and I were obviously bone-tired and maybe a little in shock.

When the lights and sounds of official vehicles were finally gone, so was the last of our stamina. We looked at each other, wordlessly calling it a day.

"I think I'll just— should I head upstairs? I can only assume that you— what? Slept down here last night? The guest room is in a bit of a shambles, but it always is. So."

"A second ago?" she said sweetly. "You called me by my first name."

"I did?"

"You did," she affirmed. "It was nice. Earlier you included me in your group of friends, and finally you've called me by my first name. We're making real progress I think. Plus, yes, I've slept on your couch, so there's that."

"I— I don't think— I didn't call you by your first name," I stammered, actually taking a step away from her, "and let's quit talking about where you're sleeping."

"Because of the unacknowledged sexual tension between us, you mean?" She cocked her head slightly.

"What?" I took a few clumsy steps toward the banister.

She took off her rust-colored jacket and stretched. "Did it occur to you that I really want to go to sleep now and, since I'm actually a pretty good psychiatrist, I might have figured out that talking about sex was the quickest way of making you go upstairs so I could get some sack time?"

"No," I protested. "Because if you knew anything about me at all, you'd know that the quickest and s*implest* way to get me to go upstairs and let you get to sleep would have been to say, 'Could you please go upstairs so I can get some sleep!'"

She stopped moving for a second. "That would have been more

direct—and probably would have worked better. Hm. I wonder why I said what I said. Well." She gave me an earnest glance. "That one's on me. Sorry. I'll think about it. Good night."

"Christ," I muttered, turning away from her and ascending the stairs.

I could hear her shuffling the several quilts that were strewn about the living room. Then I heard her sigh, very contentedly, as I hit the top step.

I didn't bother to turn on the lights when I stepped into my room. It seemed like too much effort. I sat on the bed, eyes already closed, struggled with my boots and socks, wrestled myself out of my shirt and jeans, and fell back onto the pillow in no time at all. I drew the blankets and quilts to my chin, and was lifted, in a sudden dream, out of my bed by a giant swan, and into the open arms of the night.

19

I awoke in terror. I had no idea what time it was. The sky was black, the moon was hidden, the stars were gone, I couldn't see, and there was a body in my bed with me.

I twisted away from the embrace of its cold arms, fell hard on the floor, and tumbled toward the light switch.

I leapt up and turned on the overhead light, momentarily blinded by the glare. After a second I could make out her naked form. My heart hammered in my chest so violently that it thundered and shook my entire frame.

Issie sat up. She was pale as snow, her body a cadaver stuffed with crawling spiders. I could see them churning, boiling under her translucent skin.

When my eyes cleared a bit, I realized that the skin was so pale I could see her blood veins—not spiders. Still, her nakedness revolted me beyond all reason, and I felt an immediate wrenching in the pit of my stomach.

She reached out her arms, and her eyes were hollow.

I couldn't move. I tried.

"Come back to our bed, my sweetheart," she whispered. "Come back to our wedding bed, Mark."

I started to correct her, or to ask her why she kept calling me

Mark, but I knew I was about to throw up, and my mind seemed to tear away at my skull, attempting to escape. I tried to tell myself that I was dreaming, or hallucinating. My back was against the door frame. I could feel the wood and the cold glass doorknob.

She stood. I wanted to avert my eyes but I was ragingly horrified by what she might do if I looked away. I opened my mouth twice to speak, but no sound would come out. No air, try as I might, would force itself from my lungs. I realized I wasn't breathing and that I might pass out.

She took a step in my direction. "Mark? What's the matter?"

"No!" I growled, pointing my index finger at the center of her forehead. I thought it might make her disappear. It didn't.

But she did stop coming toward me. "What is it? Are you still angry with me? After all this time? How can that be?"

She looked away, seemed to stumble or lose her balance, and sat back on the bed, her hands folded demurely in her lap.

"I thought," she said, sighing heavily, "that if I just let time go by, let the river of days wash away what happened, you would— you'd forgive me. I thought."

I just stared.

"Tristan and me," she said, even softer, looking down, "it wasn't on purpose. It was a horrible accident. Horrible. But now it's done and there's nothing in this world to break the spell. I'm sorry. Is all I can say is: I'm sorry."

She didn't sob or choke or change in any way, but tears began to eke slowly down her face, past her lips and chin, and onto her bare white thighs.

"The water was harsh, Mark." She began to wring her hands. "You know how it can get. The water was wild and high, and we were both like to die, we thought. I went to my things. I got the powders that my mother had given me. I was so sick, Mark, you don't know. I got confused. I picked out the wrong ones, don't you understand? I picked out the wrong powders—it was a mistake. I didn't mean to do it!"

Slowly her voice was rising again, the way it had in the cave, to a higher, hysterical pitch. I had an odd impulse to try to quiet her, and then realized that if we made enough noise, Dr. Nelson might wake up and come upstairs. I wasn't thinking clearly enough to understand what I thought Dr. Nelson might do, exactly; maybe she would tell me I was hallucinating, maybe she would see the specter, too. I only knew that if she were there, I would be more stable.

Just as I was about to call out for Dr. Nelson, Issie stood. I realized that if I did call out Dr. Nelson's name, there was no telling what further madness Issie might visit upon the already incoherent moment. I was still trying to decide what to do when Issie continued her rant.

"We took the powders," she said, breathing strangely, "and they were a wonder. My body flushed and my mind gave way. I felt a pain I'd never known before, but it wasn't in my body, it was in my spirit. My body was alive and miraculous, and every sensation was a revelation. The pain in my spirit was want, raw want, desire of the flesh so splendid and fine that no force on earth could stop it. No force on earth. I took the wrong powder, Mark. I didn't take the medicine for sea distress. I took the love-philtre. Do you understand?"

She asked the question with such force that I was compelled to answer, "No. I don't understand what you're telling me."

"I took the love-philtre," she repeated, louder than before, "and I gave it to Tristan too. By the time we realized the mistake, it was too late, we were locked in each other's embrace. Locked. There wasn't a thing we could do, not a thing in this world. By the time we made land in Cornwall, it was done: we were for each other, mind, body, spirit. It's a terrible burning, Mark. Few ever know it.

There's not a second of the day goes by that I don't waste in blood-yearning. But I'm trying, now, don't you understand, trying to be a good wife, like I was meant to do. Trying to be your wife in spite of the fate that's spoiled us all."

My wits were slowly returning. My heart only bordered on attack, and my mind was beginning to be more than mere timpani and thunder. Presented with Issie's delirium, my own madness seemed tame.

I realized that if I just talked to her, perhaps stomping around loudly, or encouraging her to raise her voice, Dr. Nelson might awaken and come upstairs. That was the extent of my mind's ability in those moments.

"I think I understand a little," I said guardedly. "You didn't take the medicine for seasickness, you took some sort of aphrodisiac."

She didn't seem to hear me.

"I knew when we got to Cornwall I had to find you, but I had no idea what I would say. I stayed with you and the others there at the fairy stones, but all the while I was longing and burning to go back to him. Do you remember the little stream that ran close to the place you camped out?"

It took a moment, but I did remember that I'd camped in a tent for a few days, or a week, close to the Crick Stone. There may have been a stream nearby. It would have made sense.

"I sat by that stream every day," she said longingly, "waiting for a sign from him. Whenever I wasn't with the others, I'd sit and hope past hope. And when he thought he could see me, he'd float an apple bough down the stream. That was my sign. I could go to him then, and we could steal precious hours clutching and rending and rolling in desperation. It was a glorious pain. Glorious. And you never knew."

I took hold of the doorknob, as if to steady myself. "No. I never knew."

"You were too intent on your work. That was good. Good for you to do. And Tristan and me, we'd lie together in the apple orchard upstream, close to the hillocks and the roving sheep."

"Stop." I pretended to lose my balance and stumbled, opening the bedroom door.

She stood once again, and took a step my way. "Mark!"

I held up my free hand, as if to tell her I didn't want or need her assistance. "I'm all right."

I slammed the door hard, as hard as I could, but I looked at Issie. I looked her in the eye.

"I think I understand," I told her, doing my best to sound simultaneously hurt and noble. "It wasn't your fault. It was the love potion. You came to Cornwall to be with me, but you mixed up the— wait."

My neck snapped around with such a sudden discovery that I actually did lose my balance then. I miscalculated where the wall was when I went to steady myself, and nearly toppled to the floor.

Issie took another step in my direction. "Mark!" she cried, very loudly.

"Wait!" I demanded. "Tristan, Mark, love potion, Cornwall— now I know your name!"

And just at that moment, Dr. Nelson barreled through the bedroom door nearly knocking me over and breathing frantically.

We stood, the three of us, for a moment like a surreal sideshow tableaux. Then, without a word of warning, Issie bolted. She shot to the window, tore it open, and leapt out, naked, down two stories, into the snowy moonlight.

I ran to the window, Dr. Nelson close behind, and watched as Issie rolled in the snow, gathered herself up, and ran like a spirit-deer into the woods.

Dr. Nelson and I stood, I don't know how long, gaping out the window, the icy air blasting us.

At length Dr. Nelson seemed to rouse herself and she closed the window. Then she turned to me and stuttered a few meaningless syllables before giving up and sitting down on the bed. Only then did I notice that she was fully clothed, the sturdy sweater, khaki pants, even her Russian-looking army boots.

I suddenly felt very ill-at-ease in my boxers and T-shirt. I tried not to look at her while I fetched my jeans. As I was clumsily pulling them on, standing to one side of the bed, she finally mustered human speech.

"What in *the* hell was *that?*" she demanded.

I hopped and zipped and then skittered to the chair, swallowed, and tried to manage a facsimile of coherence.

"I know who she is," I began, trying to hold back the excitement at my revelation. "I know what that woman is. I mean, she actually was in this room just now, right?"

"Fever," Dr. Nelson exploded, "she was in your bed naked and then she jumped out a two-story window without being hurt and ran away—again, I say: *naked*—in the snow!"

"So, she *was* here," I said again.

"Christ!"

"Good." I swallowed again. "Good. That means that what she told me, what I found out, what's going on—it's real. And it's really, really great."

She shook her head at me, amazed. "Great?"

"Wait until you hear this." I was no longer able to contain my excitement. It was the same ecstasy I always felt when I made any great discovery in my research, as if I'd discovered treasure or some ancient, perfect secret. "Do you know who that woman is? Or, I mean, who she thinks she is?"

"What are you talking about? What's the matter with you?" She stood up. "We have to call the police."

"Yes," I agreed happily, not moving, "but first I have to tell you who she *is!*"

"Is there something wrong with you?" She looked into my eyes. "Did she hit you or— or do anything else?"

"No. Please just sit down and listen to what I've just found out; what I've just put together. It's so obvious. I would have gotten it long before now if I hadn't been confused by the names."

"The names?" She squinted, entirely exasperated.

"It's the thing we both knew, the clear thing we were missing, about all of this. Do you want to hear it or not?"

My unusual enthusiasm must have been a bit contagious, because she did, indeed, sit back down. She stared at me with a perfect mixture of concern and anticipation.

I sipped in a breath, unable to keep from grinning. "Her name. Let's start there. I know her name."

"We— we already know her name, Fever," she said hesitantly.

"Not really. Not her real name, her full name. God, this is amazing." I nearly lifted off my chair with excitement.

"What is it?" she asked breathlessly, leaning forward.

"Her name," I said slowly, "is Iseult—and she thinks she's *living* the story of Tristan and Isolde!"

20

Dr. Nelson nodded. Then she breathed in through her nose, a sort of calming breath. Then she smiled and leaned toward me. Then she reached out her hand. I thought she might be about to take my hand and congratulate me on my brilliant scholarship. Alas, instead, she took my wrist between her thumb and two fingers and looked at her watch. She was taking my pulse.

I started to speak, but she shushed me with such finality that I didn't say a word. Then, satisfied with her reading of my vital signs, she placed the back of her hand on my forehead. After a second she looked deeply into my eyes.

"Fever," she said slowly, soothingly, "I'm going to ask you some questions now, and I want you to answer them right away, without thinking. Can you do that?"

"Look," I protested, "you don't seem to understand what's going on here."

"Fever," she repeated in the same hypnotic tone, "I'm going to ask you some questions."

"Damn it, Ceri!" I said, standing up. "I'm not crazy. This woman is living in—in a fugue state, as you've said about me, apparently."

"Please sit down," she said calmly.

"This woman, she thinks she's living out a cycle of stories from

181

at least as old as the Middle Ages, probably older. She thinks she's *Isolde!*"

"Why don't you just answer a few of my questions," she said, smiling, "and then we can talk about what just happened up here."

"Nothing happened." I could feel my ire mounting. "There may be nothing on this earth so maddening as not being believed when you know the truth."

"So you know the truth?" she asked. "You're the only one?"

"I'm Copernicus in a flat-world universe."

"But, see, the problem with the truth," she said, dropping into a little of her hypno-tone, "is that it's subject to so many interpretations. For every Copernicus who knows the orbit of the earth, there are a hundred madmen who know that Satan lives in their hair follicles. You understand that, right?"

"This isn't an abstract construct, *doctor*," I snapped. "I'm telling you what's going on with this woman. And if you'd take a second and hear me out, you'd be dying to figure out *why* she thinks what she thinks. I mean, don't you want to figure out what makes a person *that* crazy? Really?"

She looked away, and then sat back a little. "I had a call once, this was awhile back, about a person, a Russian Orthodox priest, actually, who kept taking his clothes off in the streets. He was a bit older, and it was assumed he was succumbing to dementia or Alzheimer's, but I discovered that it only happened on a certain street."

"What are you talking about?"

"I'm talking about a case I had a number of years ago," she went on, her face betraying deep concern of some sort. "So I followed the guy. I stayed with him. He was completely all right until he hit the corner of something and something else—don't remember the names. Then, slowly, he began to speak in a different voice, walk a different way, and eventually strip down to his underpants."

"Why are you telling me this?" I demanded to know.

"Don't you want to know why he did it? Don't you want to hear what a brilliant psychiatrist I am?"

"Ceri, I'm trying to tell you about a very immediate situation," I began.

"About the fifth or sixth time he did it, when I was following him," she went on, "I saw him moving in a pattern that I'd seen before, a kind of ritual dance. I had to consult a guy from the anthropology department, but it was confirmed that this Russian Orthodox priest was performing a food and fishing dance from certain tribes found only in South Pacific islands. There's absolutely no telling where he'd seen it, but when I knew that's what he was doing, I began to ask him questions about the dance, and the work he thought he was doing, and what do you think I found out?"

I shook my head. "What?"

"This scrawny, pale, priest—he thought he was Queequeg, from *Moby-Dick*. He thought it was his job to harpoon the white whale. He wanted to kill God. He wanted revenge."

"Jesus." I sat down. "How did you figure that out?"

"I'm good," she said easily, "and I'm lucky."

"I see the connection now. That's a hell of a case."

"No kidding," she agreed.

"Why did that one street corner trigger his transformation? What was the street name?"

"No idea. Turned the case over to someone else."

"What?" I glared. "Why?"

"Something more interesting, and more pressing came up."

"What could possibly have been more interesting than that guy?" I asked.

"You." That's all she said, but her single syllable lingered in the room for a moment, not quite an echo.

"You started— what, you started working on my case, or whatever, two years ago?" I couldn't believe it.

"That's when Lucinda first called me," she confirmed. "She told me enough about what had happened to you since you'd come back to Blue Mountain, the kind of things you'd done for the sheriff, and for the town, and the sort of strangeness that you've attracted. It was a hundred times more interesting than some crazy old guy who was mad at his parents for making him be a priest. Then you had your post-coma episodes, and I kind of stepped up the work. Plus, you and I? We're very much alike, I'm afraid. We have a lot in common."

"We do?"

"Which is why I would very much like to ask you several questions now," she said, shifting her weight, "and I would like for you to answer quickly so that we can dismiss the possibility that you're having another episode and move on to your theory about this woman, however nutty it might be. Got it?"

I had to let all of that sink in. "Oh. Okay."

"Good," she said, looking deeply into my eyes once again. "First, breathe in through your nose and tell me what you smell."

I think I blinked or twitched or something, but her gaze didn't waver, so I closed my eyes and did what she'd asked me to do.

"Dust, cold air, wood smoke, apple brandy, and rosemary that I think is probably from your shampoo," I reported after I'd exhaled.

"Wow," she said. "Okay. I did, in fact, have another little sip or two of that apple brandy after you went upstairs, and my shampoo does have rosemary in it. Nice."

"What were you looking for?"

"Sometimes people who are having an irrational moment," she told me, "say that they subsequently smell vanilla or almonds. But your senses seem to be hyper-observant, so that's impressive."

"Next question." I settled back. "I'm anxious to tell you about Iseult."

"Which is it," she asked, "Isolde or Iseult?"

"Iseult is the Irish name," I answered, "Isolde is from Wagner's opera, mainly."

"Fine. Question two: do you see any bright jagged edges out of the corners of your eyes?"

"No."

"Good. That sometimes happens before migraines and after some hallucinations. What's your middle name?"

"Don't have one."

"Your name's not really *Fever.*"

"Yes, sadly, it is."

"What was wrong with your mother?"

"How much time do you have?" I asked, "Because I don't think you're going to want to camp out on the sofa that long. And by the way: really? My mother? You're going to keep on with that?"

"Why shouldn't I?" she asked, but she sounded as if I'd caught her shoplifting something.

"It's just another useless tool in your ridiculous arsenal of clichés," I insisted, shaking my head.

"You do talk about her a lot, though—your mother."

"No I don't," I snapped—before I realized that *snapping* told her more than I'd wanted to reveal.

"And there we are," she declared. "Freud wins again. It's always something to do with the mother. God help all women, I say; save them from Jesus H. Freud."

"I don't know what that means," I said, "but are we done? Can I tell you what I know about this woman, or not?"

"I still think you're nuts," she said, "and your bizarre theory that she's living out some medieval story cycle is *way* too folklorey."

"It's not too— that's not even a word, and I know what I'm talking about."

"I am interested in hearing about it," she went on, "but mostly because it will tell me something about *you*."

"God!" I seethed as briefly as possible, and then soldiered on. "Let me lay out the facts. First, Issie is short for Iseult."

"It is?"

"Yes. Second, Tristan, Mark, and Iseult are the central characters of the story cycle. Third, the longing for forgiveness, the love-philtre, the Cornwall setting, and the trip to Ireland *in a boat*—all motifs of the story."

I sat back, well pleased with my presentation. Ceri was, alas, less than moved.

"Mark?" was all she asked.

"Oh, right," I stumbled, "you weren't in the room when she was calling me Mark. She kept calling me Mark. And I think she's called me that in your presence, hasn't she?"

"I don't really know what you're talking about," she began, "but if I played that back, all of what you've just said? If I played that back to you on a recording, you'd see just how weird it sounds. Really."

I nodded. I gathered my thoughts. "Right. Missing steps."

"What?"

"I've followed a very logical path, from A to Z, in my mind," I explained, beginning to bite my lips and grind my teeth, "but I've left out several, or many, really important steps along the way as I've given my little presentation. So, let's start at the very beginning."

She drew back from me a bit, and suddenly acquired a completely inappropriate air of playfulness. "A very good place to start."

"If you interrupt me, especially with *The Sound of Music*," I snapped, "we'll never get anywhere."

"We'll never climb every mountain."

"Stop it," I sighed.

"Or forge every stream."

"Do you want to hear this or not?" I sneered.

"Okay, go."

I rubbed my forehead. "Why do you do that?"

"Do what?"

"That. What you just did: quoting those song lyrics. It was just weird."

She straightened her posture and took on a deliriously haughty mien. "I'm a serious, psychiatric professional," she intoned. "Everything I do has a clinical purpose."

"Really?" I chided. "Because it really has the appearance of— just . . . messing with me."

"Well, yes, that, too," she said, tossing a hand in the air. "It's really fun to do."

I started to say one thing, something about her lack of professionalism, I think, but that thought collided with this: "Actually? It is a little fun. Kind of fun. I'm really starting to enjoy— I don't know. Being with you. Just a little."

"Plus," she said confidently, "you've started calling me by my first name most of the time now, have you noticed that?"

"No."

"Well, you have." She touched my elbow for a second. "It's nice. So. How're you feeling?"

"What?" I tilted my head. "How am I feeling?"

"Yes, how are you feeling?"

"I— wait." I took in a breath. "I'm feeling all right, I'm feeling calmer. A little calmer and less frantic. And frankly, less frightened than I was a few seconds ago. How did you do that? You did that. With your magic voodoo voice and your stupid song quotes."

She just smiled.

"So, about these missing steps."

I resisted the temptation to go on about what she was doing and how she was doing it, and, instead, settled on my remarkable discovery about Issie—if that was her name at all.

"Issie Raynerd," I began, "was a student of mine when I taught at the university, at least fifteen years ago. She took a class called world mythology, a survey course that usually had over a hundred students in it. I enjoyed teaching it, because I enjoyed the performance of it: I sang with a very loud voice, I told stories in a greatly animated fashion, and deliberately flirted with different people at different times during the semester. Even though she was an undergraduate and I was about to achieve my doctorate, we were about the same age."

"Because you're a braniac who started college at sixteen," she supplied.

"Yes. And one especially popular story was about the love of Tristan and Iseult. It's tangentially related to the Arthurian cycle. The Tristan stories, I think, are older than that. There are plenty of variants and declensions, but certain basic motifs run through every story."

"And those are?"

"Well, it's essentially about a love triangle." I shifted comfortably in my chair. "Tristan is a great knight, and the nephew of King Mark of Cornwall. He is wounded in battle and is dying. Because he is so valiant and beloved, King Mark sends him to Ireland, to the castle of a renowned healer, Iseult's mother, also named Iseult. There his life is saved, and he falls in love with Iseult, though he says nothing to her. When he is well enough to travel, he returns to the king, and begins to wax rapturously about Iseult. Before long, King Mark determines that Iseult should be his bride. Tristan can say nothing, of course, if the king wants a bride. So Mark sends Tristan to fetch Iseult, which he does, but in Ireland Tristan confesses his love for her, and she admits that she feels the same for him. Iseult's mother chides the couple. They cannot thwart the king's wishes. So the mother creates a love potion that Iseult will take, and give to Mark, on their wedding night. Tristan vows to abide by the marriage vows, though sick with love, and they begin the sea voyage back to Cornwall. All might have been well, might have ended there."

"But something happened on the crossing," Ceri guessed.

"It did indeed," I went on. "The sea crossing was rough, and the couple drank wine to steady their nerves. But Iseult's hand-maiden, Brangaine, confused the potion with the wine, or deliberately put the potion in the wine, because she had no wish to see true love foiled. Tristan and Iseult drank the love elixir and were instantly and forever smitten, incapable of loving anyone or anything else but each other."

"But there's still the matter of King Mark," she said.

"Exactly. The lovers are now impossibly locked, but cannot run away. Unable to bear the idea of sleeping with the king, Iseult persuades Brangaine to give Mark another potion to make him drowsy, and further persuades the handmaiden to take her place in the nuptial bed."

"The maid slept with the king?"

"Yes," I went on, "and Mark was never the wiser. Tristan and Iseult slipped away whenever they could to be alone. Including finding a cave where their trysts would be hidden. Whenever Tristan was free, he would send an apple bough floating down the tiny stream past the place where Iseult pined, close to her castle. She would see the bough, and rush upstream and into his arms. And again, all might have been well, might have ended there."

"No it couldn't have," she disagreed. "Guilt, jealousy, betrayal—that's always a part of the love triangle, the deceit of love."

"Exactly," I agreed. "Often Mark suspected, and just as often Tristan and Iseult denied their love. But eventually the lovers' hiding place, their cave, was discovered by a dwarf, whose name was also Tristan, and he was loyal to the king."

"A lot of double names," she interrupted.

"Just wait," I told her, "there's more of that. The dwarf Tristan told Mark where the cave was, and the king at last discovered the lovers in carnal embrace. Tristan was banished to Ireland. Brangaine was sent away. Iseult resigned herself to a loveless marriage. Mark lived out his days in misery, separated from his beloved knight by the Irish Sea, and from his wife by a wider gulf: her indifference. And once again, it might have ended there."

"There's more?"

"Tristan roamed, inconsolable, through the cold and bitter winter of Ireland's Christmastide until he came upon a castle whose chief occupant was a pale, wan girl *also* named Iseult. Though she was nothing like his beloved, Tristan married her simply because she had the same name. But he pined and his health declined until he was near death. The pale Iseult, hopelessly in love with her husband, could not bear the idea that he would die, and sent, against her better judgment, for the true Iseult, the only person in the world who might cure Tristan. The true Iseult agreed instantly and set out for Ireland. But when the pale Iseult told Tristan that his beloved was coming to save his life, he was so overjoyed that the pale Iseult became jealous. In the end she lied to her husband and told him that the true Iseult had refused to come. Tristan turned his face to the wall, sobbing and moaning, and there he died. Alas, that very instant, the ship carrying the true Iseult landed near the castle. The true Iseult ran up the lee, tore through the gates and up the stairs, only to find her love dead and the pale Iseult unconscious from grief, and lying in a corner. The true Iseult came to her love, put her hand on his brow, settled in beside him in his coffin-bed, and there she expired too. Still, in spite of death, their bodies glowed with golden warmth simply from the mutual touching of their skin."

Ceri was silent for quite some time.

Finally she said, softly, "Yeah. Jesus. There's a certain kind of girl in this world who would give anything to live in that story. And who wouldn't fall in love with the person who told it to her?"

"I would have put it all together sooner, as I was saying," I said, sidestepping her question, "except for the misdirection—the classic magic technique trick that I actually played on myself—of the name *Tristan*. All I could think about was Tristan Newcomb, the man who owned the Ten Show."

"The man for whom your parents worked," she added, "and the man who might have been your father. I can see why he might have been on your mind instead of a medieval story."

"He wasn't my father," I said, only a little sullenly. "I thought I told you that."

"All right," she answered, in a very unconvincing manner. "So, about the story: you've said it was only tangentially related to the Arthurian cycle, but to me, what you've just said—Arthur, Lancelot, and Guinevere are just slightly more Christian versions of Mark, Tristan, and Iseult. It's the same love triangle, exactly."

I nodded. "Yes. It is."

"So why does she think you're King Mark?" she asked clinically.

"Because I was the authority figure, the king," I answered, because it seemed obvious to me. "I was the person who told her the story, I was the one in charge of the class, I was the professor, she was the student. Right?"

"So what now?" she asked, sidestepping *my* question.

"What now?" I stood again. "We have to find her. Don't you want to know why she's gone around the bend about this? Isn't this at least as interesting as your Father Queequeg story?"

"It is," she assented reluctantly, "but mostly, once again, as it relates to you."

"To me?"

"It now seems possible that you're the progenitor of her madness," she said firmly, "the object of her fixation, and the interpreter of her fantasy—all in one."

"What are you talking about?"

But I knew what she meant. She meant that the very fact that I had discovered what I believed to be the source of Issie Raynerd's illness is exactly what implicated me in its origins.

She read the realization on my face, and went on. "So we do have to find her. But we apparently have to do it without much help. Skidmore's down for the count, I'm afraid, and I'm not certain how much more Melissa Mathews can take."

I shook my head. "Don't dismiss her quite so easily," I said. "She's been shot at more times than I have, and threatened in the line of duty in ways you can't even imagine. Her looks are deceiving. She tougher than almost anyone I've ever met."

"Yes," she said briskly, "I believe that. What I meant was that she's got her own problems dealing with Skidmore. She's in love with him."

"No she's not."

"I don't mean romantically," Ceri hastened to say. "I mean— well, in the more chivalric sense, in keeping with the current mode around here. She loves him chastely, and with purity of heart. But it's still love and she can't stand that he's suffering and she can't avoid thinking that his suffering is partly her fault."

I thought about it for a second. "Oh."

"And, for a change, I don't recommend calling Lucinda at this point. She's worried enough as it is."

I nodded. "I think you're right about that. And Andrews is— he's already made it clear he won't be able to help for a while."

"And the state patrol," she began.

"They already think I'm crazy." I took a deep breath. "Plus, I'm more of a do-it-yourself kind of person anyway."

"So." She stood and looked me square in the eye. "We're on our own."

21

Downstairs, coats on, gearing up for a cold winter's night, I began to have a kind of sinking feeling. Although the moon was low, it was still quite dark outside. We would, of course, go back to the cave first, but unless she was completely out of her mind, Issie wouldn't stay there.

"It's a bit supernatural the way that woman jumped out of your window and into the snow without anything on," Ceri said, pulling on her gloves and shivering already, despite the nice warm embers in the fireplace. "You know that I'm still not entirely convinced she's a real person."

"And I'm still not entirely convinced that you're a real psychiatrist," I told her, adjusting my black knit cap a little over my ears. "Especially when you give out with that kind of a pronouncement."

"Okay." That was all she said.

"Cave first," I said, "but then if we don't find anyone there—"

"And we avoid being shot to death by the very bizarre David Newcomb," she interrupted.

"Right, good point," I went on, "but I'm saying if we don't find anyone in the cave, what do we do after that? Just wander around in the snow and hope for the best?"

"Let's examine this for a second."

We were both standing right at my front door. It had begun to snow again, and the flakes were thick and slow to fall, nearly impossible to tell from the thousand stars in the sky.

"So far," she continued, "we've had no luck following Issie and David into the depths of the cave."

"But," I brightened, seeing where she was going, "we now have newfound knowledge about the other end of the cave, given to us by the only slightly dazed Melissa. We might actually be able to find our way in there, or even come across another hiding place, deeper in the mountain."

"Good thinking," she agreed, hand on the doorknob.

"Right, then, let's head for the other cave entrance, by the squad car wrecking tree."

"Sold." She pulled the door open and we stepped onto the porch, and then into the night.

The air was razor cold and once we were out of the buttery glow from the windows of my home, dark as an unlit cave. The crescent moon that had only a short while before lit Issie's retreat had now sunk low enough to be obscured by tall pines and higher mountain peaks. Occasional stripes of pale light only emphasized the shadows along the road, and in the deeper woods.

We made our way along the edges of the road, flashlights out, scarves pulled tight. The wind that was blowing the snow all around us found any opportunity to invade the slightest opening in our clothes. My face was already stinging, and I pulled the wool cap down over the rest of my ears, nearly over my eyes.

After what seemed a half an hour we found a pine tree with damaged bark and low-hanging broken limbs. The snow had obscured the wheel ruts and errant gravel, but as we slipped off the road and down the slope, I found enough faulty footing to support our assumption that this was indeed the place where Melissa had wrecked her squad car.

The flashlights seemed feeble swords against the demon night,

DECEMBER'S THORN | 195

like looking at the world through a pinhole. And if we moved them back and forth to cover a wider area before us, the sensation quickly became unnervingly dizzying. A sense of vertigo set in that, alas, threatened a return of the impulse to throw up that had so nearly capsized my attention when Issie had invaded my bed.

I stopped for a second, trying to regain equilibrium, and Ceri came to a halt a few feet in front of me. We were both breathing hard, and the woods around us were incredibly obscured.

Just as I was trying to think of a better way to search for an invisible doorway to an underground cave in all that snow, Ceri started her trek again. Loath to appear less than her equal, I forged ahead, still trying to catch my breath.

I decided that the best I could do would be to take a few steps with the flashlight pointed to my left, stop, survey a little to the right, then move a few more steps. It seemed more methodical, less thrashing, and it certainly was easier on the nausea.

It did, however, have the unfortunate effect of widening the gulf between my compatriot and me. After a very short while, Ceri was, perhaps, thirty feet farther down the hill than I.

After the briefest of considerations, I felt it best to catch up with her, so, I switched off my flashlight, let my eyes become a little more accustomed to the darkness, and then picked up my pace in pursuit of her lighthouse-precise position.

I made my way easily past trees and larger rocks, but after ten feet or so I hit a stump with my foot, and it nearly toppled me. I grabbed for a nearby limb and wrenched my side, slipping and sliding down the slope like a cartoon character.

"What the hell are you doing?" Ceri called out, sweeping her flashlight my way.

As she did, the light caught a flash of steam or fog, I thought. And then I went down, face-first into the snow.

Ceri floundered upward toward me. "Fever? Are you all right?"

The genuine concern in her voice, all lighthearted humor

gone, was sincerely touching, but I scrambled to my feet, embarrassed, before she made it all the way to where I had collapsed.

Partly to defer further examination of my clumsiness, partly because I was curious, I pointed in the direction of the curious steam.

"Just over there," I said, squinting, "was a patch of smoke or fog or something that you caught in your light for a second. But it might be heat or air from the cave entrance."

"You fell down," she pointed out.

"And now I'm up," I said firmly, "and walking toward what might be the other entrance to the cave."

I lumbered down the mountain, switching on my flashlight again.

"Look." I shook my flashlight to indicate the place I meant.

There was a distinct plume of smoke or something rising from behind a patch of rhododendrons.

"That's it!" She seemed elated.

We rushed to the site, and indeed, if one got down belly first and crawled, it would have been possible to fit through the small, horizontal opening. Barely.

"I don't think that's it," I said.

"It could be it." She didn't sound at all convinced.

I suddenly remembered that we'd had an easier time finding the other entrance from below, and turned around. I raked my light slowly side to side and steadily upward. Ceri saw what I was doing and joined in.

After five shivering minutes, we saw something. It was another rock outcropping, small and squat, obscured by small evergreens. It could have been something, but some of our vigor and enthusiasm had been undermined by the previous false alarm.

We made our way toward the huge stones without speaking.

Then, as we drew nearer, it became quite obvious that we were in luck. There was a small, flickering light coming out between the two main boulders. I switched off my flashlight and Ceri followed suit.

The light coming from inside the cavern seemed to be from a fire or maybe a torch. It was flickering but didn't appear to be getting any closer to us, or farther away. We stood close to the entrance for a few moments, neither quite certain what to do.

Then Ceri leaned my way and whispered into my ear.

"If David Newcomb is in there with a gun and baling wire," she told me, "maybe I'd just rather go on back to the house."

"But if Issie Raynerd is in there," I countered, nearly soundlessly, "we have to go in and get her."

She let out a silent breath. I watched the ghost it made as it swirled in the air around her head.

Without further discussion, I turned and rushed toward the entrance holding my flashlight like a short club.

Ceri, surprised by my sudden move, reached out for my arm to stop me, but I was just a little too far gone.

I shoved past the evergreens, turned sideways, back to one of the boulders, heavy snow pelting my face, and edged my way quickly into the cave.

There was a burning wooden torch set in a handmade column of rocks. Beside the torch were a sleeping bag and some cans of soup. Otherwise, I was alone—until Ceri nudged in beside me.

I put my finger to my lips instantly. I was afraid that the sleeping bag belonged to David and that he'd heard us coming toward his hiding place. I imagined that he stood just out of the light, gun pointed at us, finger on the trigger.

Then there was a tumble of stones and a low growling from ten or twelve yards deeper into the cave. For a second I believed that my fears about David had been confirmed. Then I heard the growling sound again, and turned to Ceri.

"Run." I began shoving her out of the cave.

"What?" She resisted.

"Run!" I insisted. "Bear!"

A split-second of registration produced an astonishingly fast exit. I was close after.

As I emerged from the cave, I saw Ceri making for a nearby tree from which depended several low limbs. It was obviously her intent to try to climb.

"Go on," I shouted. "I'll give you a boost up."

Behind me I could hear the bear complaining as it squeezed out of the cave. It sounded big. Ordinarily, I wouldn't have been so alarmed. Black bears were plentiful in the hills; I'd seen hundreds of them in my life. And as far as I knew, there had never been a bear-related fatality in our community. Ever. But tell that to the bear, whose knowledge of statistics might have been, I felt, less accurate than mine. I was fairly certain that the bear ought to have been in hibernation but if someone like David had awakened me from a long winter's nap, I'd be in a foul mood, and willing to bite just about anyone.

This thought flashed like lightning through my brain in the seven or eight leaping steps it took for me to catch up with Ceri. She already had her gloves locked onto a low branch. I put my hands together and she stepped into them, lifting upward to a higher branch. I grabbed onto another limb and jumped. Both of us were making gasping noises a little like prizefighters. I was, perhaps, ten feet off the ground before I dared to take a look downward to see the bear.

When I did, I was attacked by a confusing mixture of embarrassment and irritation. The bear was a cub, all by itself, and, I guessed, not yet a year old.

"Hey, Hieronymus," I called to Ceri, "have a look at the menacing beast."

She stopped scrambling and, after a split second of observation, gave me her assessment of the situation. "Oh, for God's sake, we're morons."

"Well," I admitted, "we are a little."

She started down.

"Hang on," I told her. "Just because it's a little one doesn't mean it can't bite or claw or otherwise give you a very unpleasant nature experience."

"Oh." She stopped moving.

"It is very curious, though," I went on, "that this little thing would be in a cave where people have been living, and would be awake, and would be this mad."

The bear was at the bottom of the tree growling like an animal three times its size. Still, seeing its size greatly abated my worst concerns.

"He was in the cave already when David and Issie moved in," Ceri surmised. "He was hibernating. Then, somebody woke him up, the same somebody who put the sleeping bag and the torch and the chunky soup cans by the entrance. That person took off because the bear was upset, and still is. Obviously."

The bear was, indeed, impatient with us. It had begun to claw at the tree and was attempting to climb up our way, all the while snarling and snorting.

"Or," I offered, "what if David, or Issie, trained the bear? What if it's a watch bear?"

"A watch bear." She wasn't asking a question, she was offering derision.

"People used to use geese as watch animals," I continued.

"That's not a goose," she pointed out. "It's a bear."

Then, out of nowhere, Issie appeared. She was standing at the bottom of the tree, dressed all in black, with an old-fashioned taper holder in one hand. It was as if she'd appeared out of thin air.

"It's my bear," she said softly, looking down at the animal. "Aren't you?"

The bear seemed confused for a moment, then sniffed and sat down in the snow.

"Your bear?" I asked. "Like a watch bear?"

She looked up at me, but didn't answer.

"Can we come down?" Ceri asked.

"If you want," said Issie. "I was afraid it was David coming into the cave there. That's why I set the bear on you. I'm afraid of David. He might be out of his mind. David tied up the sheriff with wire and hurt him bad."

I glanced up at Ceri, who stared right back.

"You're sure that bear will let me come down?" I asked Issie.

Issie started back toward the cave and the bear followed her, and then Issie called out, "It's a bear, Mark. It does what it wants to."

"It seems to do what *you* want it to," I countered.

"All right," she said.

"Why is that?" I asked, venturing down the tree a little.

"David shot her mother. For no reason. I took care of the cub. She's all on me, you understand that?"

"Yes," I answered, "sort of."

I found it was harder to understand why David might have killed a female black bear, but I thought of the abandoned deer and felt very uncomfortable.

"Well," Issie called over her shoulder, "come on, then."

Wary that the bear might decide that I was worth a nip or a snap, I nevertheless continued my way down the tree and stood ready to help Ceri. She did not, as it turned out, need said help in any way.

She jumped. She landed in the snow a few feet in front of me and started talking to Issie.

"You're not hurt?" Ceri asked.

"What, me?" Issie said, not looking back.

"You hurled yourself out of a second-story window into a snowbank—naked," Ceri said, hurrying to catch up with the woman in black. "You weren't at least a little chilly?"

"I don't seem to feel the cold the way some others do," she said as she stepped inside the cave.

The bear turned around, gave Ceri a sniff, and then disappeared.

I made my way toward Ceri, speaking as softly as I could. "Are you sure you want to go in there?"

"You're the one who said we had to find her and figure her out," Ceri answered. "We found her. Now we have to go in there if we want to figure her out, right?"

"Let me think about it."

Ceri didn't even bother to look at me; she just plunged headlong into the cave.

I followed, straining for any sight of a crouching bear cub.

That part of the cave was colder than the other entrance. The torch didn't put off much heat. Aside from the soup cans and sleeping bag, there was nothing to indicate that any human being had been there. The smell, on the other hand, significantly warned of an ursine presence, though the actual bear was nowhere to be seen.

Issie stood with her back to us, fiddling with something in her hands, or maybe rubbing her hands together for warmth. She turned around to face us, and in the light of the torch I got my first good look at her in a while. When she'd been in my bedroom, I'd looked at her as little as possible. Now, I studied that face. The eyes were sunken, her skin was pallid, her hands were skeletally white. The black clothes she wore seemed, at that moment, more a costume, rags and scarves and— something very theatrical, the *Madwoman of Chaillot.*

I was surprised to find her expression frightening until I realized that most of my reactions to this woman had been a result of fears. Her expression was dazed and vague and more than a little mad, with a hint of a smile at one corner of her mouth. Still, I'd seen crazier people. I'd probably *been* crazier people at some point or other. Why did this particular person fill me with such primal dread? I couldn't make sense of it.

"Here's the potion." Issie held out a bony hand to reveal what she'd been fussing with: a small paper packet, yellowed, in which there was secured a white powder.

"The potion?" Ceri asked.

Issie looked down, ashamed. "I know I ought to leave off taking it. But once you feel the love of it, it's hard to put it down. David tried to take it away from me at the hospital, but he didn't get it all."

I couldn't tell if she was holding out the packet so we'd take it, or just holding it out, like a child, to show us what she had.

"You were in the hospital in Milledgeville," Ceri said carefully, "and then David came to get you."

"Yes," Issie answered, not moving. "But he didn't come on his own accord, he came at the behest of others."

I decided to take a different approach. "You weren't raised around here, were you?" I began. "Your speech mannerisms are like ours, but there are subtle variations I can't quite place."

"Well, you always had a keen ear," she sneered, "and I never told you where I was raised up at. I don't have a New Orleans accent at all, but I guess something like it rubbed off on me when I was a little girl. My mother was— well, you know she was from here. But we went to New Orleans when I was just little. Don't know exactly how old, but I remember the city well. It was hot all the time, and I loved the smell of chicory. Then we moved again. You know that mother wasn't much for staying in one place."

Clearly she assumed that she'd told me much more about herself and her family than I could remember at that moment, but playing along seemed the right thing to do.

"That's it," I said lightheartedly. "New Orleans."

"Do you want me to take that packet?" Ceri ventured.

It seemed a clumsy interruption.

Issie thought so, too, apparently. Her hand snapped shut like a mousetrap and the packet disappeared into some hidden, black pocket.

"Do you want me to call your mother for you?" Ceri went on in the same curiously inept manner.

"Call my mother?" Issie laughed. "That'd be a trick. Tell her, Mark."

"I—I think it would mean more coming from you," I said quickly.

"Mother's dead, *doctor*," Issie sneered. "If you can arrange that call, I'd take it."

"Oh," Ceri said. "Well. Can I sit down?"

It occurred to me then that Ceri might have hurt herself when she jumped out of the tree, and I went to her without thinking.

"Sit by the torch," Issie encouraged. "You might need to warm up."

I caught Ceri's eye as I helped her to sit down. There was a strangeness in her gaze I hadn't seen before.

"Issie," she said, "will you sit down with me? I don't feel so good."

Ceri gently pushed me away.

Issie took several quick steps toward us and sat immediately by Ceri, close to the torch.

The rest of the cave was black, but the torch gave a circumference of light that made our little area seem like a room. I stood apart, a little nervous about the bear.

"What is it?" Issie asked Ceri. "What's the matter?"

"I shouldn't have mentioned your mother," Ceri said, swallowing.

"What?" Issie asked, leaning in toward the doctor. "Why?"

"Because I may have disturbed her energy," Ceri answered. "She's all around you, your mother is—all the time, you know."

Issie gasped and drew back. "I know!" she whispered violently. "All the time!"

"But she doesn't want anyone else to know that," Ceri went on. "She doesn't like it that I can sense her presence. She also has—she has secrets."

"God," Issie said, suddenly shivering.

"She has secrets that should have been told," Ceri intoned, beginning to use her hypnotic sound palette. "She should have told them when she was alive. Now, she can't rest until those secrets are uncovered."

"Oh, my Jesus." Issie shuddered and began rocking. "Help me."

"Your mother is in terrible pain," Ceri pressed. "And she's visiting that pain on you."

"It's like a weight of chains," Issie sobbed.

"Take my hand," Ceri said, removing her gloves. It wasn't a gesture of compassion. It was a command.

Issie obeyed.

I felt a return of the churning nausea the second their hands touched—with no idea why that had happened.

"Your hands are hot," Issie whispered.

"Yours are ice," said Ceri.

Issie continued to rock, but seemed somewhat comforted by holding Ceri's hand.

I, on the other hand, had no idea what was happening. I could tell that Ceri had figured something out, and was playing her own theatrical scene in order to get Issic to do or say something, but otherwise I was completely lost. I was watching a piece of theatre in a foreign language, from another time, about a story I didn't know.

Unfortunately, before any great discoveries could be made by anyone, or catharses delivered, there was a great, sudden chaos of snarling and cursing out in the darkness beyond the torch's glow. The bear had attacked a person, and I was almost certain that the person was David.

22

Issie was up in a flash.

"Don't you dare hurt that baby, David!" she shrieked. "If you shoot that little thing, I swear to God I'll kill you slow, and you know I can do it!"

There was a rifle blast.

Issie screamed and disappeared into the darkness. Ceri and I jumped as if we'd both been hit in the stomach. I swooped down, took Ceri by the arm, and dragged her behind me as I ran out of the cave.

The night was darker until my eyes adjusted to being out of the torch's light. Ceri shook off my grasp and stood, shaking, right by the cave entrance. Then, from deeper inside the cave, there was another rifle shot.

"Come on," I said firmly. "We're going back to the house to call the state patrol."

She shook her head. "We're not any safer in your house. Why didn't we bring a gun?"

Her voice wasn't hysterical, and both of her sentences seemed like correct responses to our situation, they just didn't sound like her normal parlance. It was hard to make out her face in the darkness.

"Maybe you should take a couple of deep breaths," I suggested. "And maybe you should put your gloves back on."

Ceri nodded and began a slow, calming inhalation. "Except that I left my gloves in the cave."

"We could just go on back to the house and you could put your hands right next to the hot coals in the fireplace."

She shook her head. "We came to get Issie."

"I know," I told her, "but there's a maniac with a gun *and baling wire* in there. Not to mention a bear with a grudge. Do you really want to go back into that cave?"

"Did you see Issie when I started talking about her mother?" she asked in what seemed a curious turn of the conversation.

"Yes," I said hesitantly.

"And her pulse almost doubled."

"That's why you were holding her hands?" I asked.

"Lots of reasons to hold her hands," Ceri said absently.

"Well, it was a good ploy, I'll give you that."

"Ploy?" she asked.

"Talking about her mother."

"It wasn't a ploy," Ceri said, turning back toward the cave's entrance. "Her mother's spirit, some of it, is attached to her like cobwebs."

I had no idea what to say to that.

"We have to go back in there, Fever," she said. "That's what we do. Both of us. You look in the caves for archeological evidence of eternal stories; I investigate the caves until I know what's down there, and then I try to find a way out."

"You speak as a psychiatrist, metaphorically," I said, only a little derisively.

"Are you going in there with me or not?" she demanded.

I considered what she'd said: we weren't really any safer in my house. There wasn't a magic barrier between the madness of the two escaped lunatics and my own front door.

"I do have a hunting rifle somewhere," I said, "in answer to your question a minute ago. Remember? The hunting rifle that Skidmore gave me?"

"Sorry I mentioned it," she said. "The last thing we need is a gun battle. I was just— I was a little disoriented for a second there. I'm fine now. Let's go."

And without further ado, she vanished back into the cave.

I stood for a second, completely at a loss, and then plunged into the cave after her.

The torch was gone, unfortunately, and the cavern was pitch black. A splinter of light was stuck in a bend deeper in the cave, but it was fading so quickly I didn't feel we could catch up. I bumped into Ceri without seeing her, but I could smell her hair.

"Flashlights," she said.

"No!" I snapped. "I think it would be better not to alert David. A flashlight makes a perfect target in the dark."

"Then how do you propose we find our way?" she asked, irritated.

"Something Melissa said," I answered, "or reminded me of. Stand still for a minute and feel the flow of air."

Several heartbeats passed in silence before she said, "Oh."

The draw of air was clear as the needle of a compass.

"One hand on the wall to your right," I told her, "and one up toward the ceiling. I'll take the left and the ceiling, and there's a good chance that we can feel our way along if we go slowly enough."

She took a moment to understand, and then locked her left hand onto my right elbow. "Got it. Let's go."

We made our way like sightless moles, locked side by side, feeling our way along. I tried not to think about the things I'd found as a child in caves like this one: mutant flesh-eating grasshoppers, leeches, bats the size of pheasants. I also tried not to think about an encounter with David Newcomb. I only wondered what earthly relationship the Newcomb family could have to this poor, terminally troubled girl.

So I performed my version of whistling in the dark: I reminisced. I traveled backward through time.

I was beginning to remember things about Issie Raynerd. She'd been, I suddenly knew, the kind of person other students couldn't help but make fun of. Her enthusiasms were odd to most people her age. She liked old music, European puppet theatre, and thrift store clothes. She'd been an A student in my classes, but not the sort I'd favored. She always seemed to retreat when I would ask her a specific question. She'd been shy to a nearly pathological extent.

"Funny," I opined aloud at last, "but I'm beginning to remember Issie as she was when I knew her at the university. Why would that happen now? And why didn't I know her when I first saw her?"

"She looks different?" Ceri ventured. "No. You said she looked about the same, and then when we saw the photograph—she doesn't look any older now than she did then."

"Right," I agreed. "That in itself is eerie. But tell me, if you can, doctor, why are these images of her coming back to me now?"

"That's the right question," Ceri said. "What's your answer?"

"I have to answer?" I demanded. "Who's the psychiatrist and who's the patient here?"

"Yeah," she sighed, "that's hard for me to tell sometimes."

"What?"

"I mean I'm finding out things about myself *while* I'm finding out things about you."

"I don't understand what that means," I mumbled. "But I don't understand a lot of what you say, if I'm being frank."

"Don't you— or, didn't you sometimes have the impression," she asked, "when you were teaching, that you were learning more than the students were?"

"Oh." I slowed just a little. "Well. Yes. I've said that before.

Saying something out loud lets you hear what you really think. You see it new again, even stodgy old ideas or objects you've had on your desk for years—they can take on a brand-new . . ."

I trailed off because I suddenly felt something crawl over my hand. Then several things pelted my arm, my chest; something hit my face. Ceri must have felt these sensations, too; she let out an involuntary gasp.

"Christ," she swore.

"Yeah," I agree, "let's just go."

I quit touching the wall and ceiling, crouched low, and tried very hard not to picture what might be all around us. We both shot forward blindly. I was absolutely convinced that we would run headlong into a rock—until a thin hope presented itself. I saw a tiny thread of light in the distance.

I could hear voices coming from the direction of the light, but there was no way to make out what they were saying.

Without thinking, I began moving slowly toward the light. Ceri was moving forward, too, and as we both progressed, the light grew, slowly, stronger; the voices came more clearly. Issie and David were arguing, but it wasn't a violent confrontation. They were having a disagreement about—unless my hearing was playing tricks—what to have for dinner.

"I can't eat that goddamned Ramen noodle packet one more night, David," Issie was saying.

"If you mix it with the Campbell's soup, the chunky soup," David whined, "it's *good*."

"No," she said. "It's not. It's slop."

"Well," David countered, "we could have had venison stew if you'd let me take that deer like I wanted."

"In the first place, deer stew is greasy," she said, "and in the second place, that bloody carcass did us more good than anything else we've tried so far. You should have seen what it did to Fever. Lord, he was shook up."

They both laughed.

I stopped all forward motion. Ceri did, too.

I could hear the difference in Issie's voice. I could hear that the winsome lost girl was gone. Hers was now the voice of an extremely calculating tactician.

I had an odd sinking sensation in the pit of my ennui: Issie Raynerd was taking me for a ride. Everything I'd thought about her until that moment had been wrong. Nothing she'd told me was true. I'd been made an unwitting player in some incomprehensible machinery of theatre.

I found that the sensation had a profound effect on my body. As silently and discretely as I could, I turned away from Ceri Nelson, took a few steps, and threw up for several minutes.

When I was finished, I discovered that Ceri was at my side. I hoped that I hadn't been too vociferous in my evacuation. I felt light-headed.

"Fever?" Ceri whispered.

"I've been wanting to do that," I whispered back, "since I found Issie in my bed. I actually feel better now."

"Except for the fact that we've been completely wrong about everything," she said.

I nodded. "Except for that."

"What now?"

I straightened up completely and drew in a long breath through my nose, then out my mouth.

"Now," I said as softly as I could speak, "we have an edge. We know she's lying."

"I don't see how that—"

But Dr. Nelson's querulous exploration was cut short by my shouting: "Issie! Issie, are you all right? We heard gunshots!"

And then, absent better thought, I ran headlong toward the lighted cavern. I have no idea what Ceri did, but within ten or twelve long strides I found myself in the cave with Issie and David. They were both seated at one of the makeshift tables, oil lamps were lit, and the fire pit was blazing close to the entrance.

David was entirely startled, and nearly fell off his perch. Issie was calmer. She collected herself in seconds, softened her facial expression, and clutched her clothing at the neck.

Behind me Ceri spoke up. "David, did you kill that poor little bear cub?"

"He did!" Issie shouted. "Then he dragged me back here with him! Do something, Mark! Why don't you do something?"

David, obviously rattled, did his best to assume his part. He slid off the chair, reached behind the table, and produced his rifle.

"That's far enough!" he barked. "I don't mind if I kill either one of you!"

That, unfortunately, had the ring of truth.

Ceri was beside me, and touched my hand only slightly, but enough to let me know she had something in mind.

"You both know I'm a psychiatrist," she said in her most soothing, hypnotic tones. "I can help. I can help you both. I can."

The repetition of words seemed to have an odd soporific effect, even on me.

"We had enough of your kind of help in the hospital at Milledgeville," David snarled, but some of the bite was out of his voice.

"I want—more than ever—to see what help I can be to you both." Ceri smiled.

I turned to look at her. Whatever plan she had in mind included being completely honest. I could tell—anyone in the world could have told—that she genuinely did want to help these two people.

That unexpected attitude filled up the room. There was a benevolence emanating from Ceri Nelson that was palpable and warm. I was certain that David and Issie felt it, too. And it made me reevaluate my fear.

I was steeped in my own fears about Issie Raynerd, I recognized then. I was afraid of what I'd find if I completely remembered her. I was afraid of what I'd know if I learned why she was doing what she was doing. I also realized that these fears were almost entirely intuitive. I had no conscious, objective evidence to support even the smallest pebble of the mountain of dread under which I found myself—deep in a cave made entirely of overwhelming angst.

But the fact that Ceri wanted to help, sincerely wanted, more than anything, to bring an end to whatever suffering was causing Issie and David to behave the way they were behaving—that was helping me, too. That fierce, concentrated compassion was entirely sustaining, and healing. At least a little: it was enough to keep me, for a while, from collapsing onto the stone floor.

"I—I don't know if anything can help me," Issie stammered.

It seemed a genuine sentiment, not an actor's line; David had lowered his gun.

"I just want to talk," Ceri said, taking a cautious step toward the troubled couple.

I watched as Ceri made her way, very slowly, almost floating, toward the table. David and Issie stared, blinking, as if they were watching a great light approaching, or a distant comet across the starry sky.

"Let's sit," Ceri said gently.

Without appearing to think at all about it, Issie and David moved to their seats. I felt likewise compelled to find a chair and join them. Within seconds all four of us were seated around a crate that served as a table. The oil lamp in the center of it gave our faces a ruddy glow, and a warmth, and we were all so close to one another that our knees touched, and hands could have.

"Mark is ready to forgive everything," Ceri said after a moment of silence.

It seemed an odd start to me, and jarred me out of my peaceful stupor just a bit. I could see a flash in Issie's eyes, too, as if she were waking up and feeling an advantage, a realization of having the upper hand. David only seemed confused.

"Tell her, Mark," Ceri encouraged, looking my way.

That she was calling me Mark and encouraging me to indulge in the play of Issie's creation was obvious. With no time to understand why or to think things through, I fell back on my old theatrics from the university: storytelling as teaching. What's the end of any story? That which was lost, or most desired, is finally found at last.

"I—I realize now that you've come a long distance," I began, "over rock and stream and stormy sea. That's how this story goes. You've come to me for just one thing. Every quest has an end when the grail is found, and here's your prize: you're forgiven— with a full heart and an open mind. That's your chalice, and I genuinely hope, Issie, that it brings you peace."

They were mostly lines from a later medieval grail ballad whose anonymous author had imagined Tristan finding, in a land between this and the next, the absolution he required to enter into heaven. The words seemed appropriate.

"There," said Ceri quickly, apparently a little concerned that I'd go on longer. "Now we can begin the healing."

Which was another odd phrase, to me.

"Yes," Issie answered, clearly a little confused.

It came to me then, seeing Issie's momentary consternation, that Ceri's gambit was brilliant. She was playing the part of the fringe psychiatrist, a new-age metaphysician—though I was not entirely convinced it was much different from the person she really was.

Now, I thought, if only I knew what we were really talking about.

"So," Ceri continued, leaning forward almost conspiratorially, "let's return to the moment of crisis. The sea crossing, as Mark just mentioned. What happened?"

There we were, the four of us, in another one of the surreal vignettes that had so frequently plagued me of late. A witch, a ghost, a dwarf, and I, all in a cave underneath my ancestral home, gathered around a battered wooden crate in the eerie glow of an oil lamp. What manner of Christmastide, I was forced to ask myself, was this?

I was shaken from my somewhat self-pitying musing by Issie's strangely honest reply to Ceri's question.

"I was sick," she said very genuinely, all acting gone, it seemed.

"Yes," Ceri encouraged. "The sea crossing to England, going to Cornwall to be with Mark, because you were afraid to fly."

"I was afraid to fly," she repeated. "It was awful, that storm. It was awful. I thought we would die."

"You and the chaperone," Ceri said softly.

"Yes," she answered.

"And who was the chaperone?" Ceri asked.

"It was Tristan, I told you," Issie said, sighing, a little irritated, more like a real person interviewed by a psychiatrist and less like an actress playing the part of Iseult. More, in fact, the way I sometimes responded to Ceri's questions to me.

"Yes, Tristan," Ceri said, nodding. "And you took the wrong potion."

"I did that," Issie said ruefully. "It all went wrong then, I can tell you."

"Issie," David ventured, as if he were not certain what was happening.

"Hush," Issie told him imperiously. "Can't you see that me and the doctor's having words?"

David licked his lips. I thought he might be worried that Issie was giving herself away a little, but it was impossible to tell anything except that he was frightened.

"You took the wrong medicine," Ceri went on, relentless, staring right at Issie.

"I did," Issie confirmed.

"You took the love-philtre," Ceri said firmly. "And you fell in love with Tristan."

Issie grinned and blew out a mean, nonverbal curse. "Not exactly."

"Issie," David ventured again.

"I said you to hush," she snarled.

All pretense that Issie was afraid of David had gone, which may have been some of Ceri's intention, but to what end was still a mystery to me.

"You fell in love with Tristan, you said," Ceri pressed, "and it ruined your marriage to Mark."

"It was ruint all right," Issie said. But there was a rude, raw pornography behind her words.

"What happened?" Ceri asked softly.

Issie started to respond, but David pounded his fist on the table. The oil lamp bounced and threatened to topple. Ceri reached out to steady it, and quickly surveyed everyone's face. Alas, the spell had been broken, as had been David's intention. Everyone leaned slightly back, and Ceri seemed shaken.

"I was lost," Issie said, back to the winsome ghostly girl who had first knocked on my door. "And the sea was wild."

"The love-philtre was taken by mistake," I said, hoping to allow Ceri a moment to gather her wits. "And you and Tristan were locked together—locked for the rest of your lives."

"Yes." She closed her eyes.

David folded his arms and couldn't hide a tiny grin. His work had been done.

"And then you came to me in Cornwall," I went on, attempting to blend what I remembered of reality into the conversation. "I was there, at the Crick Stone."

"And I was there to help you," Issie said, "as best I could. But the damage had been done. I could never be a wife to you, not a real one."

I noticed something then in Issie's eyes, and realized that while I was doing my best to combine reality and her fantasies, she was also trying to do something very similar. She was weaving strange facts and believable fiction into a fabric that she hoped would— hoped would *what*, exactly? What was she trying to do? Now that I knew it was a trick, that she was up to something more cold and calculated than it had ever appeared, I was at a complete loss as to what to do.

But what I had seen in Issie's eyes, I thought, might begin to offer a clue. When she'd said that something had happened on the sea voyage with Tristan—that was true. Something had happened. And that was where the damage had, indeed, been done.

There was the key. I was absolutely paralyzed with dread at the prospect of what was behind any door that key might open.

23

Ceri began her questioning anew. I had no idea at that moment if she'd seen the secret layers, truth upon lie, that I'd seen in Issie's eyes. That was impossible to tell from the odd questions she began to ask.

"Do you have any hot chocolate?" Ceri wondered, looking around the cave as if she were surveying someone's living room.

David could not prevent his face from registering disbelief. "Hot chocolate?"

Ceri nodded and said, directly to Issie, "You've made this place cozy, considering the circumstances, and I just wondered if you had any hot chocolate. I'm still cold from being in the snow. I don't know how you did it—running through the cold like that in your all-together."

"I don't feel the cold like others do," Issie said, turning up the winsome quotient to its highest setting.

"I know," Ceri said, a little less warmly than she had spoken before. "Sometimes the fugue state helps you to ignore the nerve endings. That's dangerous, though. You could get frostbite really easily, and lose a foot, or worse."

Ceri had made her medical pronouncement staring hard into Issie's eyes, penetrating through some invisible barrier, I imagined.

Issie was momentarily at a loss for what to say, but I did notice that she glanced, involuntarily, toward her feet. She was wearing boots of some sort, but they were battered and thin, and I wondered if she might, in fact, have a touch of frostbite. She had a strange sort of limping walk, which I had first attributed to her great madness, then to her actor's skill.

Ceri was trying to undermine Issie's resolve, to break through the layers of fabrication and get to the truth—the way, as I understood it, an analyst might do.

So I thought I'd help. "I got frostbite when Lucinda buried me in the snow. I lost one of my little toes, a patch of my backside, and the tips of both elbows last year. Last year about this time. The backside's healed over, I don't notice the elbows so much anymore, but I miss my little toe."

Issie glared at me. "I don't know what you're talking about."

"Okay." That was all I said.

Ceri picked up the thread. "Frostbite is nothing to ignore, Issie. It can turn gangrenous and fester something awful. I mean, at the worst end of it, you could die. And another example? When David pounded the table just now and nearly knocked over the lamp, I noticed that a bit of hot oil splashed onto your hand, but you didn't even know it. Your nerve endings are beginning to atrophy, I'm afraid. The worst end of *that* is that you could catch on fire."

"What are you two going on about," Issie snapped. "I'm talking about Tristan and the love potion."

"Oh," Ceri said quickly. "Right. So go on. What happened?"

Ceri leaned forward, so I did too. We were both suddenly filled with rapt attention. It seemed an attempt to further dislodge Issie from her concentration.

And it worked a little. Issie spent precious seconds collecting herself. In those seconds I could see the further marriage of madness and reason.

"The water was wide," she began, as if she'd momentarily forgotten her lines, and had been prompted from off stage. "The sea was wild. We were both sick. Sick to death. And I went to take the seasick medicine that my mother had give me for the long crossing. But I made a mistake. I picked out the wrong powder. I give it to Tristan and I took more than my share. In seconds my blood was pounding. My skin was hot. I thought I could see clear for the first time in my life. And what I saw was Tristan, sitting on the bed. I wisht you could see him the way I did then. He was a handsome man, no matter his size."

Ceri seemed to choose that precise moment to interrupt. "Yes, Fever— oh, I mean, Mark met Tristan. Am I correct?" She turned to me. The look in her eyes somehow told me to be honest.

"Yes," I said. "I was little, but I saw him fairly often, though at a distance, when my parents were first working for the Ten Show. After only a short while of being with him, you forgot his size entirely. You were more impressed with his ability to engage in conversation with anyone: a mayor, a street cleaner, a magician—the magician's assistant. He was, from afar at least, one of the most charming people I'd ever seen."

"That's him, Lord," Issie agreed, some of the actor gone from her voice.

So that was part of Ceri's plan, not unlike my own resolve: to begin to blend fact into Issie's fiction and see what her reaction might be. In this particular case she didn't think to object to the honest facts about Tristan Newcomb, though it was nearly impossible for me to imagine how she might have known him at all.

"When I left Blue Mountain," I mused, possibly against better judgment, "I tried to put my entire childhood out of my mind. I don't really know much of what happened to my mother, and I have no idea when Tristan died. I kept in touch with my father only sporadically. My friend June Cotage—she and her husband were my parents' friends really—June wrote to me that my father had died only after she realized that I might not know. He'd been dead for nearly a year at that point. A year. As I say, I tried to put most of Blue Mountain out of my head when I went to the city."

"But you came back," Ceri said very softly.

I nodded. "I came back. Joseph Campbell says—and, I mean, it's not that I can blame everything I do on Joseph Campbell—but he did say that you explore the world, dabble in religions and philosophies all you want, but at the end of the dance, you have to go home with the one you came with. He went back to Catholicism. I came home to Blue Mountain."

I glanced at Issie. She was completely thrown off balance. What had been her storytelling time had become something of a bizarre group therapy session. Ceri thought that too, apparently.

"What about you, David?" she asked. "Tristan Newcomb must have been something of a force in your life. From what Fever's told me, he was quite famous in certain circles."

"What?" David looked around as if someone had shaken his chair. "Me?"

Issie gave him a powerful look, which did nothing for his composure.

"Oh, my God." I gasped, very genuinely. "I just realized something—speaking of someone quite famous in certain circles."

Everyone turned my way as if I'd interrupted a church service.

"Maybe it would be best," Ceri began cautiously.

But I wouldn't let her finish. "Do you remember the loaf of bread we ate?" I asked Ceri.

"What?" She was just as off balance as everyone else at the table.

"The loaf of bread from Paris? You loved it?"

"Yes," she answered with extreme hesitation. "What about it?"

"Would you like to know who sent it to me?" I asked, grinning.

"Would I like to know who sent it to you?" She squinted. "Are you all right?"

I turned to David. "Who do you think sent me a loaf of bread from Paris. He does it every other month or so. Because we're friends."

"What?" David actually looked a little afraid of me, afraid I might be as mad as Issie Raynerd. "Paris?"

I looked around the table, making certain that everyone saw a slight look of madness in my eyes. I was hoping my revelation would have some significant effect, though I was uncertain what that effect might be.

"Orvid," I said softly. "Orvid Newcomb sent me that bread."

Ceri tilted her head, Issie squinted my way, but David actually jumped out of his chair and took several steps away from me.

"Orvid Newcomb," I repeated.

"Um," Ceri said, a little impatiently. "Who's that?"

"David knows," I said, using my most conspiratorial tones.

"Okay, so tell me," Ceri went on.

I settled back into my chair. "Several years back, a crazed preacher named Hiram Frazier came to Blue Mountain, or, really, wandered aimlessly into our town. He killed two lovely young girls who were favorites of one of our citizens, a woman named Judy Dare. Orvid was Judy's boyfriend, and he helped her get revenge. He killed poor Hiram Frazier, although it was always my impression that Hiram was already dead: his spirit had gone and only his body was left. Orvid killed that body, and then he and Judy vanished. Orvid was a cousin or a nephew or something to Tristan Newcomb, and admired Tristan greatly. He was among those who were convinced, in fact, that Tristan was my father. As I've said, that was incorrect but rumors persist to this day. At any rate, I thought David, here, might like to know that Orvid Newcomb is a good friend of mine who sends me expensive fresh bread from Paris on a regular basis."

David continued to back up.

"What is it, David?" Issie asked, irritated.

"Orvid is what is sometimes called, in the movies, a *hit man*," I said ominously, "isn't he David? And he's very, very good at it."

David's face was a mask of confusion, and he began shouting at Issie. "You never told me he knew Orvid! Goddamn it, Issie. He knows *Orvid*!"

"So what?" Issie barked.

"I'm not afraid to die," David said, beginning to quiver slightly, "except if I die at the hands of Orvid Newcomb when he's angry. And he'd be right spit-mad at me if Fever Devilin is a friend of his."

"Orvid is very protective of his friends," I assured all present. "Tell Issie, here, why you'd be afraid of Orvid's brand of outrage."

That was a gamble. I'd only seen Orvid kill one person, Hiram Frazier, and that had actually been, in its own way, very gentle.

"Who do you think taught me that trick with the baling wire?" David whispered. "I saw him kill a man that way, and it took three days. The longest three days of my life, God in heaven."

"David," Ceri asked, "you studied with this person, Orvid? He *taught* you?"

David's eyes were vacant. "He made good money. I didn't care about the blood—I thought. Seemed like a good idea. I had an advantage. He said so. You know Orvid, how he looks? He stands out—that long white hair and them bow legs. But me? If you don't look too close, you'd think I was a child. Who thinks a child is coming to kill you? That was my advantage. You understand? Tristan always told us, all of us little 'uns, that our size could be a benefit or a burden, but it was up to us."

I was still stuck on David's earlier pronouncement. "Orvid killed a man with baling wire?" I asked. "The way you were about to kill Skidmore?"

"I thought I could do it." David swallowed and closed his eyes.

"I'm confused," Issie began in an obviously desperate attempt to bring the group back to her topic. "You say David tried to kill a man? But—David's here to help me."

"Oh, for God's sake, Issie," David moaned, "please stop it. He knows *Orvid*!"

"And Orvid would come here if I asked him to," I said plainly. "He'd do that."

David rolled his head and staggered a little.

Ceri patted Issie's hand. "It's all right," she said sweetly, "I still want to hear the rest of the story. I still want you to tell me what happened. We were on a boat, on the ocean."

Issie was about to crack, it was obvious. Her eyes shot to David, then back to Ceri. She licked her lips and appeared to be at a loss for words.

"By the time you made it to Cornwall," I intervened, "you and Tristan were locked together, and there was no hope for a marriage with me. But you did your best. You tried."

Issie squeezed her eyes shut. "I tried. Yes. I tried. But—but the love elixir, it had done its work."

"And when I went to Ireland to see where my ancestor had lived, you followed me?"

"Yes." She nodded, regaining a bit of her composure.

I reflected then on a perennial observation of mine: most people never realize how transparent they are. They think that their fabrications are opaque; they think that their lies are impenetrable armor. But they're always wrong. Nothing could have been more grotesquely pathetic than Issie Raynerd's insistence on playing out the poorly written drama in her mind.

And on, indeed, she did go. "I followed you to Ireland. I watched and waited. And when the moment was right, I came to you and begged your forgiveness. But you seemed surprised to see me. As if a wife's place were not beside her husband, however troubled the marriage bed might be."

I tried to dig and churn up some memory of seeing Issie in Ireland all those years ago. I barely remembered her in Cornwall—one of a dozen students on the same study trip. But there was nothing in my mind, that I could find, to tell me that I'd seen her in Ireland.

So I decided to give up, almost entirely, on playing the play. Torpedoes be damned.

"I'm very sorry." I sighed. "I think my recent difficulties might have erased some of my memory. I really don't remember seeing you in Ireland."

Truth is a beacon that penetrates any darkness. Issie Raynerd was lost in a black, moonless night. Maybe a beacon would help.

"But, I was *there*," she said, again losing a bit of traction. "Really."

I shrugged. "Sorry. I mean, you do realize that when you first came to my door, I didn't know who you were at all. I had no memory of you whatsoever. Whatever it is you're trying to do may be, when all is said and done, entirely in vain, because I lost a part of my memory—along with my little toe—in a snowbank a year ago. Your whole little play here can't hope to have the desired effect if—if I don't know who you are. I'm very sorry, I truly am. I don't know what you want. I don't know why you're here. I don't know who you are."

Ceri was sitting stone still, obviously waiting to see what my newly minted honesty would buy.

David was still breathing in sobs, unable to calm himself.

Issie's eyes were desperate, and it seemed to me that she might be about to break, somehow.

"The end of the story," I went on, as if I hadn't noticed anyone's delicate state, "is that Iseult and Tristan continued their affair for quite some time until Mark finally caught them together, in a cave much like this one, only with a crystal bed. He would have found them sooner, but Iseult did something that at first she thought was clever. She substituted her handmaiden for herself in the marriage bed. You left that part out of the story."

Issie started to speak, then stopped, slumped, shook her head. "You don't remember when I saw you first how I mentioned Brenda Gain? When you called Lucinda on the phone?"

I thought hard. "Maybe. Gee, if you did, that would have been really clever. *Brangaine* is often the name of Iseult's maid, and that does, if slightly mispronounced, sound a little like *Brenda Gain.*"

"Explain," Ceri said uncomfortably.

"In the story," I told her, "it's usually this handmaid who confuses the potions at sea. And the maid substitutes for Iseult on the wedding night with Mark."

"Ah." Ceri nodded.

I turned back to Issie. "You actually did listen in my class. That's so great. What happened to that part of the story, the part about the maid?"

"What happened?" she snapped. "What *happened*? You were too goddamned stupid to get all the references. You're supposed to be so smart. I said Brenda Gain and you didn't even bat an eye. I dropped a lot of hints that you didn't get until tonight, it looks like. Christ!"

"Well, in my defense," I began, glancing at Ceri, "I *was* in a coma for three months."

"And, if I may point out," Ceri added, "you seem to have dropped the whole 'we had a child' element of the plot awhile ago. What was that?"

"Maybe she just thought that up to explain David's presence," I responded, deliberately adopting Ceri's derisive tone—seemed like the right thing to do. "There's no child in the stories at all."

"Shut up!" Issie exploded.

Instantly she was on her feet. There was an odd little pistol in her hand.

David backed away. That seemed like a bad sign. If the man who was trying to kill Skidmore with baling wire was afraid of what this woman might do with her pistol, that would be cause for alarm.

Ceri appeared to remain calm. "Well, now we're getting somewhere. Something happened in Ireland."

Everyone looked at Ceri.

She continued. "If you shoot someone now," she said calmly, "you'll never get to the bottom of this. You'll never get Fever to remember what you want him to, or do what you want him to do. He'll never understand what you're doing here, and a lot of work and planning will have gone for naught. But most importantly, *you'll* never know what it is that's eating you up from the inside. Because *something* is. And if you don't fix it pretty soon, you'll be gone. You might not be dead, exactly, but there won't be anything of *you* left."

Ceri's words unfurled in the dank air of the cave like the wings of some giant invisible bat that might devour us all. It took me a second to realize that she had somehow pitched her voice a way so as to induce the maximum amount of fear-inducing body chemicals. It was a tremendous trick, and I found myself wanting to learn it.

Issie was only slightly stymied by the effect. The pistol lowered for a moment, but did not leave off pointing in our direction. David, on the other hand, looked as if he might explode at any moment.

"But if I shoot you now," Issie said directly to Ceri, "I could go on with my work, and Fever would suffer for it. And then I could kill him and be done."

"Good," Ceri countered, "you've started calling him *Fever* again. No point in dragging out the scene when someone's turned on all the lights in the theatre."

"I knew it wouldn't work forever," Issie said ruefully. "But I thought I'd get more mileage out of it than this."

Almost all of the character of the "ghost wife" was gone.

Standing there before us was a hard, damaged, small-town mountain girl—with a loaded gun in her hand. Ask anyone: that's infinitely more dangerous than a supernatural creature.

For the first time in a very long time, I was genuinely, consciously afraid for my life. This woman would shoot me. I could see that.

And I knew, with absolute certainty, that I'd be dead—this time—for good.

24

"Why are you doing all this?" I asked Issie.

The time for any sort of pretense was gone. I wanted plain answers to plain questions—no more analytic babble from Ceri; no more mythic folklore from me.

Issie appeared to be mildly surprised by that approach. "You really don't know who I am, do you." It wasn't a question; it was a realization.

"No," I told her. "I do remember your being in my class; I vaguely remember seeing you along with the rest of the group in Cornwall. I don't think you were in Ireland at all. That was a personal trip, the diversion to Ireland. It really didn't have anything to do with the university study group."

"But something happened in Wales between the two of you," Ceri said softly, "that made you both go to Ireland—or made Fever go to Ireland and Issie to follow."

Issie and I both looked at Ceri.

"That much is obvious," Ceri went on. "My favorite theory at the moment is that Fever discovered something about the Cornwall stones. He actually stepped through the hole in the stone and into another world. But the truth is probably something less fantastic and more—what's the word?—*mundane.*"

"Mundane?" I prompted.

228 | PHILLIP DePOY

"Sex," she answered straightaway.

I felt the same biochemical revulsion at the sound of that word as I'd had when I'd thrown up moments before in the interior of the cave. I was surprised to have such a sensation at the mere mention of the word *sex*, a word that ordinarily provoked delight—or something like it.

Issie was grinning, a ragged, leering expression.

I looked away.

"Well," Ceri said, almost to herself, "apparently there's something to that. Fever shivers, Issie grins."

"You got to know what Fever was like back then," Issie insisted. "He *wanted* you to fall in love with him. He did everything he could to make it happen: sing the songs, tell the stories, make a joke, touch your arm just right, so that it don't seem forward, but you feel the burn of it."

I started to protest, but a split second of reflection prevented objection. I did want everyone to be in love with me back then.

Issie saw all that on my face. "You see he don't deny it."

Ceri looked down to hide a shadow smile. "I see that."

"That's how it all started, really." Issie's eyes grew so cold I thought she might have suddenly been possessed by another personality.

"Look," David said nervously, "I'm not so sure this is a good idea anymore. I mean, I'm all for screwing with this guy's life for all kinds of reasons, but we got the law on us something awful now. State patrol, Issie. And worser than that: Orvid! You ought to leave off. Come on back to the hollow and lay low for a while. Really."

His entreaty had no effect on the woman at all.

But I saw that David had dislodged himself from the entire matter, and was ready to bolt. With him out of the way, maybe Ceri and I could gang up on Issie and overpower her, gun and all. At least that was my thinking.

"I don't know any hollow where you could hide from Orvid," I said calmly. "You think he couldn't find you?"

David's eyes acquired a faraway look. "I guess he could at that. If he wanted to, he could find me anywhere in this world."

"And how do you think you'd do with baling wire wrapped around your head?" I asked. "Getting tighter and tighter—hour after hour."

His faraway look intensified. He was watching Orvid torture the man about whom he had spoken earlier. I knew that he was.

Unfortunately, seeing David's face in such pain and distress only made me pity him. So I was not entirely surprised to hear myself ask, "What had the man done, David?"

He knew exactly what I was asking. "That man that Orvid killed in such a way? He'd—he laid hands on Issie."

Issie's head snapped in David's direction.

"She was a young'un," David went on, "about thirteen, I'd have to say. This man, he got her and was feeling of her. She ain't have no trouble get him to leave off—kicked him in the nuts real hard. But when she told her mother, her mother got tore up about it. I don't know exactly how it happened after that, but Orvid got involved. I was a lot younger then, and I wanted to go with Orvid to kill this man. So I did."

"You and Orvid were going to kill a man because he touched Issie for a second or two?" Ceri asked, apparently unaware of certain maternal instincts abroad in my hometown environs.

"Well, that's the thing," David went on, "the mother, Issie's mother— she said that this man— said he had his way with Issie. Said Issie was, you understand, *with child* on his account."

"What?" Ceri asked, astonished.

Issie closed her eyes.

"I knew it weren't so," David mumbled, "but I didn't want to get on the wrong side of Issie's ma—nobody did. You'uns can see that."

Ceri looked at Issie. "You didn't try to stop it? You didn't correct your mother?"

"He'd laid his hands on me!" she hissed. "I *wanted* him to suffer."

I wished at that moment that I could somehow, by telepathy or even some secret note passed between Ceri and me, share my instinct about hard, damaged, small-town mountain girls. I wanted to make Ceri understand that we were in danger of our lives.

"Your mother," Ceri went on, clearly not receiving my psychic bulletin, "she's someone you've mentioned a lot. She helped you to go to the university; she paid for your trip to Wales; she gave you the love-philtre. Which was actually what, exactly?"

"Shut up talking about my mother," Issie warned.

"Okay," Ceri said quickly, "but there was something on that boat trip with Tristan. Something your mother gave you that made you both behave incorrectly."

"And *shut up* talking to me like a *doctor*!" Issie shouted. "Damn!"

Without warning Issie pointed the gun straight up and fired a single shot. The sound of it was so loud that it deafened me for seconds. David hit the floor. Ceri flinched and covered her head.

"Next one goes right in your big mouth," Issie whispered to Ceri. "You understand me?"

Ceri nodded, still covered up.

David was up and headed for the cave entrance.

"Where the hell you think you're going?" Issie growled.

"I got to pee," he answered, picking up his pace toward the exit. He was clearly making an escape.

"David!" Issie warned.

"I got to go!" He began to sprint, crouching low.

Issie fired another shot. The bullet hit David's thigh and blood spattered the fire and the stones. David leapt forward, into the tarp that covered the cave opening. He didn't make a sound. He flailed at the tarp, and tried to swim across it to the edge where he might escape.

Another bullet hit him square in the back, and I thought I could hear it crack his spine. He was dead before his body stopped moving.

"There." Issie turned back to us.

Ceri sat. I stared. David's body bled slowly into the snow on the floor around it.

"Now," Issie told us, the gun steady in her hand, "I kind of liked David. He got me out of the Milledgeville. On the other hand, I don't care a thing in this world for either one of you. Does that give you an idea of where we're going? You asked me, while ago, Fever, why I was doing this. Have a seat. Maybe now it's time to let you know what happened."

"David needs help," Ceri said, but all of her confidence was gone.

Issie's upper lip curled back in a grotesque parody of a grin. "He's past any help you can give him."

"Issie," I said, trying to steady my voice, "you just shot and killed David."

She looked confused for a second. "What? Why are you telling me that? I know I shot David. What's the matter with you? You really did lose your marbles when you's in the hospital."

"I—I think I must have," I murmured vaguely. "A lot of this doesn't seem real to me—a lot of what's happened since you came here."

"Oh," she coughed, laughing, "it's real all right. Real as rot."

"You pretended to be Iseult, thinking that would mean something to me," I began, "but it wasn't ever clear to me, not at all, what you were doing."

"That's the part makes me laugh," she sneered. "You supposed to be so smart! I use some soggy old story you told me once, and you don't even figure on it, not 'til it's too late. *Doctor* Devilin."

"Do you hear your voice?" I asked quickly.

"What's that?" She wrinkled up her nose.

"Your voice, your diction, your vocabulary," I went on, "in fact, your entire way of speaking—it's all quite different from the way you spoke when you came to my door."

"No it ain't," she protested.

"The woman I met a few nights ago," I demurred, "would never have used the contraction *ain't*, for example."

"Yes she would have," Issie railed. "Shut up!"

"Her accent was more genteel," I continued, "and her voice was pitched at least two tones higher."

"I don't even know what that means." She was simmering.

I knew that I was doing something entirely foolhardy. I was poking a crazed wild animal. Eventually one of two things would happen: she would crack and cry, or she would shoot her gun. My reasoning was that she was planning to shoot her gun anyway; I was only trying to give us another option.

And then, mirabile dictu, Ceri was back.

"I think you're right on this one, doctor," she said to me, as if we were in some sort of academic consultation. "This person we're seeing now? That's another personality."

"Shut up!" Issie shrieked suddenly. "I had all that I could take at the Milledgeville! I can act a hundred different ways! That don't mean I'm a hundred different people! Christ on a cross!"

And she fired her pistol.

The bulled grazed the outside of my right upper arm.

For a second I was so startled that I didn't feel it at all. Shock is actually a very strong ally in a situation such as that one. It absented me from pain long enough for me to flip the crate-table forward and upward, directly into Issie's arms and midsection.

She toppled backward, dropping the pistol. She landed hard and cursed more vilely than I had ever heard another human being speak.

She scrambled, but I was up and managed to kick the pistol away toward the back of the cave.

Issie was on her feet and swung her fists, as if they were a single club, directly into my wounded arm. That hurt. That hurt a lot. My vision went white and I dropped to my knees.

The next thing I knew, Ceri threw the chair she'd been sitting on, and it connected with Issie so forcefully that Issie hit the floor again and slid across the cold stones toward David's still-bleeding body.

Ceri grabbed the back of my jacket and hoisted me to my feet.

"Time to go," she whispered firmly.

"Absolutely," I assented.

We headed toward the back of the cave. I searched the floor and found Issie's pistol, scooped it up as we passed, and plunged into the darkness beyond the open cavern.

"You had to get the gun?" Ceri asked, gasping as she ran.

"Yes I had to get the gun!" I told her, irritated. "First, I don't want her to shoot me again. It really hurts. Second, I'm not convinced we won't run into that damned bear again."

"You're not going to shoot the bear," she said firmly.

"Not if it leaves me alone I'm not," I assured her.

We were now in total darkness.

"Wait." She switched on her flashlight.

The passage was illuminated—unfortunately. All around us, on the walls, on the ceiling, on the floor, there were thousands of brownish-red cave crickets, camel crickets—humpbacked, jack-legged nightmares. I hated them. They were skittering and jumping all around us. Obviously we'd felt their grotesque bodies pelting us when we'd been feeling our way along the cave earlier. They were not poisonous. I knew that. But they were revolting, extremely unnerving in such numbers. They appeared to be blind, or had no eyes, but they could feel our movements, and they jumped toward us. Ceri was apparently as disconcerted as I was.

"What I would like to do now," Ceri said slowly, "is to run as fast as I can until I'm in your living room. Can we do that?"

"At least," I whispered.

Without further consideration, we both exploded forward, down the crawling stone hallway, past other disturbing insectum and fauna too fleeting to consider, until we found ourselves near the other opening to the caves.

Slowing only slightly, I saw the bear near the entrance. Ceri saw it, too. It was waiting for us, crouched and motionless.

"Don't shoot it," she commanded.

"If it comes at us," I disagreed, "I'm going to shoot it."

"No!" she insisted firmly.

We slowed to a cautious, tentative walk. I had the pistol pointed at the animal, but Ceri was in front of me, apparently intent on blocking my shot.

"Get out of the way!" I whispered.

"Stop pointing that gun!" she countered. "You're not going to shoot at that bear."

"I'll aim to wound it," I said, "just to stop it."

"No!" she barked.

A second later it was obvious that the point was heartbreakingly moot: the bear was dead. David had, indeed, shot and killed it. Or maybe Issie had, there was no telling at that point.

"Goddamn it," Ceri said softly.

"Let's get to the house before I bleed to death, could we?" I insisted, stepping over the carcass and into the snowy bank in front of the cave's entrance.

"You're not going to bleed to death, you're barely grazed, but okay."

I trudged up the hill, my arm aching and beginning to twitch. I was shivering, an aftermath of the shock more than a product of the frigid night.

The snow had stopped falling, and the stars were burning

above our heads, more than I could ever remember seeing, as if the sky were mostly starlight, only occasionally interrupted by a benevolent black peace.

I slowed down to stare up at all that stunning illumination. It seemed to be drawing my attention upward, lifting my weight and my every intention. I thought how wonderful it would be to take a few moments to lie on my back and stare up at the astonishing brilliance, a sensation I hadn't felt since I'd been a child, alone at Christmas, out on the snowy lawn in front of our house, making snow angels and staring up at the burning Nativity, the holy night, the bleak midwinter sky.

Just as I was about to fall backward, Ceri took my arm.

"Fever?" she said firmly. "What are you doing?"

I realized then that I'd been about to lie down in the snow. "Shock," I managed to say. "Adrenaline. Not good."

"Right." She put my good arm over her shoulders and wrapped her arm around my waist.

Up the hill we staggered.

In what seemed several hours to me, the house came into view.

But what I saw was not exactly my house. It was a rare glimpse of the expanded *Now*. I didn't see my home simply as it was at that moment, I saw the house in all times at once: as it was being built, long before I'd been born, and I saw it as it was when I'd been a child, then the abandoned house of the first days after I'd returned to Blue Mountain—even the renovations that would happen to it after I died. I could see the entire history of the house, shifting in the nighttime air. It was an eternal moment, and it was beautiful.

25

I have no recollection of what happened next, but moments later I found that my feet were on my front porch.

"I'll get it," I said giddily, fishing in my pocket for the keys.

I unlocked the door and turned my face toward Dr. Nelson.

"Won't you come in?" I asked her politely.

"Okay," she said, helping me past the threshold and into the kitchen. "Let's get your coat off, wash out the wound in your arm, and patch you up."

"Good," I agreed, making my way toward the kitchen table. "I could use some patching up."

In a dream of a dance I moved across the kitchen floor and sat in a kitchen chair. I watched as my mother and Lucinda and Melissa Mathews and Dr. Ceri Nelson all went to the kitchen sink, as though they were all one woman. I dizzily recalled the Wallace Stevens metaphor: "Twenty men crossing a bridge, into a village, are twenty men crossing twenty bridges, into twenty villages."

"I'm Billy Pilgrim," I mumbled, half-distressed.

"What?" she asked absently. "I don't know who that is."

"I've come unstuck in time," I explained.

"Okay." She was humoring me.

In relatively short order, however, I felt a cold cloth on my arm, then a bandage, a piece of cloth that looked remarkably like one of my kitchen towels.

Dr. Nelson handed me a glass of water.

"Drink," she commanded gently.

I did.

"Take about ten slow, deep breaths, right?" she encouraged.

I did.

Somewhere around breath number seven, she sat down beside me.

My head began to clear. The white mist that had filled my house, and my mind, was evaporating. My arm hurt like hell.

"All right." I nodded. "Thanks. That was close."

"You were going to pass out."

"Yes." I looked toward the phone. "We have to call the state patrol now. And we should call Melissa Mathews, too."

"Are you sure about that?" she asked, obviously testing my cognition.

"Yes. She'd be offended if we didn't."

She thought for a moment, and then nodded her head. "Right."

"In fact," I said, getting to my feet, "I'm calling her first."

I strode to the phone and dialed the Blue Mountain police number, which I knew, of course, by heart.

No answer.

I had to look through a small paperbound book beside the phone to find Melissa's private number.

That phone rang only once.

"Mathews," she said sharply.

"Melissa," I shot back, "it's Fever. There's been another incident in the caves down from my house, and David Newcomb is dead."

"How?" was her first question.

"Shot by the woman, Issie Raynerd," I answered.

"Right," she said, "but that's not her real name. You know that, right?"

"I— it does seem like a fabrication. What's her real name?"

"Have you called anyone else about this?"

"No," I assured her. "This is my first call. But I thought the state patrol—"

"I'll call them," she said.

"Good. Look. How's Skidmore?" I held my breath.

"He'll be fine." I could hear the weariness in her voice then. "He's hurt bad, though. And mad as the devil. I never heard him cuss before today."

"It's a rare occurrence," I agreed. "Melissa?"

"Yes?"

"What's Issie Raynerd's real name?"

"Where is she now?" she asked.

"Down in the caves, or, really, probably on her way up to the house. I'm calling from my house. She also shot me. Did I mention that? In the arm."

"You'uns had to keep running back and forth between your house and them caves. You was bound to get hurt."

I glanced at Ceri. "Melissa says we were bound to get hurt running back and forth between my house and the caves. Why were we doing that?"

"That's therapy," Ceri answered, "in a nutshell."

"Get a gun," Melissa said instantly. "You got a gun, right?"

"Skid gave me one for Christmas some years ago, a hunting rifle." I looked aimlessly around the house. "I have no idea where I put it."

"You have Issie's pistol," Ceri reminded me.

"Oh, right," I said to Melissa. "I've got a little pistol I took off of Issie."

"What kind is it?"

I pulled the pistol out of my coat pocket and stared. "No idea."

"Well point it, but try not to use it, okay?" She sighed.

"Right," I agreed. "But look, Melissa? Why won't you tell me this woman's real name?"

"I'm not sure we know her real name," she said, but I could tell she was hedging.

"But you think you know who she is."

"Yes."

"Then?" I demanded

"There's a lots to it, Dr. Devilin," she answered uncomfortably. "Best right now for me to get to your house with the state patrol. You'uns lock the doors and get some kind of plan, hear?"

"Yes, ma'am," I told her.

She hung up without further comment.

"Well," I announced, "the cavalry is on its way. But there's a wrinkle."

"Issie Raynerd is not the girl's real name," Ceri said. "I heard. Should we look for your hunting rifle? That way we could both be armed."

"I'd rather not," I answered, heading toward the front door.

"Why not?" she asked, following me into the living room.

"I'm not that comfortable around guns," I answered honestly. "I don't know where this particular rifle is, and I would rather, at this point, clobber Issie—or whatever her name is—in the head with a big stick. More direct. More satisfying."

"More caveman."

"Ah. Metaphor. Nice. I was just thinking of this great poem by Wallace Stevens," I began.

"Christ," she interrupted. "For a guy who didn't really take to academia, you certainly are an academic. Poetry, really? Now?"

I had it in my head to argue that dire situations were the only real excuse for poetry in the human experience. But then I realized that such a line of conversation would only prove her point concerning my conflicting feelings about the academy.

Instead, I went to the front door and bolted it, glanced at the living room window locks, and went to the fireplace, there to take up a very solid iron poker, and place the pistol on the mantel.

"Here's my weapon," I told her, hefting the poker. "What's yours? You want this pistol?"

"No, my weapon is my mind," she said, only half-jokingly.

I started to say, "Now who's the academic?"—but a pane of glass in my living-room window exploded.

Ceri dropped low, behind one of the chairs. I stood, stupidly, right where I was by the fireplace.

"Fever?" Issie's voice came from my lawn. It was gentle, even flirty.

Then I heard the bolt action eject a shell and put another in the barrel.

"Yes?" I answered, and then instantly moved away and to my left.

The gun fired, broke another pane of glass, and a bullet struck the mantel. That told me what I had intended to discover by answering her call: she was a very accurate shot.

The bolt clicked again.

I stayed low and made my way to the door.

After a moment I could hear my porch steps creak. Then the boards in front of my door groaned. Then I could actually hear her breathing heavily and sniffing several times.

My plan was to hit her as hard as I could in the shins, a move I was certain would dislodge the gun from her hands and render her helpless for a while. I crouched low, right by the doorframe, and waited.

After another few seconds I was quite startled when she knocked on the door. I jumped a little and hit my elbow on the table near the window.

"It's me, Fever," she said, her voice soft and simple. "It's your Issie. Your wife."

I glanced toward Ceri. She took in a breath, but obviously had no idea what to do or say.

"I have the wedding ring to prove it," she said, almost at a whisper. "Remember?"

I actually did remember, with odd clarity, that she had showed me a wedding ring the first night she'd appeared at my door. And the words she had just spoken were, I thought, identical to some of the first words she'd said to me. That gave me a very uncertain idea.

I stood up to greet her, though the poker was still in my hand. I unlocked the door. I turned the handle. I pulled the door open.

There she stood, her eyes vacant, the gun pointing downward, toward the porch floor.

"You must be cold," I said.

"I'm not," she said, stone still.

"Please come in."

"Do you know me?" she said.

"Should I?"

She held out her hand, and there it was: a golden wedding ring. Why did it look so familiar? Then Issie crossed over the threshold into my home. She didn't look right or left. She took three strides and stopped, eyes closed.

"It smells like home," she said.

"Issie?" Ceri began softly, "would you like to sit down."

Issie seemed surprised by the sound of another voice. She looked at Ceri and then back at me. It seemed clear to me that she had begun to repeat her first visit to me, nearly word for word. Something seemed to be looping in her brain. I realized that I ought to be extremely careful—she'd made some kind of odd shift. Again.

"Please," I said calmly, indicating the sofa with an oddly formal gesture.

"Here," she said absently, handing me the rifle, "I brought your gun back."

I took it from her hand quickly, and looked down at it. I shook my head. No wonder I had known some of the specifics about the gun. It was, in fact, the very one Skidmore had given me years before.

"David took it when we broke into your house while ago," Issie continued, drifting. "I see by your face I don't need it now."

"You broke into my house?" I asked, before I thought better of it.

"Uh huh." She sat down. "It was David's idea. He thought we should grab you in your sleep and take you down yonder, you know, to the caves. But you looked so sweet lying in your bed asleep that I told him no. He took your gun and some liquor—a few other valuables. We didn't really think it out. We just—catch as catch can, so they say."

Ceri nodded. "And now you're here to tell us the rest of the story. The real story."

"I am." She sighed. "None of this worked out the way I thought it would. Not a bit of it."

Ceri moved around the sofa and took a seat in one of the chairs across from Issie. I stood by the door, apparently frozen, with a gun in one hand and a poker in the other, just watching.

Ceri sat back. "Where would you like to start?"

"Wait," I interrupted, "you just said that you took some other valuables."

"That's right," Issie answered serenely.

"What, exactly?" I wanted to know.

"Found what I wanted," she said, not looking at me. "Precious keepsakes, I might say."

"For instance?"

"They're mine," Issie answered, a hint of anger touching her words.

"Yes," Ceri interceded quickly, "they're yours and they're safe."

She shot me a warning glance.

"Right. Good." I looked around the room for a second as if I'd never seen the place, and then laid the gun and poker against the wall by the door.

"Why don't you have a seat, too," Ceri said to me, very pointedly.

"Yes." I moved instantly and sat.

"Well," Issie began, "it all started when I was just a little girl way back in the woods, over there in Fit's Mill."

I couldn't hide the obvious fact that I was startled by the mention of that place. It was a terrible, dead patch of kudzu and Klansmen, only occasionally enlivened by misery and despair. And it was the last resting place of my mother: her grave was in Fit's Mill.

"You never knew that's where I was from," Issie declared with some satisfaction. "I never let on. Changed my way of talking. Just like you. You did that when you left here and went to that university."

That was true enough. I learned very quickly that I'd been admitted to the university only partly because of my IQ and aptitude. I'd fulfilled a very specific niche in the institution's enrollment records: token poor white mountain boy.

So I sanded down my accent and my vocabulary every day until the rough-hewn edges were all gone, and the colorful colloquialisms had vanished. I spent lots of time making a five-word sentence into a twenty-five-word declaration, the way I heard most of my professors speaking. And when all the work was done, though I was still the odd Appalachian boy with the *interesting* family and the *fascinating* stories, people took to me, and I settled in.

"Maybe," Issie went on, "for people like me and you, Fever, there's no real home, no real place to call our comfort. Not in this world, at least."

It was, at that point, impossible to tell if the wavering accent and the wistful demeanor were contrived or genuine. Was she the actor, again, or had she been shocked backward into her real self?

"You were a little girl," Ceri said, attempting to return Issie to her story.

"I was just a little girl," she said, and appeared to be on the verge of tears. "Away back in the woods."

Then, slowly at first, with growing intensity, we all heard the sirens coming. Apparently Melissa's plea to the state patrol had been sufficiently insistent, and several cars were on their way up the mountain.

"Police?" Issie asked, stunned. "You'uns called the police on me?"

Ceri stood so suddenly it startled me, and Issie jumped.

"You killed David, you shot Fever, and you tortured the sheriff!" she shouted. "Now you're surprised that the police are on their way? Get up! I want to smack you into the wall until these policemen pull me off your *unconscious body*!"

The words were so viciously pronounced and so loudly expressed that I was afraid Ceri might have snapped.

Issie's face was a mask of terror. For a moment. Then her entire mien shifted frantically, and she began to laugh.

"All right," Issie said after a moment, shaking her head. "You're good."

Ceri shrugged. "Sometimes it works and sometimes it doesn't."

I glanced back and forth between them several times. "What in the hell are you two doing?"

"I was seeing, or trying to see," Ceri explained, "if I could scrub away all the veneer and get to the real person, whoever was running the Issie Raynerd Show."

"And here I am," Issie offered, presenting her arms as if she were accepting applause.

"I—I'm confused," I said.

The sirens were approaching quickly.

"I believe that the doctor has seen through most of my disguises," Issie admitted. "Men doctors are always easier to fool than women doctors are."

Most of her zaniest accent was gone, and all of the winsome quality had left with it. Once again she was the hard, damaged mountain girl, her most honest role.

"Looks like you won't ever get the whole story, with the police taking me away," Issie continued, actually winking at Dr. Nelson. "That'll be frustrating for both of you."

The sirens were in my yard. A car door slammed.

"They'll take you back to Central State," Ceri said.

"It's not as bad as it used to be," she answered, but some of the vigor had left her voice.

"Since 1842? I should hope." Ceri was moving slowly around her chair, to put the chair in between her and Issie.

"Central State?" I asked them both.

"The hospital in Milledgeville, remember?" Ceri answered. "Among other things, it provides psychiatric evaluation and treatment services for people referred from Georgia's criminal justice system."

"Insane asylum," Issie said plainly.

"I know what it is," I assured them both. "I'm just wondering why she wouldn't go to jail instead of to the hospital."

"Because I'm crazy, Fever." Issie laughed. "Anybody can see that."

"It's just an acting job," I objected, then looked to Ceri. "Right?"

"Oh, no," Ceri said firmly. "She thinks that she's acting, of course, and fooling lots of people. But something happened. I think it happened to her on that trip to Wales and Ireland all those years ago. She's very seriously disturbed."

There were footsteps on the porch, and, a second later, a pounding at the door.

I backed toward the door, for some reason, even under those circumstances, not wanting to turn my back to Issie.

I opened the door. Several men with guns drawn flew into my house. Behind them, Melissa Mathews strode in and glanced around, noticing the rifle and poker by the door.

"Well," she said softly, "this is a better situation than I thought it would be."

Issie looked at me. "Did you happen to see those camel crickets in the cave while ago?" she asked casually.

"I did," I answered, baffled.

"Did you know," Issie asked, smiling, "that they live out all their lives inside those caves? And when it's a long time without food, down there in the dark, do you know what they do?"

I shook my head, staring at her.

"They eat off their own feet and legs," she said, obviously enjoying the idea, "even though they know it'll never grow back. I've watched them do it."

At first I just assumed she was raving, then I thought she might be deliberately trying to disgust me, but I finally arrived at the very clear notion that she was trying to tell me something—maybe something important about who or what she was.

"Where's David Newcomb?" Melissa asked, all business.

"His body is down at the entrance to the cave," I said. "What we might call the front entrance."

Melissa turned to the two state patrolmen. "Would you'uns mind going on down there with the ambulance men? You know where it is. I'll stay here with her."

248 | PHILLIP DePOY

Without further exchange, the patrolmen were out the door and down the steps. I could hear them speaking with other people, presumably the ambulance men.

"Why don't we all have a seat?" Ceri asked as if we were about to begin a group session, or so I imagined.

Ceri and Issie sat on the sofa. I took one of the chairs opposite; Melissa took the other. She put one boot up on the coffee table in between her and Issie, and very ceremoniously drew her pistol.

"Just so we all know how I'm doing," Melissa said, "I'll tell you, *Issie*, that I'm looking for any excuse to shoot you dead. Any excuse. If you go to sneeze, you'd best to warn me before you do. You hear me?"

Issie nodded, not remotely intimidated.

"Good," Ceri said. "Now. Issie was just about to tell us something important. Let's start in Wales."

"Let's not," Issie said sharply. "Let's start on the day I fell in love with Fever Devilin. That's the fatal autumn day."

We were all silent, waiting. The sound of voices trailed off down the mountain toward the dead body of David Newcomb. Then Issie began to talk.

26

"In the autumn of the year, many years ago," Issie began, "my mother packed me off to school. She told me she knew of a man from our part of the world who taught at a great university in the city. She said to go study with him, that he was a good man. So that is what I did."

I was suddenly cold, and thought about going to stir the coals, or add another log to the fireplace.

"That first day I felt a rush of wings up in my breast," Issie went on, her voice mild and serene. "His looks were familiar to me, like a dozen other mountain boys I knew. But his voice and his ways were new. He filled up a room—the way a hot fire does, or a morning sun through the window. Honest to God. That's what he was like to me."

Melissa let go a breath, mostly to demonstrate that she was not being taken in by Issie's persuasive admissions.

"By November I was in love with him all the way," Issie confessed. "I had no one to tell. Momma didn't like it when I talked about boys. I didn't have a father, nor sisters to talk with. I was an only child who'd never met her father. He was never mentioned in Momma's house. So I kept it locked up, how I felt. But when I heard about the trip to Wales, and how some students could go, I was so happy. You can't know how happy I was. I would go on that trip, I would tell him about my feelings, he would see that we were meant to be together, and everything would be fine after that. No more long weeks and years alone. No more feeling like I was the only one of my kind in this world. That's what would happen and I knew it."

"But the special tickets for that trip were only for graduate students," I said, deliberately interrupting what, to me, was a very uncomfortable line of the story.

"Yes," she said, "I found that out. I cried and cried when I went home at Christmas break, and Momma finally asked me why. I told her I just had to go on the trip to Wales to be with you. I thought she'd be happy, since she was the one who told me about you in the first place. But she wasn't. She was troubled in her head, I could tell. Still, I cried some more, and she agreed at last to pay my way. But she wouldn't let me go alone. She got someone to go with me."

"You said you couldn't fly," Ceri interrupted carefully. "You had to make it an ocean voyage."

"We drove up to New York City," Issie said, nodding, "Momma and me. We met this man there. His name was Tristan. He was very sweet to me, and Momma told me to be nice to him. We stayed at a real hotel. It was nice. Then we got on the ship and headed for London."

"But it was a difficult crossing." Ceri leaned toward Issie.

"No," Issie said, her face contorting. "It was Hell."

"Why?" Ceri asked gently.

"That's when it happened." Issie let out a shuddering sigh. "It was a very bad storm. We both got sick, me and Tristan. I went to the bags that Momma had packed. She had given me three medicine powders, one for seasickness, which she knew I was prone to; one for female complaint, which wasn't necessary because it wasn't my time; and one—one she said to give to Fever when I met him, that it would help him to hear my complaint of love."

"The love-philtre," I said.

"That's what I thought it was." She closed her eyes. "God. How was I ever that young?"

"What was it?" Ceri asked.

"I didn't know then," Issie went on. "I just mixed it up the way Momma said to do for the seasickness, put it into a syringe like she taught me, and gave myself a shot, and Tristan a shot. It wasn't but seconds later when I knew something was wrong."

"You took the wrong medicine," Ceri said softly.

"Medicine," Issie repeated ruefully. "It burned in my thigh where I shot it in, then it burned in my whole body. I was flushed as a doe in heat, I was. I was sick with it, and hot, and filled up with desire. I knew right away what I'd done, but it didn't matter to me then. I just wanted him."

"Tristan," Ceri prompted.

Issie began to shake; her black shawl fell from her shoulders, exposing milk-white skin.

"Yes." Issie creaked. "Yes. Tristan. I'd given him the shot, and he was clearly taken with the fire as I was. I stretched out to him, and put my arms about his neck, and went to kiss him. I was ready to give him everything and all at once. But he cussed and hollered and drew away something fierce. I was wild with it. I grabbed him and drew him to me, but he took my shoulders and shook me hard. 'Listen to me!' he shouted. He shouted at me. I was shaking and crying and tore up with wanting him, wanting him bad. Then. Then he told me."

Issie was beginning to cry, although I don't think she knew it.

"What did Tristan say?" I asked, or was compelled to ask.

"He said we mustn't touch that way," she answered hoarsely, "because he was my father! Tristan Newcomb was my father!"

Ceri sat back, her hand over her mouth. I blinked several times, partly in disbelief, partly at the slow awakening of some subconscious terror that was, at that moment, unnamed.

"What was the drug?" Ceri asked, her hand still at her lips.

"Cocaine," Issie whispered, heartbroken. "I know that now. My mother had given me cocaine to take to Fever. My mother. I guess she thought we could share it and get to talking. I don't know."

"God Almighty," Melissa managed to say.

Issie reacted to Melissa in an unexpected way. "But that wasn't the worst of it," she snapped, clearly filled with a sudden rage. "I felt so ashamed that I'd lusted at my own father, I was like to die. He was good to me then. He did his best to calm me down. He knew after a while, or figured out, that we'd taken cocaine. It wasn't the first time he'd had some. He was hopping mad at Momma. He couldn't think why she would give it to me. So I told him, because I didn't know then what cocaine was, that she'd given it to me as a love potion, to take with Fever, so that Fever would fall in love with me when I got to Wales—the way I was in love with him. Tristan got real quiet then. He cursed again, and his hands began to shake, and said that wasn't Momma's intention, not at all. I didn't know what was the matter with him. I was a little afraid."

"You were in shock," Ceri said quickly, "from— from Tristan's news."

"I guess," she responded vaguely. "It's hard to remember how I felt then. It was so long ago. I told Tristan all about my love for Fever, but he kept stopping me and telling me not to talk. It was hard—the cocaine made me want to tell him everything."

"Well," Melissa began, without a hint of empathy, "that explains one thing, at least."

"What?" I turned toward Melissa.

"Now you know her real name," Melissa said coldly. "It's Isolde Newcomb."

Issie smiled then. It was the single most chilling facial expression I had ever seen.

"There's more," she said, in a completely new voice.

I stood, for some reason. "That's what happened to her," I muttered, going to the fireplace to stir the coals. "All of that, it's what made her fall apart. Who wouldn't?"

I looked around, foolishly, for the poker, taking moments too long to remember that it was by the door.

"What more?" Ceri asked gently.

"I think she's told us enough," I said insistently. "Taking cocaine, feeling sick on the ocean, finding out that the man she made a pass at was her father, realizing some fairly unsavory things about her mother? That's enough to send anyone over the edge. No wonder she ended up in the state hospital."

"There's more," Issie sang, the same hideous grin plastered to her face.

"Fever?" Ceri said, realizing my distress.

"I just don't think this is the right thing to do," I said to Ceri, as if no one else could hear me. "She's been through a lot, she's obviously out of her mind. Let it be. Let someone at the hospital take care of it."

Melissa leaned forward. "Maybe you'd better sit down, Dr. Devilin," she said. "You don't look right."

I could feel that my face was clammy, and my eyes burned. I felt cold in my bones, and my mouth was dry. Was it further shock from the gunshot wound? Or witnessing a murder? How was Ceri so calm? Why was I so disconcerted?

"Something's wrong," I mumbled.

"Here it comes," Issie said, relishing my distress.

"Seriously," I said, to no one in particular, "I think we've had enough for one night."

"Take a look out your busted window—*Doctor.*" Issie laughed. "It's coming on sunrise. You're about to see a new day."

My eyes glanced out the window. The horizon was dimly red. The morning star was rising.

"Why don't you sit down, Fever," Ceri encouraged.

I made it to my chair again, but I kept up my protestations. "This woman—don't you see that Isolde Newcomb actually *has* lived part of the Tristan cycle? I mean, it's an amazing bit of ironic poetry on the part of the universe—she *is* the woman in the story."

Ceri nodded. "I see."

"So," I began.

"I see that you're trying to put her back in the realm of myth," Ceri continued. "I see that you're having— I mean, sorry, but I can clearly see that you're having an intuitive episode. I know because you're exhibiting behavior I've experienced myself. You know something that you don't know."

I cocked my head. "I *what*?"

She smiled. "Good. That shook you loose a little. Look. Here's what's happening. Issie is about to tell us something significant. You already know what that is, and you don't want her to say it out loud."

"I already know what that is?" I shook my head. "You're as demented as she is."

"Maybe," Ceri admitted lightheartedly, "but I know what you're going through this second because I've gone through it, too."

"You think I know something that I'm repressing?" I asked. "You think that because you're a psychoanalyst—"

"I don't think that," she protested. "I think you're having a precognitive episode. I think you know what she's about to say based on your intuition."

"No." But I was already feeling the creeping cold of her words, and they did seem terrifyingly correct.

"Issie?" Ceri said, turning to face the crazed woman by her side.

"It took rest of the week," Issie said. "Tristan wouldn't talk to me much after that night. He drank a lot. I stayed in my cabin. I had my own cabin. I slept for hours on end. I was so tired. Finally when we got to London, I was so glad to get off that ship that we decided— Tristan rented a car. I drove. He didn't drive, Tristan didn't."

"Are you going to get to the point?" I heard myself snap.

Everyone looked at me.

Issie smiled. "Yes."

"You drove to Wales," Ceri said.

"We did. And on that trip I learned the rest of the family secrets." Issie sat back and folded her arms with immense satisfaction. "I want to get a good look at Fever when I lay this little package down in front of him, what I'm about to tell him. I want to see it sting him like nettles and bees, the way it did me."

I stared at her and steeled myself, but my heart was thrashing wildly and I was experiencing a panic that threatened to rip me out of my chair and toss me off the top of the mountain.

"When Tristan told it to me," Issie said, "I ran the car off the road. I got out and threw up for what seemed like an hour. I couldn't stop screaming. He was scared. We stayed there, on the side of the road, for most of the rest of that day, him trying his best to comfort me, but it did no good. The damage was done, and I was done in with it."

"What is it?" I demanded. "Just say it!"

"All right," she responded primly, "I will. Fever? Do you know who my mother is?"

I ground my teeth so hard that I couldn't see. "No."

"Yes," she said immediately. "Yes you do. Because my mother, Fever, was your mother too. You? You're my brother."

My head split open, along with my chest. I thought for a second that my body might have broken apart, exploded into white, burning streams. But that sensation only lasted for a second or two, and then, astonishingly, everything was calm.

Everything was calm because Dr. Nelson had been correct: somehow, I'd already known what Issie had just told me. My alarm at hearing her say it out loud was not, in fact, dismay, it was the shock of recognition. Issie Newcomb was my half sister, and, in some way or other, I had always known that. To be sure, the realization had always been just out of my grasp, in the shadows between conscious thought and dreaming. But now that the magic words had been pronounced, I had an unexpected feeling of peace.

I stared at Issie's face, amazed that I hadn't seen my mother's eyes there before that moment. Instead of the burning terror that I might have expected, and that Issie had clearly anticipated, I felt nothing but sadness and a yearning compassion—for my mother, my poor, lost mother—and for this woman whose life had been capsized by sexual shame and a particularly vicious brand of family confusion.

I could see Ceri smiling; I didn't know why. I could tell that Issie was waiting, but for what, exactly, I had no idea. Melissa slowly put away her gun. Everything seemed suspended in time for a while.

Then I reached out my hand toward Issie. "I'm sorry," I said. "It'll be all right now."

Issie stared at my hand for an instant and then burst into tears, great gasping sobs and hysterical muttering. She collapsed toward Ceri, and Ceri responded by taking her in her arms and holding Issie, rocking her, slowly petting her hair.

27

Melissa Mathews snapped her firearm into its holster and rubbed her face. "I don't understand."

I nodded. "Well. It is a lot to take in, all at one sitting."

"She went insane because she was in love with Tristan and you," Melissa said slowly, trying to piece it all together in her mind, "and so she pretended to be somebody from a story?"

"She's not insane, I hate that word," Ceri said, still rocking Issie. "She might be all right after a while. Now."

"Now?" Melissa's face wrinkled up. "She killed her cousin. She's either going to jail or to the insane asylum."

"She's not insane, Melissa," Ceri insisted. "Please stop saying that, all right?"

"But what did she think she was doing," Melissa asked, "coming here, pretending to be Dr. Devilin's wife? And then trying to kill Skidmore? Why did she do all this? It is crazy, you have to say that."

"Well," I said to Ceri, still a little light-headed, "this does have to be, at the very least, the worst case of sibling rivalry on record."

"That may be part of it," Ceri said. "It'll take awhile to unravel. But, have you ever had an unpleasant experience, say, an argument with someone, and then wished, later, that you had said or done something that would have made it turn out better—better for you? Like, you think of what you should have said, or something you should have done? You play it over and over in your mind, hoping it might come out different, trying, in fact, to make it come out different? And try as you might, you can't let go of it? Do you know what I'm talking about?"

I let out a long breath. "I only have, maybe, ten thousand moments like that in my life."

Melissa nodded. "I had a couple of tough arrests—I think about it all the time."

"So, while part of Issie's problem is that she experienced some *serious* sexual trauma," Ceri went on, "and part of it is that after the trauma had a chance to sink in, she also began to envy her half brother—I mean it's a very complex series of events and emotions she's been dealing with. But the odd behaviors, the inability, sometimes, to distinguish fiction from life, and the little play that she's been putting us all through for a few days? That's actually a product of her brain trying to work it all out. She's trying to make everything turn out better. It's the opposite of insane. She's been trying to fix herself in the only way her miswired consciousness could figure out to do. These events of the past couple of days or months, however misguided, were an act of healing."

Issie had grown quiet.

I realized then that I was hearing men's voices, the patrolmen and the ambulance people coming back up the slope with David's dead body.

"And as to the killing of David Newcomb," I said to Melissa, "Issie did that in self-defense, and to protect Dr. Nelson and me from David. I mean, you saw what he did to Skidmore. We were in fear of our lives, and Issie saved us."

Ceri avoided eye contact with anyone, but Melissa stared me down like a lie detector.

"Skidmore told me that David Newcomb was in the mental hospital," I continued, "because he was, quite possibly, responsible for seven murders. And if you'll recall, you couldn't identify Issie's fingerprints. Why would that be?"

Melissa nodded, her eyes still locked on mine. "Because she's not in the criminal database."

"Exactly," I said.

Issie sat up, still leaning a little on Dr. Nelson's shoulder. "David was a voluntary commitment at the Milledgeville," she said. "He came to get me."

"Why?" Melissa asked.

Issie smiled heartbreakingly. "Family," she said, sighing. "Somebody or other in the family told him to come get me out. I don't know why that happened now, after all this time."

"How long had you been in the hospital?" I asked.

"Near five years," she said.

"Why?" Ceri wanted to know.

"What?" Issie said, sniffing.

"Why were you put in the hospital? You were committed?"

"Oh." She nodded. "Momma put me there."

Melissa turned to me. "Your mother was alive five years ago?"

I shook my head. "Don't know. Don't know when she died—or even if she's dead now. I've seen her grave. It's in Fit's Mill. But it wouldn't be the first time she'd lied about something important, would it?"

"You saw her grave?" Issie whispered.

I nodded. "There's a wild native azalea growing beside it. Smells like honeysuckle."

"Okay." Issie leaned back a little, her eyes still rimmed in red. "Reckon that's why she never come and got me."

"She committed you?" Ceri asked.

"Me and her," Issie answered, "we spent long years in that piece of crap house over there in Fit's Mill. I spent lots of time alone there, too, even as a little tiny young'un. She'd come back and never tell me where she'd been. Days. Weeks sometimes, she was gone. Had to fend for myself. Got used to it. But when I came back from over there in England? I lit into her like a house afire. We tussled many a time. She hit me. I hit her. It went on for some years that way. 'Til one day I tried to kill her with a carving knife. She smacked me good then. Real good. I woke up in the trunk of a car. Next thing I know, there I am in the Milledgeville."

I felt a stinging sensation in my sinuses and realized after a second or two that I might be about to cry. I didn't. I could count on one hand the times I'd cried in my life. But the fact that the impulse was there at all, that was significant. I could only think, then, that biology had won out over every other option. My empathy for my sister seemed to be expanding.

"I mean," Issie went on, "I realized after I came back from England that she'd been coming here when she left me alone. To this house. To her real family. A husband. A son. You can't know how many times I stood out there in those woods, after I came back from England, staring in at this house. Walked all the way from Fit's Mill, and it's a good piece from there to here, just to watch you in the kitchen, Fever. And every time I'd come back to Fit's Mill, from here, Momma and me would bicker—or worse."

"You're not finished with what happened in England," Ceri said awkwardly. "There are a few moments missing."

"Missing?" She turned toward Ceri.

"Maybe we've had enough for one day," I interrupted.

"You stopped by the side of the road, you said," Ceri explained to Issie, ignoring me, "and stayed there for a long while with your father. Then what happened?"

"After that?" Issie let out a long, slow breath that seemed to exorcise minor demons. "We drove on, and I went to Fever. I was set to tell him everything. I was burning up to tell him. But he was all caught up in his work, and couldn't nobody get next to him."

I tried to think. "That's probably true. I was obsessed with the work there. I concentrated for hours every day on the stones, the stories about them, and even the incantations I'd heard or read. I don't remember much else about being in Wales."

"But you left at a key moment," Ceri said pointedly. "Why?"

"Why? I think I've already told you why. I wanted—I wanted . . . wait."

In a very sudden slap of light, I saw with impossible clarity a single moment in Wales. I saw myself winding around and around the stones in Cornwall, mumbling words and phrases. I was about to crawl through the stones, on my hands and knees, when I had a shooting pain in my head and a violent sense of panic. I instantly thought of my great grandfather, Conner Briarwood, in Ireland, and had a nearly overwhelming desire to leave, that second, from Cornwall, cross to Ireland, and see the place where he had killed a man in a fit of jealous rage, the act that produced our American family. I realized, as I was sitting there in my home in Blue Mountain, that the sensation then was a duplicate of the sensation I'd had coming up the mountain only a short while earlier: the faint, timeless, visionary rapture that had tried to warn me about Issie's impending revelation.

"I don't want this to sound completely insane," I announced, before I thought better of such a phrase, "but I think I knew Issie was coming, Issie and Tristan. I think I left at the so-called key moment because I knew she was coming and I wanted to avoid her. Does that sound crazy?"

Melissa looked away.

Issie shook her head.

Ceri told me, "Not to me it doesn't."

The voices outside told us that the men were packing David's body into the ambulance, and several people were headed toward my front door.

I stood. "I'm saying now, officially, for the record, that Isolde

Newcomb killed David in self-defense, and in defense of Dr. Nelson and me. Except for her action in that regard, we'd all be dead now, and David, a known murderer, would be on the loose."

"The best thing for this woman," Ceri chimed in, "would be to get her back to the state hospital in Milledgeville and then let me come down there and take over her case."

I stared at Ceri Nelson, then, with a nearly overwhelming sense of gratitude.

Melissa hoisted herself out of her chair just as an insistent pounding came to my front door.

"Okay," she said, making certain to display her complete reluctance to believe us.

I went to the door. Two state patrolmen stood silently, staring into the house.

"This one goes with me," Melissa said to the patrolmen, inclining her head toward Issie. "I need to get her paperwork for Milledgeville. That's where she escaped from while ago."

The two men stared.

"Take the dead body over to the mortuary," she went on. "I'll take Ms. Newcomb to the lockup with me until we can get it all sorted out. Okay?"

"Will the sheriff be—will Skidmore be all right with that?" one of the men asked.

"He will if I tell him he will," she said, her voice made of steel.

Both men looked down. One said, "Yes, ma'am."

Melissa Mathews was a deputy sheriff, and these two men were state patrol, but it was clear who was in charge.

"I'd like to go with Issie," Ceri began.

"Nope," Melissa said with complete finality. "You can come visit later. But right now, me and her's about to have a talk. Step over here, please, Ms. Newcomb."

Issie closed her eyes for a second, and then stood. I was hoping she'd glance my way, but she didn't.

Melissa put Issie in handcuffs before I knew what was going on.

"You'll sit quiet in the back of the squad car," Melissa said, as if she were explaining the rules of some game to a child, "and I'll sit in front. And when I ask you a question, you answer it like a straight shot. We clear?"

Issie nodded, not looking at the officer.

"When can we come to your office?" I asked Melissa.

"I want to question this person," she said, "then process the paperwork, and then talk to the sheriff. So it won't be until later this morning. You'uns ain't tired?"

I suddenly felt every muscle in my body. "God, yes," I said. "I am."

"All right then," Melissa said.

"Issie?" I said suddenly.

She did not look at me.

"What keepsakes?" I asked. "What is it you got out of this house that was important to you?"

"The wedding ring I showed you, for one," she mumbled. "It belonged to Momma. She took it off when she left your father for good. That was in her room, along with some poems I wrote for her when I was little. I used to like to write poems. They're still down in the cave. And a sweater you used to wear when you were teaching. Smells like you."

I started to respond, but Melissa took Issie by the elbow and began to ease her out the front door. I watched them leave, still hoping Issie would look back my way, a quick flash of kinship. She did not.

The door was closed. Suddenly my house was silent, and seemed empty.

28

Eventually Ceri stood, groaning and rubbing her neck.

"If there's any of that apple brandy left," she said, "I could certainly have some."

"Me too," I agreed, shuffling toward the kitchen.

The sun was past the horizon, and gold mixed with red, shot through bare black tree limbs. That light made the woods outside my house look like a set from a lavish play, not remotely real at all.

"Should you cover the windows in your living room?" Ceri asked, still standing at the sofa.

"You could pull the curtains to," I suggested, not looking back.

She did. The room was significantly darkened.

I continued on my important mission, the immediate acquisition of alcohol.

In no time, Drs. Ceridwen Nelson and Fever Devilin, doubtless charter members of the Oddest Names in the World Club, sat at my kitchen table drinking locally made calvados from short plain glasses.

After the second glass was finished, and the third was poured, I began to ask the questions I wanted to ask.

"So, by way of discovering why, exactly, Isolde Newcomb came to my house five nights before Christmas," I said, staring at my glass, "we think that she was trying to heal herself of sexual trauma and bad mothering?"

Ceri smiled. "Not exactly. I think foremost in her mind was revenge."

"Revenge? For what?"

"For the fact that you had the happy family and childhood that she didn't."

I laughed until I coughed and felt light-headed.

"I know," Ceri said, "but that's what she assumed. You got a father and a mother, a nice house, a college career. She got slapped around by her mother, never knew her father, didn't know she had siblings, lived in Fit's Mill, for God's sake. Blue Mountain is Mayberry. Fit's Mill is— I don't know, Kudzu Hell."

"How do you know Fit's Mill?" I asked.

"I know the area," she said, somewhat evasively, I thought.

"So my sister, my half sister, wanted revenge." I reached for my glass.

"And she wanted to make you suffer as she had suffered, for years, with shame and remorse, and head-splitting pain. I mean, if her chronology is correct, her own mother slapped her in Milledgeville and then died, leaving her in a state hospital forever."

"But why did David come to break her out?" I wondered out loud. "I mean, if that part of her story is true."

"Someone in the Newcomb family must have known that your mother died, and wondered what had happened to little Isolde. I mean, from what I know about the Newcomb family, odd as they are, they do watch out for their own. Witness the vengeance wreaked on some poor idiot who grabbed Issie once. He got the Orvid Wire Treatment from her mother. Your mother."

"Probably not," I said. "There were plenty of things wrong with my mother, and she was prone to hysterical exaggeration. I can see her calling up Tristan and telling him that his daughter had been menaced by some toothless, backwoods ape. But dispatching Orvid to take care of it? That would have been Tristan's doing. Not mother's."

"Oh." Ceri took a sip of her brandy.

"Still, there are plenty of unanswered questions here," I said. "Why was David— why did David do that to Skidmore?"

"Remember how we said that sometimes things get stuck on a sort of loop in your brain, and you keep playing those events over and over again, hoping to make them right, or to exorcise them?"

"Yes, God."

"David was deeply affected, as a young person—who knows how old—by watching a hero of his destroy a man in that manner. My bet is that David has done that before, reenacted that event with other people as the victims, in an effort to fix himself, to stop nightmares, or to quell overwhelming fears. Something like that."

"So, your take on every bit of insane behavior is that it's an attempt, on the part of the lunatic, to correct himself, or herself?"

"Yes." She drank back the rest of her brandy. "Yes it is."

At that exact moment, my front door burst open and Lucinda came charging in, still dressed in her nurse's uniform, hat and all.

"Fever!" she shouted, before she saw us in the kitchen.

I stood and turned, only a little unsteadily. "Hey."

"Lord." Lucinda closed her eyes and exhaled. "I saw the ambulance and the state patrol on the road coming from here, and they didn't stop when I waved, and—Lord."

"I'm all right." I went to her.

She threw her arms around my neck. I could feel how frantically her heart was beating. I put my arms around her, too.

"I'm all right," I repeated.

We stood there for a moment. Then she seemed to realize that Ceri was in the kitchen, and let go of me.

"Come on in," Ceri said, still seated. "We're having a nightcap after a very, very long night."

"You're finished with your shift?" I asked Lucinda.

"Just got off. I called you, but you didn't answer." She noticed my bandage. "What happened to your arm?"

"A lot's happened." I blew out a long breath. "A lot to tell."

Lucinda went first into the kitchen; I followed.

We all sat at the table. I poured another glass for Ceri and one for myself, and then looked at Lucinda.

"Not for breakfast," she said.

Then Lucinda studied my face. After a moment she turned to Ceri and studied hers. She nodded, her eyes slightly closed.

"You two are peas in a pod now," Lucinda said finally. "I can see that. You're just alike. I mean you have so much in common. In some ways, you're meant for each other."

I had no idea what kind of feminine intuition or psychic power Lucinda had employed, but she was absolutely correct. Ceri and I had grown completely comfortable with each other. We were, in most objective ways, made for each other, and we both knew it.

"You're right," I said plainly. "I think we've found that out over the course of this very long, very weird couple of days and nights. In almost any way you can imagine, we belong together."

"Oh," said Lucinda, looking down at her hands. "I see."

"Except for one thing," I said, leaning toward Lucinda, my elbows on the table. "I'm in love with you. And that's really the only thing that matters. By the way, you're in love with me, too. That's what you and I have in common. And it beats everything else."

"By a mile," Ceri added, smiling. "And besides, Fever and I are more like— more like brother and sister."

The brandy, in combination with a very long night and a significant number of shocks to the system, took over completely. Ceri and I dissolved in ridiculous, drooling, gasping, uncontrollable laughter.

It wasn't fair to Lucinda, who was baffled, and uncomfortable, maybe even embarrassed, and certainly feeling left out. But there was nothing for it. I could not have stopped laughing if there had been a gun to my head.

At last I managed to say, "I have a long, odd story to tell you. And I don't even know the whole thing. But you'd better keep your seat. And I'd recommend that you join Dr. Nelson and me in the conspicuous consumption of this beverage. I think you're going to need it."

"The good news," Ceri chimed in, still breathless from laughing, "is that Fever is not crazy. In fact, given everything I know now, it's kind of amazing just how *not crazy* he is."

"Hey," I said, "that means I win the bet!"

"What bet?" Ceri asked.

"You know what bet," I said, grinning.

Lucinda's head tilted, and she stared at me. "What the hell happened here?"

Just at that instant, the phone rang.

Hoping it might be news about Skidmore, I nearly jumped at the phone and snatched up the receiver.

Before I could speak, a strange voice said, "Fever?"

"Yes," I answered tentatively.

"It's Orvid. Orvid Newcomb."

"You have got to be kidding," I said, eyes wide. "I've just been talking about you! And thanks, incidentally, for the most recent loaf of Poilâne—"

"Look, Fever," he insisted, "I've just gotten some very disturbing news."

"Are you calling from Paris?" I asked, a little shaken.

"Yes."

How, then, I wondered, could he have found out about David and Issie so quickly?

"What's your news?" I asked.

Lucinda and Ceri were staring at me. I mouthed the name *Orvid* but I don't know if they understood me or not.

"I think you might be in some danger," Orvid went on. "I've just learned that a relative of mine, David Newcomb, fetched one of our weirder cousins out of the state mental hospital over there in Milledgeville, about a month ago, maybe. This David? He's very, very troubled. And the girl?"

"Before you go any further," I said, "I want to tell you that I genuinely appreciate this call, Orvid. But everything is fine now. David and Issie were here. They almost killed the sheriff, tried to kill me, and David is dead. The girl's in custody."

"Oh." The line went so quiet I thought we might have been disconnected.

"David tortured the sheriff with baling wire," I went on clinically, "something that he claimed he learned from you."

Again: "Oh."

"Orvid?" I prodded.

"David was a kind of— I don't know," Orvid mumbled into the phone. "There was a time when we were close."

"I see."

"And the girl," he began slowly. "How much do you know about her?"

"I know that she's the daughter of your hero Tristan Newcomb, if that's what you mean." I didn't want to reveal the nature of my relationship to Isolde Newcomb in front of Lucinda. That would take a bit more time and thought.

But Orvid didn't know that. "You know who her mother is?"

"Yes."

"Fever?" His voice betrayed a genuine concern that I found oddly touching at that moment.

"I— Lucinda's here, and— and a friend of ours," I stammered.

"Ah," he said quickly. "Understood. How are you holding up?"

"Oddly well."

"Good," he drawled. "It's not like you haven't had plenty of other bizarre revelations in your life before now."

"No," I agreed. "It's not remotely like that. But look, I'm serious about your trying to warn me: I'm very grateful."

"David," Orvid said, "is very dangerous. *Was* very dangerous."

"Did he," I began. "Did he learn that trick with the baling wire from you?"

"Yes." Orvid's voice was placid. "Did he tell you what happened that day, way back when?"

"He said that you and he killed a man by winding the baling wire so tightly around him that he— I don't know, bled to death, or worse, I suppose."

"Ah, well, not exactly." Orvid sighed. "Your— Issie's mother learned that Hector Graves over there in Fit's Mill had grabbed Isolde and tried to get fresh. Issie defended herself and got away, but Issie's mother was outraged. She knew if she complained that Issie had been menaced and gotten away relatively unharmed, no one would do anything about Hector's advances. So Issie's mother did what she did best, I'm told."

"She lied," I said quickly.

"She exaggerated," Orvid corrected, then lowered his voice. "This was a period in your mother's life when she was drinking and using a *lot* of cocaine. But anyway, she called up Uncle Tristan—which, just let me say: our family has a flair for odd names, wouldn't you say? Tristan, Fever, Isolde—Orvid."

"But to continue with your story," I prompted impatiently.

"But to continue with my story," he responded, "your mother called Tristan and told him that Hector had raped Isolde. She wanted revenge. Tristan said he'd handle it and called me. He told me to put a good scare into Hector. But that's all."

"So what happened?"

"I went to get Hector," Orvid went on, "and David wanted to come along. He was a teenager then, and kind of looked up to me the way I looked up to Tristan, I guess. But anyway, he said he wanted to learn from me, and I was younger then, too, and kind of enjoyed the adulation, I suppose."

"So the two of you got this man," I urged.

"We got him in his home, middle of the night. We tied him to his bed with the baling wire. I told him that I was going to tighten it until his brains popped out, I think that was my exact phrase. He was more terrified than I'd ever seen a man. Can you just imagine waking up to me and David in a situation like that?"

"He must have been out of his mind," I said.

"Yes, and that was enough for me. I told him we were going to leave him in his bed like that until he realized how he'd made a young girl feel, how frightened. And then I sent outside for— well, frankly, for a bump of coke. I did a lot of that in those days, too. I didn't realize what was happening until I heard the screams coming from Hector's house."

"Wait," I said, "it was David who killed that man?"

"I went tearing into the house and found David laughing and crying and shaking," Orvid said quietly, "and Hector unconscious with baling wire imbedded into his head so deeply that you could see bits of his broken skull popping out his forehead."

"Christ," I exhaled.

"I grabbed David," Orvid went on, "and we were gone. I called the cops, anonymous tip, but it was way too late for Hector. I tore into David. Told him I never wanted to see him again, and that he ought to avoid me. I may have said that I'd kill him if I ever saw him again, and that he should leave town. Which he did."

"Where did he go?"

"Not sure, but he must have ended up in New Orleans with that branch of the family. I just know that he had himself committed to Milledgeville a number of weeks ago, not sure how many, and that he sprung Isolde. That may have been his intention all along, or it may have been a weird coincidence. Are you familiar with the concept of folie à deux?"

"Actually, I am. It's a madness shared by two people."

"Folie à deux," Ceri said, actually slapping her forehead. "God. Of *course*. Damn it."

"What is it?" Lucinda asked, glancing apprehensively between Ceri and me.

"That's what I was worried about," Orvid continued, unaware of the secondary plot unfolding in my kitchen, "when David and Issie got together. David, see, was sweet on Issie. I found that out. He had been for years. He would do anything she said. When I heard they were together, I knew you'd be in trouble."

"I was," I said. "But it's over now. How did you find out that David had gone to Milledgeville?"

The phone was silent for a moment. "Family" was all Orvid would say on the subject. "Look, I'd like to hear all the details of this thing, but I sense there's a situation there in your home that needs your attention right at the moment."

"God, yes," I agreed.

"So you'll call me back later?"

"Absolutely. And Orvid? Seriously, thanks."

"Don't mention it. That *is* good bread."

"No, I meant—"

"Good-bye, Fever," he said, and I could hear that he was smiling.

"Hey to Judy," I told him.

I could hear the phone shuffle and Orvid's slightly muffled voice saying, "Fever says *hey*, sweetheart."

I could barely hear Judy's lilting voice. "Hey right back."

"Call me," he said into the phone, and then hung up.

"Well," I announced to Lucinda and Ceri, absently replacing the receiver, "that was Orvid Newcomb calling from Paris to warn me about Issie and David."

"Only a couple of days too late," Ceri said affably.

"But he did relate some valuable information," I told her, returning to my seat.

"All right, look," Lucinda said strongly, "I've had just about enough of not knowing what's happened here. I want to know and I want to know right this minute."

"That's fair," Ceri said, standing.

"What are you doing?" I asked Ceri.

"I'm going to borrow your beat-up old green pickup truck," she answered, "and drive on down to the sheriff's office, see if I can talk Melissa Mathews into letting me stay with Issie, who should *not* be alone right now."

I started to protest, but if anyone could have talked Melissa into something, it would have been Ceri. And the look in Lucinda's eyes made it clear that she and I needed to be alone.

So I fished in my jeans pocket and produced the keys to my truck.

"Watch second gear," I advised her.

"Like I've never driven an ornery truck before," she said, taking the keys from my hand. "I'll be back tonight. You guys should get some sleep after you talk."

And within the next few seconds she was gone out the door.

29

I rubbed my eyes and sighed, just as I heard my truck starting up.

"I guess I never thought to ask her how she got to my house in the first place," I said absently, "or where her car was. I assume you brought her here. Did you know that her first name is the same as the Lady of the Lake in some of the Arthurian stories?"

"You mentioned that," Lucinda said tersely. "And her car's at the hospital. I brought her here. This is not what I want to talk about now, especially *not* what her name is."

"It's just that it's a coincidence because of what happened subsequently," I began.

"Fever." She gave me her most commanding look. It worked.

"I know," I said. "I have a lot to tell you, but should we sleep first or talk first? I'm just about as tired as I've ever been in my life and my bones hurt."

"I'm tired, too," she admitted, "but I don't know that I can sleep until I know at least a little about all this mess. I can wait for the details, I guess, but you've got to let me in on some of it now."

"All right." I nodded. "Where to start?"

And with that, the phone rang again.

I sighed.

"Go ahead," she told me, looking away. "It might be about Skidmore."

I dragged myself over to the phone again. "Yes, hello?"

"Fever!" Andrews bellowed. "It's me."

"Timing is everything," I muttered.

"Yes," he shot back, obviously not listening to me, "I'm done with my grades and all my committee work so now I'm ready to come up there and help you with whatever it is that's going on. Something to do with that Issie Raynerd, right? Man, was she a weird girl. I assume you want me to come right away. You can't really take care of these things by yourself at this point. The car's packed, I've had a bit of something to drink, but say the word and I'm set to shoot up there and settle the situation for you. Just in time for Christmas."

"Andrews," I interrupted, because it was clear that he'd had more than a bit to drink and was prepared to go on talking for a while, "everything's fine here. It's all taken care of. I genuinely appreciate your calling, but my advice to you is to hit the hay, sleep until tomorrow—and then come on up here for a bit of Christmas. I'll have a pretty great story to tell you."

"Oh," he said, clearly stymied. "Well. Brilliant. Good. In fact, I could very well log a substantial number of Zs. I may have had a touch of some very good Armagnac that was a present from someone or other, and, well, there you are. Fine, then. I'll ring back when I wake up, right?"

"Perfect," I assured him. "And Andrews?"

"Hm?"

"Thanks for the offer." I smiled.

"What? Of course. I know how you can't really manage these things without me. See you in a bit."

"Right," I said. "Good-bye."

And that was that.

"Andrews," I said.

"I gathered," Lucinda said.

"How about if you and I trundle on up the stairs and I'll hit the stupendously strange highlights of the past several days."

She sat for a moment, glanced at the plywood covering the kitchen window and then at the bandage on my upper arm. I could see that about a dozen sentences were forming themselves in her brain, but each one was so eager to express itself that it prevented the others from breaking into words.

At last she gave up and just said, "I'm taking off all day Christmas Eve *and* Christmas day."

"Oh, thank God," I told her and was suddenly very grateful she was there, and would be there. "When is that, exactly? I've kind of lost track of time."

"Let's head upstairs," she said wearily. "I'd like to have a look at that arm. What happened with that?"

We stood and began to shamble out of the kitchen and up the stairs. "This? Gunshot wound. Just grazed. It's stopped bleeding completely. I got dizzy though."

"We should go to the hospital," she said, putting her arm around my waist. "Get you some stitches."

"Let's get some sleep first, really. It's not bleeding and I think I need sleep more than anything."

"Because you need to stitch up the raveled sleeve of care more than you do your arm," she told me, yawning.

I stopped dead still at the bottom of the stairs.

"That's Shakespeare," I said, amazed.

"Hamlet," she answered. "I'm a small-town girl, Fever, but I learned how to read a long time ago and I have a wider range of tastes than, frankly, you ever give me credit for. I also know just about everything there is to know in this world about American hummingbirds, for example."

I grinned and stared into her eyes. "You do, huh?"

She started up the steps. "Family Trochilidae," she began.

"The smallest is the Bee Hummingbird, in fact the smallest of all birds, only two inches long."

"I have a sister that I didn't know about," I responded as we began our way up the stairs.

She froze on the steps. To her credit, she was only stunned for an instant.

"I'd expect that's one of those *highlights* you were just mentioning," she said.

"One of them," I agreed. "You're not bowled over by this strange revelation? You don't seem that surprised at all."

She inclined her head a bit, thinking. "Sweetheart, there's so much about you that's odd, I believe I've come to think of any *strange revelation* as your *normal day.* That's just you. And I like you just fine that way. That shouldn't come as a surprise to you, should it?"

In that moment I felt that Lucinda and I were, for all practical purposes, already married, and that state paperwork didn't really matter. I found the feeling intensely comforting.

"I guess that your news *is* going to be more interesting than hummingbirds," she went on, "but I would appreciate your recognizing that I am, in fact, an expert on the subject."

"We'll have to engage in a bit more investigation before I agree to use the word *expert,*" I told her, "but I will say that the initial evidence is very impressive."

"Is it that woman," she asked as we continued to ascend the stairs, "Issie? She's your sister?"

"Yes."

"She does favor your mother, around the eyes." Lucinda shook her head. "Lord. Your mother."

"I'd say *amen* to that."

"So she's not your wife."

"She is not," I assured her.

"Short few days ago you had an invisible wife," she said as we achieved the top of the stairs, "and this morning you've got a real live sister."

"Half," I corrected.

"Still family."

"Her real name is Isolde Newcomb."

That stopped her. "Oh."

"Her father was Tristan."

"Lord," she said, breaking away from me, "you've got to be kidding, like the opera? *Tristan and Isolde*? Really?"

I was about to comment on Lucinda's knowledge of Wagner when it hit me that my mother's naming her out-of-wedlock daughter *Isolde* was a perfect example of what my mother always did with the facts of her life. She'd been trying to tell her daughter, from birth, who her father was without actually saying the words out loud. That way, mother could think to herself, "I did everything I could to tell her who her father is. You can lead a horse to water." Except that a poverty-stricken girl in Fit's Mill with a strenuously debilitated mother could hardly have been expected to connect those dots on her own.

"I know," I finally responded to Lucinda. "I think that was my mother's sadly twisted way of trying to tell Issie who her father was. But I'd have to say, once again: impressed with your wide range of knowledge. Opera *and* hummingbirds. Have you always been this eclectic in your interests?"

"Why else do you think you're in love with me?" she said, smiling sweetly. "You don't realize that we have, over the course of the many years we've known each other, talked about everything under the sun? Twice? What else do you think there is?"

"Well," I began, heading toward the bedroom, "you *are* extremely attractive. Plus, there's your proven ability to save my life. That always makes a nice addition to a comfortable relationship."

"Oh, that." She dismissed my pronouncement with the wave of a hand. "I had to do that. I'm a nurse. We have an oath. I take it very seriously."

"The same way you take being engaged to me very seriously," I offered.

"Damn right."

We made it into the bedroom, and the sudden sight of my bed made me so tired I almost collapsed.

Then something occurred to me, admittedly the product of a sleep-deprived mind.

"Look," I said, "I know you were worried about me, and called Dr. Nelson to see if I had lost my entire bag of marbles, but was there something else at work in your bringing her here? Was there some ulterior agenda?"

"Such as?" She yawned, sitting on the bed and getting out of her white shoes.

"Was it a test?" I demanded

"A test? Of what?" She slipped off her hat and tossed it onto the nearby chair.

"Did you introduce me to Ceri Nelson to test my commitment to you?"

She stopped undressing and glared at me. "What? Your commitment to me was *tested* by that woman?"

I realized that I had somehow maneuvered myself into a stupidly dangerous patch of emotional landscape, and resolved to obviate any argument.

"I think I made it clear downstairs at the kitchen table a few moments ago," I said clearly, "how I feel about you. And in front of 'that woman.'"

"Yes." She nodded. "I guess you did."

"Well, then."

"Okay," she acquiesced. "Any other major points before I collapse? I didn't realize how tired I was until I sat down."

"That's exactly why I'm still standing," I agreed. "If I sit, I'll be out."

"So? What else?"

"Did I tell you anything about the child? I can't remember whether you know about that or not?"

"There's a child?" She woke up a little.

"Not really," I said quickly, "I just thought he was. It was David Newcomb, another little person in the family. Issie's cousin, and a very troubled soul."

"Where is he?"

"He was in the ambulance you passed coming up the mountain," I told her. "Dead."

"He's the one who shot you in the arm," she assumed.

"No," I corrected her, "that was Issie. Turns out she may, at this point, be several people. Or one really great actor. Or a combination of the two. By the way, did you know there was a cave down the slope from this house? It's a big cave with an entrance and an exit. I can't understand why I never knew it was there."

Lucinda stared at me with all the intensity her exhausted eyes could muster. "Sweetheart, you knew that cave was there."

"What?" I stared back, only confused.

"We used to—you and me, we used to go down there sometimes to spark in the younger days. You don't remember that?"

I suddenly felt very weak, and a little sick.

"We quit going down there when we caught your momma and Tristan Newcomb doing the same thing as we were about to. We talked about it all the rest of that day. You know. It was near Thanksgiving day, that year before you left town for college."

The vague feeling of nausea remained.

"I don't remember" was all I could say.

"Well, I'm not surprised. You were very upset. I'd like to forget about it myself."

"But." I blinked. I took a breath to go on, but Lucinda interrupted me before I could speak.

"Sweetheart," she said, yawning, "I thought I could hear all this before I went to bed, but I'm worn out just hearing the highlights. I'm pretty sure I have to sleep now."

"You know—you're right." I stumbled toward the bed. "Sleep first. Then talk."

She was out of her nurse's uniform in seconds, and under the covers, eyes closed.

I struggled with my shirt, and it hurt my arm, but I was already half in dreams. I sat in my chair for a moment, avoiding the nurse's hat, so that I could take off my boots, and glanced out the window at the snow in the soft morning light.

For a second I thought I saw a dark figure in the woods just beyond the yard, someone hidden in the last bits of night there, but then a deer stepped out of the shadows and seemed to look up at the house.

I thought then about the long, cold, lonely walk Isolde Newcomb—my sister—had made, many times, from Fit's Mill, over the mountain on logging roads and through thick trees and rhododendrons, just to stand in those same shadows and stare into the house, my house. I imagined her longing; her impossible fantasies about what a happy family must have lived in this house. I could almost feel her desperation and rage; it was a nearly biological reaction. And as I felt a surge of compassion for her pain and sorrow, I understood that it was my sorrow, too. I had also stood on the outside of my family, looking in, always hoping for something that had never arrived: an actual family. Because Issie's fantasies about what went on in this house were entirely fictitious. She was jealous of a mother who cared and a father who was present, and neither of those characters had ever existed. There were, indeed, figments of her imagination. And mine.

For another instant I felt what she'd felt: shivering, out there in those woods, watching the warm light in the kitchen and the white, fragrant smoke from the chimney, imagining what lovely things must be going on in that house. Then, with equal clarity, I felt her turn away from the house in silence and begin to trudge through the snow on the long, long walk back to the place over the mountain where she lived, for the most part, alone.

Thank God Lucinda murmured then, already asleep, or I might have drowned in melancholy. I somehow got out of my jeans and into the bed beside her. She sighed like a happy child when I pulled a second quilt over us, and finally settled in.

I caught one last glimpse of the bare tree limbs out my window, just as the morning sun turned them white, almost burning, like long thin candle flames. Behind them a vaguely charcoal sky was changing to the palest blue I had ever seen, and everything in the world was turning into light.

POSTSCRIPT

On the last day in January I returned home from a long, solitary walk in the woods to find that a parcel had been delivered to my door. From a distance I thought it might be a new loaf of bread from Orvid Newcomb, but as I stepped onto the porch it was obvious that the package was too narrow and square for that.

I picked it up with no small amount of curiosity. Special delivery events have always been rare and suspicious commodities to me. I was all the more puzzled to see that it had come from Ceri Nelson.

Stepping inside, I tore open the bundle. I switched on the lamp beside the door. Late afternoon was about to turn into evening, and the house was dark and cold.

In the package there was a leather-bound book.

There was also a very official-looking document entitled "Certificate of Sanity" suitable for framing. It had my name on it, in bold letters, and it was signed by Dr. Ceridwen Nelson. That made me smile—she was acknowledging that she had, indeed, lost her bet to me.

Finally, there was a short, typed note, obviously also from Ceri:

Fever,
I hope this note finds you well. Enclosed please find the
diary of Isolde Newcomb. I have her permission to send
it to you; we both agreed that you might want to read it.
More anon.
                    Best,

She had neglected or forgotten to sign it.

I examined the accompanying book, flipping through its pages. It was nicely worn, and had no words of any sort on the cover, or lock, as some diaries have. It took me a minute to recognize the handwriting, but I realized finally that it was the same as the scrawl on the back of the photograph of Issie and me. It also came to me then that the date on the picture that we had all assumed to be her death date was, obviously, right around the time she must have discovered that Tristan was her father, and that I was her brother—a death of another kind. Many of the pages were blank; several had been torn out.

I turned to the first page and read.

Dear Diary,
Mother gave you to me this morning for my tenth birthday, and
then taught me how to write on your pages, and I am very proud to
have you. Mother brought it to me from New Orleans, where I
lived until I was five but do not remember it much because I was
sickly. She has told me that it was a hot and humid place. She
was gone for almost two months. I am glad that she is home. I
have eat the last of the turnips and was wondering what might be
my food in December.

Dear Diary,
I am sorry I did not write you for over a year but I have been put
up at another house and did not have you near. Mother was gone

for eighteen months, but she is here now. I stayed with a man name of Ramsey. He works in the gas station but he also makes good liquor. He's a nice man, and even when he was drunk, which was most of the time, he was never mean to me. I asked Mother if he might be my father and she just laughed so I guess not.

Dear Diary,
I have spent all summer with Mother and I was glad of it for a while. She showed me how to cook and what to put in some of her potions. She told me not to tell anyone about her potions, but I guess it is all right if I tell you, because you are a book and not a person. But Mother is sad now, and I do not know what to do. She drinks all of Ramsey's shine and it does her no good, because she cries or argues with me about little things such as which way the toilet paper goes on the roll, over or under. I cannot see how it matters, but she is very strict about things now. I do not know why.

Dear Diary,
I am writing a history essay for my school. I like school. My sixth-grade teacher is Mrs. Barksdale and she likes me. I will write my essay here for practice on penmanship, which counts.

WORLD WARS, A HISTORY REPORT
First there was World War I. The I *is a Roman Numeral. That stands for* One. *It was about the Kaiser and the dreaded Hun. A Hun is a German person and a Kaiser is a man in a pointed helmet. That war was in 1917.*

After it was over there was a party that lasted ten years called the Roaring Twenties because everyone in America was twenty years old, or acted like it. There were flappers then. A flapper is a girl who cut her hair a certain way and rolled her stockings down. They drank gin from a bathtub and danced all over town.

Then there came the Great Depression, when everybody felt

really bad for a long time. People were lined up in straight lines, like for the cafeteria, just to get a loaf of bread. No one had any money, and it was very cold.

Then came World War II. The II means Two. That war was about Hitler who was the worst person that ever lived. He was also a German person. He killed about a million people and shaved off the ends of his mustache so that it looked like there was a caterpillar on his lip. He did this to frighten children. We had to stop Hitler from living in the White House where the president was, so we went to Germany and we bombed Japan with the atomic bomb. The atomic bomb is one small bomb that packs a big wallop, and when we dropped it on a city, that city turned into a mushroom. That's how powerful the atomic bomb is.

World War III, and by now you know what the III means, is a secret war. It is being fought right now by invisible men. I think they cannot wear clothes or else you would see them, like The Invisible Man *by H. G. Wells. For this reason the men who fight World War III are cold all the time, and so they call this the Cold War.*

I believe that we will keep having World Wars with lots of Roman Numerals because the Romans were a warlike people, as it tells us in our history book. We should stop using Roman Numerals because they cause wars and they are very difficult for a sixth-grader to learn.

In conclusion, I believe that we are having wars the wrong way. When I play war outside with Billy Dendy, like Civil War or Army Man, we hide in the woods and we make sounds with our mouths. These sounds are for the guns and bombs.

When someone gets exploded in our games, they make a big jump and a loud noise, but that is all. And then when it starts getting dark, Billy's mother calls us and we go inside and have dinner.

I believe that we should stop having wars until everyone in them can get up and go home to dinner with Billy Dendy's family when it starts getting dark.

All of these things are all true historical facts that were told to me by my Mother which is one of my three required sources, the other ones are the World Book Encyclopedia and our book, History Through the Ages.

Dear Diary,

It's been some time since I wrote in these pages but I am upset and I have no one else to tell it to. A man named Hector Graves got smart with me today. He grabbed me and tried to feel under my skirt. I kicked him as hard as I could between his legs and you can bet he let go of me quick. I came home and told Mother, but now I am scared. She had been taking her medicine, which I don't know what it is but it makes her nervous, and she was all red in the face and weepy. I thought she would tear down the house when I told her about Hector. She started screaming and sent me to my room. I heard her on the phone. I don't know who she is calling, but I can feel that something bad is going to happen. The trouble is that I flirted with Hector before he grabbed me. I knew I ought not to do it. He was drunk and laughing, and I lifted my skirt twice, just for a second. I cannot tell this to Mother because she is mad as a hornet as it is. I hope she is not calling my school. I do not want them to know about this.

Dear Diary,

Guess what! I am taking you to Atlanta! After all these years, I am going to college! Mother has paid for the whole thing, which I do not know where she got the money, but I am as happy as I can ever remember. I love school, and there is a man in Atlanta who teaches at my school who Mother says is the best teacher in the land. He has a funny name like me, and he is not too old so I hope he will not be boring. As soon as I finish writing these lines, I will pack you into my suitcase and off we go!

Dear Diary,
It is the middle of my first semester at college and I am in love. I am in love. I like to write that. He is my teacher Dr. Devilin but I call him Fever and he does not seem to mind. He told stories last week about Iseult who was an Irish princess and her name is also Isolde, like mine, in some of the stories. These are the most beautiful and romantic stories I have ever heard, and they are very old. They date to the second century AD, and have survived. Some of them are the basis for an opera by Wagner. Some of them influenced the King Arthur stories. I cannot say if I love these stories so much because I was named after the woman in them, or because I am in love with the man who is telling them to me. I will take all of his classes. He will notice me after a while. Even though I am shy in class and do not talk much, I can see him looking at me sometimes. He told us about a research trip he is taking after Christmas and I will go on that trip and he will see that I am in love with him and he will talk with me about it. I do not think I have ever been happier in my life.

After that entry there were missing pages, torn roughly from the inner spine. On the last page in the book were written the following, baffling lines:

Open up your fortresses of gold, you setting sun. Loosen and drive home the ruby leaves; now autumn's here to stay. I see the breeze in the chestnut limbs. I know the silver rising of the moon behind the pines. I hear the music of the saddest song I know. It's following behind me as across this wide mountain field I go, toward home.

Excerpt from

The Story of Tristan and Iseult

DR. F. DEVILIN

as found in

The Journal of Jungian Folklore, Vol. 173

Word of the knight Tristan preceded his coming, brave beyond measure, beautiful beyond compare. As the nephew of King Mark of Cornwall it was expected that he would find his way to his uncle's court at Tintagel. He had already slain the Red Dragon of the Tamar Valley, and solved the riddle of the stone at Mên-an-Tol.

But in the winter of his twenty-third year, he flew in between his uncle and an arrow meant to kill the king. He was mortally wounded, and would surely die. King Mark had heard, as everyone had, the stories of a great healer in Ireland, Iseult the Mother, and her daughter of the same name. He sent Tristan in a boat across the ocean to Ireland to be healed.

When Tristan arrived to that country, three women were already waiting on the salt sea strand: Iseult, her mother, and the handmaid Brangaine, all dressed in black. They had sensed his coming. They transported his near-dead body to a hidden room in their castle, where they labored nine days long without rest or food. On the evening of the ninth day, Tristan opened his eyes and saw the younger Iseult, knew she had saved his life, and instantly fell in love. She had hair as auburn as the autumn sunlight, and skin the color of milk. Iseult saw his ardor, and was, herself, stricken. The mother, too, saw their passion, but wisely prevented the new love from blossoming by sending Tristan back to Cornwall on the next tide.

Tristan presented himself to King Mark, and regaled his monarch with tales of the beautiful Iseult. The king misunderstood his nephew, thinking that Tristan was proposing a royal match, and a way to consolidate Cornwall and Ireland as allies. Mark commanded Tristan to take an offer of marriage from the King of Cornwall to the beautiful Iseult.

Heartsick, but dutiful, Tristan returned to Ireland. Once again, he saw, as his little ship approached the land, three women in black standing on the shore. They knew he would return.

Before he could even speak, Iseult's mother accepted King Mark's offer of marriage. Overcome, Iseult protested, as did Tristan, confessing their love for each other. But the mother wisely explained that a king's offer was inviolate, and instructed the young lovers to foreswear each other. This they vowed to do. And to insure that Iseult would not be unhappy in her marriage, the mother concocted a potion that would seal the bridal bed, a love philtre. Iseult and Mark would drink a toast before consummation, and Iseult would make certain that the powder would be in each cup, so ensuring mutual passion, and a lifelong love that could not be abated by any other love, nor any circumstance, not even death.

Devastated, Tristan and Iseult set sail for Cornwall, with Brangaine as their only companion. But the sea was stormy and the night was black, and Tristan called for wine against the cold salt wind, and a potion against the sickness of the waves.

Alas, Brangaine, sick herself, confused the potions and poured all of the love philtre into two cups of wine. Or was it that Brangaine, certain of the lovers' passion, wanted to see that such a love would never die? Or was it that the handmaid, jealous of such joy, would rather see the couple suffer? No one knows but Brangaine, and she is dead these thousand-and-more years.

Unaware, Tristan and Iseult drank the potion. As if struck by lightning, as if picked up by the left hand of heaven and shaken, set down again upon a different boat, they were locked in love's eternal torture from that moment on. Nothing could alter their passion, not even death.

They arrived in Cornwall filled with wild confusion.

Iseult proposed a deception. She instructed her handmaid, Brangaine, to play the part of the bride. In the darkness of the bridal chamber, King Mark would never know.

This was done, and without another thought, Tristan and Iseult repaired to a cave down the slopes from King Mark's castle. There they entwined in true love's knot until the bloodred dawn. This manner of deception continued for a quarter of a year.

Summer came. Mark took his court to Madron, as was his fashion, to the Stone at Mên-an-Tol, there to elicit the secret of the stone from Tristan. Tristan told his uncle that he must meditate nine days in the forest to cleanse his spirit before revealing the hidden meaning of the stone, but that was a lie. Each night in the forest, Tristan sent a small apple bough down the winding stream that led to a secret place where Iseult watched and waited. When she saw the blossoms, she flew upstream to her true love. They slept together in field and in forest and in hidden caves for more than the week, but on the ninth day, they were discovered, sleeping on a crystal bed, by the dwarf Tristan, a cousin of the king. The dwarf Tristan had seen the apple boughs, and wondered at their gathering in a pool so close to the King's summer court. He cast a spell on the boughs and they whispered Tristan's name, echoed as if it were in a cave. The dwarf Tristan ran instantly to fetch the king, and brought the unhappy monarch to the cave to see the crystal bed, and the deception of his wife, and his beloved nephew.

In a rage, Mark drew his sword and would have killed the lovers as they slept, but for the fact that Iseult whispered Tristan's name in her sleep, and he, in turn, kissed her hand. Heartbroken, Mark brought his sword down on the crystal bed and cleft it in half, but could not murder the lovers. He banished Tristan from Cornwall forever, and instructed Iseult never to speak a word again, not for the rest of her life.

Chastened, the lovers obeyed, and the story might have ended there.

But Tristan was sick with grief, and wandered Ireland for years vainly seeking out the places where Iseult had been: a chair where she'd once rested, a cup from which she had sipped, or a stone she might have touched on her walk along a certain road. On one of his melancholy pilgrimages, he chanced to meet another woman, whose hair was the color of wheat and whose eyes were filled with sorrow. Her name, too, was Iseult, and though she neither looked nor behaved as his beloved, Tristan sought to marry her simply because her name was Iseult.

But the marriage was not a happy one, and childless. Tristan pined for a year and a day, and then fell into his bed, like to die. Frantic with grief, the false Iseult, as she had come to be known, sent word of Tristan's illness. Within the week a letter came, telling the unhappy wife that the true Iseult would come, and would heal Tristan, as was her ability. When the false Iseult took this news to her husband, Tristan opened his eyes, and they seemed to shine. He took food, the first in days. He sat up. His cheeks flushed and his pulse quickened.

This response from her husband filled the false Iseult with jealousy, and she paced and sobbed all night. In the morning she cast her weary eyes out the window of Tristan's bedchamber, and saw a ship approaching. In that ship were three women, all dressed in black. As it neared the shore, the false Iseult panicked and ran to Tristan.

"I am sorry, my beloved," she said with a voice as cold as ice.

"News has come from Iseult, King Mark's bride. She is not coming. She will not come to you. She has refused to help."

With that Tristan's eyes darkened, his heart unwound, and his skin grew gray as the mist. He turned his face to the wall and spent his last breath whispering the name of his true love.

At that very instant, the true Iseult's foot touched the top of the stairs and she bounded into Tristan's bedchamber. The false Iseult fled the room in inconsolable despair, and the true Iseult could see that Tristan was dead.

With her mother and Brangaine standing in the doorway, the true Iseult went to the bed of her only love. She laid herself down beside Tristan and wrapped him in her arms. She broke her vow to King Mark and whispered Tristan's name into his ear. Though he was dead, his body sighed, and his cold, clay lips kissed her hand.

And when his lips touched her milk-white skin, Iseult was content, and breathed out her life, into the damp gray mist.

Tristan was buried in ancient ground, with the true Iseult on his right. The false Iseult wept on their graves for nine months and a day, and then she took her own life. She was buried on Tristan's left.

Out of the true Iseult's grave grew a white rose, out of Tristan's a red, and out of the grave of the false Iseult grew a black, thick briar. These three entwined around and covered up the graves, until no living soul could tell one from the other. But the red rose grew in a true love's knot around the snow white rose. And the briar, black and bent as night, never drew a drop of blood, not in the thousand-and-more years from that day to this.